Gem Squash Tokoloshe

RACHEL ZADOK grew up in Johannesburg. She studied fine art and worked as a graphic designer and then a waitress while pursuing a career as a writer. She lives in south London.

Gem Squash Tokoloshe

Rachel Zadok

PICADOR AFRICA

First published 2005 by Picador Africa
an imprint of Pan Macmillan South Africa
P O Box 411717, Craighall, Johannesburg 2024
http://www.picadorafrica.co.za

ISBN 1770100237

Cover design: Donald Hill of Studio 5
Printed and bound in Great Britain by
Mackays of Chatham plc, Chatham, Kent

This book is dedicated to Jane Frances te Riele,
whom I knew too briefly.

You live still, inspiring all who walk life's path after you.

Acknowledgements

I am grateful for the help and support offered by so many. My husband Julian, for living with my chaos and never expressing doubt at my crazy ideas. My mother, Sheryl Kavin, for all her love. Alison Burns, Emily Pedder and Tamar Yoseloff, for their encouragement and for sharing their skills with me. Mxolisi Phahlamohlaka for the Sotho translations. Everyone from the City University group, especially those who pooled their resources at a moment's notice to help me when I was in over my head. And Alan Gaunt, for his giant heart and generosity of spirit.

Finally, I am eternally grateful to my strong women friends for the inspirational way they live their lives. Donna, Jessica, Nadja, may all your dreams come true.

The Soul Stealer

Something wake him, stir a hunger in his guts, call. He lick the breeze, taste a morsel of fear on the icy air. His glands drip, drip, his cheeks, taut drawn, long to stretch, distort with moans and screams. There's a pain out there.

He pull away from the winter-dead tree, unfurl from its grey knots. Two gnarled roots shake off clump-hard ground, step out. Come spring the tree remain winter-naked, no rain revive a tree house where he choose to sit, to sleep. His walk is long loping, his step wide. Shadow to shadow, no eyes see, no minds believe. Dead Rex is forgotten, long gone from man's memory in this place. No one remember the soul stealer, no one appease him, no one protect himself, no more.

He lick, lick the pain, taste for screams. There's begging about, a pleading. The old souls stir in his gut, they eat at him as he ate them, hungry. He speed along, faster now, a light guide him, a single candle burning flame.

He come to a paint-scabbed door, pick a peeling flake. His fingers slide over splinters and into a crack, he twist and turn and flatten and through, drop silently into the room. Slip into the shadows.

He lick the smells. Paraffin. Fear sweat. Sick smell like dog-dead. Headless chicken spurting blood smells. Hot wet goat smells.

His eyes follow the shadows that leap over man, the light that flick over woman. He seen that man on other days, he been before to this place. Pretending he kind. Dead Rex seen into his dark place, he been expecting him, fresh rot.

Dead Rex lie his head down next to the woman, he know her too, but there be nothing there for him, until now. Now her eyes be fear-wide, all pupil black, and he see a trouble to be making in their reflection. He see more than one feast tonight.

He draw near to her lips, he long to kiss her pain. He pucker and probe and suck her mouth, draw out her screams. His cheeks distend, bulge, fill up with all her noise. The old souls clamour for fresh living, upward surge from his gut. He swallow hard.

Back under the door he slip, into the night. There trouble to be making and he ache to be hurrying up with making it. Into the house and down the passage. He peek in on the mad one, she be sound asleep. No risk her seeing him tonight. He slide up to mosetsana's door, it be open, an invitation, come in, come in. He enters.

Mosetsana sleep. Easy he slip under the covers and into her bed. He stroke her hair, run knuckle-twig fingers through fine tangles, he like mosetsana, she be still pure, blank canvas, torment not yet painted on her soul.

Mouth to ear he spread his lips. A small moan slither out, a little tease into her sweet dream. She whimper, he spill a little more, 'No, baas, no!' She stir, but still not wake. He reach impatience, feel around with wasted tongue to find a scream and flick it to the front. His mouth open full, a cavern of zigzag teeth, he scream. Like a banshee it fly out into mosetsana's ear. She sit, bolt upright. One more moan wriggle out from his lips and she recognize the voice.

She whisper a name, rub eyes, get out of the bed. From shadow to shadow he follow her until they back at the paint-scabbed door.

She listen, he listen with her. A voice plead high, it rise, it wail, the woman-lady voice, mosetsana know this voice, love this voice. She press her ear to the wood, rub her fingers against the peeling paint, she still her breath, listen hard. Someone's crying-moaning, someone's groaning-grunting. Someone speak, a hush speak, a strained speak, like a speak through gritted teeth. A deep voice man-speak.

'Open the door,' Dead Rex whisper in mosetsana's ear, 'open.' She be shaking now, her heart double beating, she feel a wrong thing here. Her small hand push against the worn wood, it don't budge.

'Push harder.' Her feet push against the cold ground, hands press the door. The door snag, and drag, and open a slice. The smells rush out, the paraffin vapours, the dog-dead, the blood smell, the fear stink.

Mosetsana gag, her eyes cry. Ball fists squeeze salt-wet eyes.

'Push, push,' he hiss. She lean her whole self into the door. The slice grow bigger, big enough for mosetsana to look in.

Now she see, the candle flame burning show her.

The fat pig-bristle buttocks, hard pumping, the trouser shackle round his ankles. The dark juice stain on his legs as he mash into woman. Woman bent over bed, dark demon shadows lick her like black dogs. Fat-fingered butcher hand push down her head, fat-fingered butcher hand squeeze her delicate woman wrists, bend her arms back behind her, like broken sticks they look. He groan-grunts, a pig-beast, hard-boiled-egg eyes bulging.

Dead Rex feel mosetsana panic, feel mosetsana pain, feel fear, feel confusion. Her soul scream what her body hold frozen. She want to run away.

'He be hurting her,' Dead Rex whisper. 'Hurt him back.'

PART ONE – 1985

Chapter One

MY MOTHER BELIEVED in magic. She told me stories of the fairies who lived on our farm as she rocked me to sleep at night. On hot summer nights, Mother left the window open, letting in the cool night breeze which carried the smell of citrus to my nostrils. That smell, mixed with the perfume of Mother's lilac-scented soap, brings Dead Rex and Tit Tit Tay into my mind, and makes me look over my shoulder to make sure they're not behind me. I'd lived on the farm from the day I was born, and as long as I could remember, I'd been surrounded by fairies. They lived on the peripheries of my vision, well hidden from my curious eyes, but I knew they were there. Mother was forever warning me about the dangers of bad fairies: 'Don't go into the orchard alone, Tit Tit Tay will steal you and turn you into a monkey child.'

I did not want to be a monkey child, and whenever I was tempted to wander off into the orchard, I only got as far as wiggling the rusted bolt on the low gate before the hairs on my neck prickled in warning, making me run off yelling, 'Shaya' and 'Suka wena' to ward off any fairies that might follow.

The orchard had been abandoned for over a year, ever since Papa had taken a job as a salesman and Moses, our farmhand, had disappeared. It hadn't rained for a long time. I couldn't remember it ever having rained, and Papa said that it was either give up the farm entirely or go on the road. 'It's only until the rains come,' he promised.

Water was the most precious thing on the farm. Mother valued water more than anything else, including her jewellery and our dog Boesman, and sometimes, I thought, even more than me.

'Water is our life,' she said whenever I suggested she turn the hosepipe on me, 'we don't waste it.' I'd watch as all the precious water got sucked up by her vegetables, sticking my bottom lip out as far as I could to demonstrate my dissatisfaction.

When Mother was not tending her vegetables and herbs for the farmers' co-op market behind the town hall, she painted pictures. Sometimes of me, making me sit still, staring ahead unblinking until my eyes burned; sometimes of Boesman, though he wasn't a very good model; but mostly of the fairies. Some days a strangeness would take hold of her, and she would disappear into the orchard for hours, leaving me alone on the farm with only Boesman for company. I didn't mind. Boesman was good company. Papa got Boesman from a man who bred Ridgebacks. He'd given Boesman to Papa free because he wasn't a pure dog; his father was a stray and the litter wouldn't sell. This didn't bother Papa. He said mongrels were stronger because their genes were mixed. Boesman and me celebrated our birthdays together. Mother said that Boesman had come the same day as me, though Papa said it was a few days after. Papa wanted a dog to keep him company after I arrived. Mother had a baby, so he got himself a dog. Boesman turned out to be more my dog than Papa's. We did everything together, he even slept in my room.

One day, when Mother was in one of her strange moods, I followed her to the orchard gate, hoping she would take me with her to meet the fairies, but she didn't seem to notice that I was there. She just closed the gate behind her and, without looking back, disappeared into the trees. I hung around the gate for a while, talking to Boesman. I told him about Dead Rex. 'Never look him in the eyes,' I said, holding Boesman's head firmly in my hands as I stared into his liquid eyes. 'He'll lock you away inside your head and you'll be able to see everyone else, but no one will be able to see you.' Boesman didn't seem afraid so I continued: 'And you won't be able to move, no matter how hard you try, not your arms or your legs, you won't even be able to turn your head.'

Boesman just looked at me. He wasn't afraid of anything and I felt safe with him.

Just then a high-pitched laugh came from the direction of the orchard, making me jump with fright. Boesman threw himself at the gate, and began to bark frantically. On his hind legs he was almost as tall as a man, but still no match for fairies. The cackle came again, this time closer, and I grabbed Boesman by the collar, pulling him away as hard as I could. 'Run, Boesman, run,' I yelled, but he pulled back, stronger than me.

'Boesman!' I screamed and ran away as fast as I could. I ran back to the house, shouting out all the magic words I could think of, scrambling over the stoep and through the front door, slamming it shut behind me.

The front room was cool and dark, getting no sun in the late afternoon. Dead Rex stared down at me from above the fireplace, his skin dark brown, slick with an oily blue sheen, eyes the same colour as the slimy algae in the water tank. I kept my eyes warily on him to make sure he wasn't moving. I knew the fairies could hide inside Mother's paintings, pretending they were just pictures until I wasn't looking. Then they would slowly move towards me, wanting to steal me away to whatever horror they felt up to that day. I edged towards the door that led into the passage, watching him all the time. Some fairies did terrible things: Dead Rex was the worst of them. He'd once stolen the bricks that raised Moses' bed off the floor, making it low enough for the Tokoloshe to get him. That's what Mother had told me when Moses disappeared last year, after Papa went on the road.

Tit Tit Tay was just as dangerous, but not because she was mean. There was a painting of Tit Tit Tay in the passage, she looked sad and lonely and she reached out with mud-brown arms towards me. Mother said Tit Tit Tay had once had lots of children, but she had lost them all, hiding them in secret places for safekeeping and forgetting where they were. Her memory was so bad that she couldn't even remember what they looked like, so any child that crossed her path she thought was hers. I ducked quickly under her, feeling her fingers brush my back as I passed out of reach. I breathed a sigh of relief. The rest of the fairies in the passage weren't so bad, and I didn't have to watch them or avoid them as I passed on my way to the kitchen. Even if they did come out of the paintings, the worst they could do was tie my shoelaces together or pull my hair, and I only wore shoes on Sunday, so I wasn't worried.

I sat down on the step outside the back door. Long ago, when we had people who worked for us, before the drought, the back step and the front stoep were polished to a red waxy shine. Now they were dull and faded, more brown than red. I wondered when Mother and Boesman would come home. Mother was the only person who ever saw the fairies. They were her friends and even Dead Rex left her alone, but I was worried about Boesman. Even though he was a big dog, he might not have understood what I'd told him at the orchard gate.

My thoughts were interrupted by a sharp gust of wind. Dust flew into my eyes, blinding me. I rubbed the grit away with fisted hands and noticed great purple clouds moving in from the south. They came quickly and my skin prickled with gooseflesh as the temperature dropped. A blue electric streak ripped across the sky, making the hair on my neck stand up, and I jumped at the loud thunderclap that followed. I'd never seen anything like it in my short life, it seemed to me as though the world was ending. Tears stung the back of my eyes, and then the sky began to cry. A bulbous teardrop hit the ground, throwing up a miniature dust fountain. Then another and another. Soon they were pelting down, loud and furious, drumming the tin roof. A vivid vein of electricity cut across the horizon, illuminating the farm in a queer neon glow and leaching the colour from things so that the world was momentarily monochrome. The sky rumbled like God's hungry stomach. Water gushed out of gutters, evicting rotting leaves and their tenants of spiders and beetles. The sky was angry, constipated by drought. Three years we had suffered under its stifled threats and rumbles, its teasing gatherings of clouds that hung pregnant in the sky and dispersed without expressing a drop. This storm had momentum built of frustration.

I cowered on the step, terrified, my arms around my head to protect me from the sting of the drops, the cracks of lightning. This was the end and I prayed to God to save me. I said the only prayer I knew, the one I got down on my knees every night with Mother to recite, always the same.

'God, please look over us with kindness, make our vegetables grow, protect us from bad fairies, bring Papa home safe and bring the rain.'

Our prayer had finally been answered, here was the long-absent rain, this was not the end but the beginning.

I stood up and faced the new wet world and stepped tentatively into the full force of the driving rain. Turning my face skywards I let the rain wash away the dust that coated my skin. My T-shirt was soaked in seconds, my hair plastered to my scalp. Rivulets of water ran off my shorts, down my skinny legs and pooled around my narrow feet, having nowhere to go but into the hard-baked ground that couldn't drink fast enough.

Now that I was completely soaked, I wasn't afraid. I ran down towards the orchard gate, wanting to share my baptism. Halfway there I met Mother and Boesman, coming towards the house. She was laughing, the wet fabric of her clothes clinging to her like a second skin, arms outstretched, holding her rolled-up painting up in one hand, gesturing towards the sky.

LATER WE SAT together, Mother, Boesman and I, towelling ourselves off in the kitchen, drinking hot, sweet coffee. The storm had dissipated; now it was just rain, gentle and repetitive. Mother spoke softly of the change rain would bring, of the new leaves that would sprout on the trees, of the oranges we would pick. She said she hoped to have time to plant some roses now, like Grandma English. She said that Papa would come home.

Chapter Two

SATURDAY DAWNED WITH a bright and steamy hope that belied the trouble it brought to my young life. The sun was not yet quarter way to noon and already it had baked the earth into a cracked red crust. Boesman lay in the sun, humiliation steaming off him. He eyed Mother suspiciously, ready to bolt should she reach for the hosepipe again. I felt little sympathy for him: his bathing ordeal was over for the week; I still had to endure mine. I sat naked on the kitchen step, watching as Mother filled the cast-iron tub she'd dragged outside into the yard with boiling water from a pot on the kitchen stove. She liked to bath outside on hot days, now that we had no farm workers. Only the chickens focused their beady eyes upon us as they pecked, pecked, pecked. We could stand naked in the yard, feeling the sun lick the water from our bodies. I much preferred it to the dank interior of our bathroom, where lukewarm water dribbled and sputtered out of groaning taps into the glacial white bath. The enamel sucked out all the heat before I got in, leaving me shivering in an inch of icy water. Out in the yard the water seemed bigger, almost filling the tin tub that kept the water warm with its sun-baked metal.

Mother lowered her hand into the water, testing the temperature. She swore as she withdrew her red fingers and poured a jug of cold water over them into the tub. After three more tests she was satisfied and, leaning over the tub, she threw her hair forward and submerged her head completely. Her white hair fanned out in the water like a strange many-tentacled animal, each one of its thousand arms reaching out to catch the light. She emerged dripping, hair clinging to her head, and began soaping up with aloe vera leaves, which she threw into the tub once she had squeezed all the slipperiness out of them. She divided her hair into long ropy sections. Using her fingers as a comb she separated each section into two and rubbed these together like she was washing kitchen rags, working out knots and dirt with nimble fingers. She worked her way around her head, tugging, separating, fingers combing, until every strand was slick with aloe, then she rinsed with cold water from the jug, which she sent me to refill twice.

I watched as Mother stood up and pulled the dirty smock she was wearing over her head. She stood there, naked in the brightness, her hair already beginning to dry in the heat, springing into life to catch the sun and form a halo around her. She looked back at me, narrowing her blue eyes. Her focus bored into me, unblinking, drilling through my skin into my gut until my stomach twisted into a knot. I looked away, trying to break her stare, but she didn't move and I was forced to look back up at her. I felt a twinge of fear as I watched her, tall and sturdy, her hair white snakes uncoiling over her shoulders. I couldn't take my eyes off her, fearing that if I did she would turn into something bad, something that was not my mother.

It's only Mother, I told myself, like those words were some sort of charm that could hold the fear that was pushing between my eyes at bay. I felt a hot prickle of tears. It would be humiliating if I cried. Mother hadn't done anything, she was just standing there.

Cry-baby, what you crying about? She would want to know.

Look away, look away – I wished she would look away.

'Well, are you coming to bath or not, Faith?' The question came suddenly, like time had stopped and started again with a jolt. Uncertainly I nodded.

'Well, come on then, Papa will be here soon.' I got to my feet and slowly walked towards her. She had seemed so strange a second ago, so far away; now it was as if nothing had happened.

I climbed into the tub, careful not to let the hot edge touch my inner thigh, and sat down in the warm water. Mother emptied the jug over my head. Then I stood up to be washed, automatically lifting my arms, angling my head, turning around while Mother lathered Sunlight soap against a rough cloth I knew was once a flour sack, although she said she'd bought it in town. She scrubbed every inch of me until I glowed, pink and raw. I didn't complain; all that would get me was a slap across my backside and a day's worth of teasing. Better to just bear it.

Once done, Mother and I dragged the tub out of the yard and tipped its soapy contents into one of her flowerbeds. The soapy water kept the aphids and the guilt Mother felt at the 'extravagance' of a bath at bay. Extravagance is when you do something you can't afford, that's what Mother told me.

Wrapped in towels we made our way to Mother's room,

where carefully chosen clothes, crisply ironed that morning, awaited us, laid out on my parents' large bed. Mother dressed with care on Saturdays, letting me brush her hair while she rubbed delicious-smelling creams into her cheeks before dusting them lightly with fine powder. I loved the sweet smell and unbelievable softness of the powder puff. Some days, when she was in a good mood, Mother let me slip my fingers through the cream satin ribbon and gently press its downy feathers to my cheek, feeling them whisper against my skin. Its heady perfume tickled my nostrils and the whole experience left me feeling dreamy, like I was floating on a soft cloud. Today wasn't one of those days, and I watched jealously as Mother closed the gold powder box without offering me the puff. She applied a little Vaseline to her lips, making them shine, before standing up to admire her reflection in the mirror.

'What do you think, Faith? Will your papa think your mother is worth another look?' I nodded furiously; Mother was beautiful, worth a thousand looks.

I SAW PAPA'S dust cloud coming up the road long before his car was visible. He'd come home earlier than usual, but even so, all signs of the previous night's storm had evaporated. Only our water tank, filled to the brim, was testament to the rain. Mother stood at the door, her lips a thin line. She watched his approach just long enough so she could see him framed in the windscreen before she turned away and disappeared inside.

Papa's shiny green Ford Cortina pulled up to the house.

He always said that a salesman's car made the sale. Most other people believed it was the suit and tie, or the gift of the gab, but Papa believed it was the car. He said that clients saw the car coming, and when it parked in their yard they would gather round before he had even opened the door. Letting them get a look under the bonnet was a good opener for new customers. Papa believed it was his car that made him salesman of the month three times running. It was out of this car that he stepped now, arms open to scoop me up.

Papa smelled of Van Dijk cigarillos, long-smoked, and his shirt, sleeves rolled up to the elbows, smelled of sweat.

'Hey, baby, look what I brought you,' he said, producing a toffee apple and a new Superman comic. I nuzzled against Papa's neck. I liked the feel of his day-old stubble and the smoky smell of his hair. Papa reminded me of a lion, his hair and moustache a yellow mane.

'The child will get sick on that,' came Mother's voice from behind. 'Besides, she is freshly bathed. That will make her grubby.'

Papa sighed. 'And what is a childhood if it can't be grubby?'

'She's grubby all week,' Mother replied. 'Not that you would know, Marius.'

Papa put me down and winked at me. Leaning into the car, he produced a large bunch of white lilies.

'Get those at the cemetery?' Mother asked, but I could see she was pleased, and Papa could see it too.

For the rest of the day Papa boasted of his sales, telling us funny stories of stupid customers and clumsy roadhouse waitresses. Mr Williamson who didn't know his arse from his elbow, Sonnet the new waitress at Henry's Burger Stop who insisted on wearing stilettos to work and kept tripping up, spilling coffee all over herself and the customers. Even tipped a plate of chips on to Papa's lap, and if that wasn't bad enough, tried to clean them off. Papa sat on the stoep in the sun, taking swigs from his bottle of Lion lager. I hung around his neck while he admired Mother's latest painting. It was of Sillstream, the water fairy who lived in the reservoir. Mother told us how it must have been her that had caused the rain, considering it was Sillstream she had been painting that day. Papa smiled and said, 'If not, why not?' and although I didn't quite know what he meant, I repeated it.

DINNER ON SUNDAY was special in our house. It was the last meal of the week that we ate as a family and Mother liked to think that the feast of chicken, roast potatoes and boiled gem squash would remind Papa that home was the best place to eat.

I didn't like gem squash.

I didn't like their dark green skins, darker than boiled spinach, an ugly, dirty green. I didn't like their stringy orange insides that tasted of nothing and bitterness and had to be mixed with butter and sprinkled with sugar just to make them edible. I didn't like chewing their skins that wouldn't soften, now matter how long they were boiled. I didn't like their pips. Mother insisted I eat the pips and the skin. She said they were full of fibre, good for me. I didn't care. I didn't want fibre. I wouldn't have eaten a single gem squash for the rest of my life, not the horrible outside or the stringy inside, if it wasn't for the Tokoloshe. We had a Tokoloshe in our cellar.

Our cellar housed vegetables, home-made ginger beer, spiders and a Tokoloshe. Mary told me about our Tokoloshe.

I didn't like Mary.

Mary worked for Mother when people still worked on the farm. She polished the stoep and made hard, chewy scones and, sometimes, she cooked dinner. Usually when Mother went out with Papa and it was only me to feed. Mary was old, older than anybody else I knew. Her face was creased, folded with wrinkles. They made her look like she was always scowling. Mary never smiled, but sometimes she would laugh, I never knew why. She had a dry raspy laugh that sounded like a cough and exposed her shrunken gums. She had false teeth, but only popped them in to eat. The rest of the time she carried them around in her apron pocket, along with her snuff. Mary liked snuff. She liked to sit outside in the sun, legs stretched out and spread apart, the yellow and black snuffbox in one hand, taking pinches of snuff between the fingers of the other. It made her sneeze. Sometimes I found discarded snuff containers. I kept them, sniffing secretively at the sticky residue until my eyes watered.

Mary told me about the Tokoloshe in the cellar. She said a witchdoctor had sent a Tokoloshe to live with us, to steal our souls while we slept. She said that the land we lived on didn't belong to us, and unless we moved and gave the land back, the Tokoloshe would stay. It would live in our cellar, eat our vegetables and drink our ginger beer.

'Tokoloshi, tokoloshi, tokoloshi,' she hissed at me through papery lips. 'Ough, ough, ough,' she laughed, her lips drawn back in gummy glee.

That night I lay awake, watching for the Tokoloshe. Shadows slid around the room, slipping through the crack in the door, across the floor and under the bed. Shapes shifted, the chair twisted monster-like, the cupboard loomed. The Tokoloshe was everywhere. I pulled the sheets over my head, clutched King Elvis and said a prayer. I woke up yelling.

Mother didn't like to cook alone. She didn't like 'slaving over a hot stove' without any company. She didn't like the idea that we, Papa and I, would gobble down our food without 'a single thought as to how much work' it was. Every day, at five in the afternoon, she would shout for me. I would have to stop what I was doing and go and help her make dinner. I thought this unfair, especially since Papa ate the most food and he didn't have to help. Helping was boring. I wasn't allowed to do any of the fun stuff, stir the pots or chop the vegetables. My sole purpose was to fetch and carry and wash things.

'Get the salt out of the cupboard, Faith.'

The salt was kept in a big tin with a picture of a little boy running after a chicken on it. I had to use both arms to carry it to Mother. I imagined the boy was kept in the tin, and that's what made it so heavy. I used to be disappointed when Mother opened the tin and it was just salt. Papa once told me that salt preserved people. Some people buried their dead in salty earth and a long time later other people would dig them out and they wouldn't be rotten. He said preserved was like being pickled. I imagined lots of little dead people in a jar, like onions, and wondered if we would find a little pickled boy when we got to the bottom of the tin. We never did.

'Get me a cup of flour, Faith.'

The flour was kept in a big white sack that was rolled down at the top and closed with two wooden pegs. I liked to stick my hands into the flour, it felt silky and cool, but

Mother wouldn't let me. Sometimes, though, I would sneak into the kitchen, open the sack and bury my arms right up to my elbows. Then I would run outside and scare Boesman, pretending to be a ghost. I didn't do it too often though: I was scared of being caught.

'Run down to the cellar and fetch me three tomatoes, Faith.'

'Uh uh.' I shook my head.

'Didn't you hear me, Faith?'

I nodded.

'Then go.'

I folded my arms. I wasn't going down into the cellar ever again.

'Do you want a hiding, Faith?' I shook my head. I certainly didn't want a hiding, but even more than I didn't want a hiding, I didn't want the Tokoloshe to get me.

'Go, now!' Mother pointed at the kitchen door. 'Out, three tomatoes, or else.'

I popped my eyes and scrunched my nose. Mother picked up her wooden spoon and waved it at me.

'You have three seconds,' she said. 'I'm counting.

'One.'

I didn't move.

'Two.'

I eyed the spoon, thinking of the sting and slap of the wood against my bum.

'Three.'

'Mary saysa witchdocta putta Tokoloshe inna cellar an its goin' tweat me.'

Mother wrinkled her brow at me. 'Mary said what?'

I took a deep breath. 'Mary said . . .' and I told her about the Tokoloshe. When I had finished Mother put the spoon down and held out her hand.

'Let's go take care of this Tokoloshe,' she said.

I followed Mother down the stone steps into the cellar, my heart bumping in my chest. A dim electric bulb cast gloomy light and long shadows that pooled around barrels and boxes. Dusty bottles lined wooden shelves; their necks gave daddy-long-legs spiders pillars to spin webs between. The cellar smelled of damp dust. Mother stopped at the bottom of the steps and looked around.

'Where's the Tokoloshe?' she whispered. I stood on the last step and looked around. I saw a shadow slip behind the tomatoes.

'There,' I pointed. Mother tiptoed over to the tomatoes and moved the wooden crate that contained them. It scraped against the floor as she pulled it back to look behind.

'There's nothing here, Faith.'

I stood on my toes to peer over her. I looked around again. I saw a round bump in a box. 'There,' I pointed.

Mother crept over to the box. 'Where?'

'In that box,' I whispered, 'I can see its head, it's hiding.'

Mother reached into the box. I closed my eyes and waited for her scream.

'This?' Mother asked. I opened my eyes and saw the Tokoloshe bump; it was a large butternut. She brought it over for me to see close up. I touched its smooth shell; it was cold, but that was all. She put it back in its box and picked up a gem squash.

'Sit down,' Mother said. We sat on the bottom step, side by side. Mother took my hand and looked at me. She held up the gem squash.

'Gem squash are magic,' she said. I wrinkled my nose in disgust. 'Tokoloshe don't like gem squash.' I wasn't surprised, only Mother liked gem squash. 'Tokoloshe won't come near you if you eat lots of gem squash. Gem squash will protect you.'

I shook my head, I didn't know whether to believe her.

'Haven't you ever heard anyone say, "A gem squash a day keeps the Tokoloshe away"?' Mother winked. She turned my hand over and placed the gem squash in my palm. 'See you in the kitchen.' She picked up three tomatoes and left. I stood up to follow, clutching the magic squash. As I climbed the steps I heard a noise, a soft rustle. The hair on my neck stood up. I turned around slowly and that's when I saw it. The Tokoloshe. Standing, partly hidden, behind the tomatoes. A shadow of a Tokoloshe, but still a Tokoloshe. I lifted my arm and aimed the gem squash.

'Gem squash Tokoloshe!' I shouted. The gem squash sailed through the air and I bolted up the steps.

AFTER SUNDAY'S DINNER I lay curled up on a big cushion on the stoep, my stomach full of gem squash. My parents sat on the swing chair. It creaked softly as they rocked, back and forth, back and forth. Mother read the letter that had come from Johannesburg, Papa read the paper. The letter was from Mia, Mother's old friend. I'd met her once; she came to the farm, 'to recover', Mother said. She didn't seem very old, no older than Mother anyhow, so I didn't know why Mother called her an old friend. Mia had cried a lot and Papa had said it was because she'd married a good-for-nothing.

Mother sighed and Papa rustled his paper and I drifted on the sounds of rustling and sighing and creaking, my eyes getting heavier and heavier.

A LOUD CRASH jolted me awake. Hushed voices, the sound of crying. It was dark, hot. I couldn't make out where I was. I tried to remember when I had fallen asleep, nothing came. I lay still, wondering what to do, when I remembered the warning Mother had given me about getting lost in fairy rings. I stiffened, straining for sounds. I could just make out someone breathing. Low voices hummed like electricity, just beyond my grasp, or perhaps it was the language I could not understand. Mother said fairies spoke in strange tongues. I knew that if I tried to move they would discover me. I was afraid, Dead Rex, the Tokoloshe, Tit Tit Tay. Now, in the dark, alone, I didn't want to see the fairies. I lay still, taking shallow breaths as often as I dared. My heart thumped, my breath rasped, filling the black. I needed to pee. I clenched and crossed my legs and held it for as long as I could. Soon the sharp smell of pee closed in, and it seemed as if the very darkness was alive with a prickly swarm.

I woke to the sun streaming into my room. Boesman lay asleep at the bottom of my bed, but woke as soon as I moved, drumming his tail on the floor in greeting. The house was quiet, strange for Monday morning. Usually, by the time I awoke, Mother had already packed her small van for the market, and I would find her and Papa in the kitchen, eating breakfast before he left for the week. This morning only the net curtain blew in the breeze. The kitchen was deserted.

The heat told me it was late, I had slept too long. The door to Mother's room was slightly ajar, a gentle push from me opened it wide enough to see Mother, lying diagonally across the top of the bed, asleep in the clothes she had worn the night before. An empty bottle lay on the floor. Papa was not there. Nor was his car in the drive. He had left without saying goodbye.

Chapter Three

WE WERE LATE for the market, but our usual stall in the coveted first row had not been taken. Mother began to unpack our goods on to the blue trestle table the market management provided for each stall. She arranged our vegetables on one half and laid out her watercolours on the other. She propped the two large oil paintings against the front.

'Môre, Bella, or should I say afternoon,' Tannie Hettie, whose stall was next to ours, greeted us with eyebrows raised.

Tannie Hettie was short, squat and geometric and the clothes she wore accentuated this. Dresses that reached just below her knees and were belted through the centre, dividing her neatly into two squares. Her grey hair was cropped and tightly curled. She sold dried and sugared fruits, a confectionery she made herself. The tiny sugar crystals caught the light and my eye, and I longed to be brave enough to ask her for a taste. Some days, when she was in a good mood, she would read the thoughts from my mind and toss a small packet in my direction. Mother said that Tannie Hettie might be stern, but under her tough exterior beat the kind heart of a true friend.

'Marius came by this morning,' Tannie Hettie said while counting out change for a customer, all the time watching Mother out of the corner of her eye, 'asking everyone if they knew of a good farm manager.'

'No surprise considering the rain,' Mother replied, her lips stretched thin over her teeth. 'We'll need someone to oversee the orchard.'

'A small orchard like that, not even fifty trees, one would think he would oversee it himself.'

Mother gave Tannie Hettie a strained smile, and smoothed an exposed area of the white cloth that covered the table under her hands.

I decided to sit out the day's heat on a blanket under the table. From below I could hear the exchanges between Mother and her customers. Voices both familiar and strange, muffled by the metallic shade, filtered down to me. I recognized the voice of Oom Piet, a man who stopped by our stall every Monday to pinch my cheeks. I was relieved he did not have the same X-ray eyes as Superman so that I could stay hidden below the table. Oom Piet was our best customer and the biggest flirt in our small town. He was something of a ladies' man, whatever that was, and I'd heard Tannie Marie say that he had been spotted leaving the recently widowed Tannie Markike Botha's house late one night, while his wife was away visiting her sister. I knew that was bad, because Tannie Marie said it in a low voice and it was met with raised eyebrows.

Mother wouldn't flutter her eyelashes when Oom Piet appeared, and it was for this reason that he owned so many of her paintings.

Everyone said Oom Piet looked like Pik Botha, with his

carefully trimmed and waxed moustache and Brylcreemed hair, but he was so dull and stupid that he made me yawn and cross my eyes whenever he came by, something that would have earned me a slap from Mother had I done it to anyone else. He used the same ineffectual line on Mother every time he saw her, claiming he knew nothing of art, but certainly had an eye for beauty. I heard this phrase now and imagined the wink that followed, with the sideways tilt of his head, his sausage-like finger tapping his cheek, and the toothy smile that made his top lip disappear into his moustache till he looked like a happy beaver.

'Well then,' came Mother's reply, 'you may want to hang this great beauty on your wall, she's only eighty rand.'

That's how Mother sold at least one painting every market day.

There were no other familiar voices that day, and by the time I crawled out from my secure cave, most of the vegetables were sold. I looked over to Tannie Hettie's stall and was disappointed to see that all her fruit, with the exception of a packet of dried bananas, was gone. Dried bananas were not my favourite, but they were better than nothing and I hoped that there was no one left in the market who would want them. My hopes were dashed when the girl whose father owned the PEP store bought them for twenty cents. My thoughts returned to the toffee apple Papa had brought me, making my mouth water with regret that I'd eaten it so quickly.

The church bell chimed four o' clock and the stallholders packed up. Tannie Hettie sat in her folding chair, watching the proceedings silently. She had nothing left to pack, but seemed in no hurry to leave. Mother finished loading the van and nodded to Tannie Hettie, who stood up and folded her chair and handed it to Mother. All three of us squashed into the front of the van. I sat between them, wondering what had happened to Tannie Hettie's Morris. After a short drive we stopped outside a small white house. Tannie Hettie opened the van door and, in their usual manner, she and Mother nodded their goodbyes. Just before she slammed the door shut, she pressed a packet of sugared fruit into my hand.

MOTHER LIKED THE sound of her own voice and would talk to me endlessly, telling me stories or singing pop songs she heard on Springbok Radio, her eyes glinting manically as she pumped her arm up and down in a rendition of the latest top ten. But the day after market Mother was quiet. We worked silently side by side in the vegetable garden, me digging up soil with the red spade and bucket Papa had given me for my birthday, adding various quantities of water and earthworms in an experiment designed to discover the perfect consistency and texture for mud cakes. While I let the slick results run through my fingers, Mother dug loamy compost into new beds, and built miniature greenhouses out of sticks and thick plastic to protect her new seedlings from pillaging birds. The only sounds to pass her lips were grunts of exertion as she plunged the rusted iron fork into the ground.

With the day's work complete, Mother retired to the kitchen table, where she sat staring into space while her coffee cooled. Boesman whined and pawed at her feet; his nails left red welts on her pale skin. She hardly noticed. That lonely day turned into a lonely week, and every night we went to bed early, without stories, without fairies, and once, without dinner.

On Friday Mother snapped out of her melancholy mood. She became tense and nervous and went about the day's chores muttering to herself. On Saturday morning the knot in my stomach was so big I vomited my breakfast up behind the umbrella thorn, catching my arm on a hooked thorn. By nine that morning, Mother and I were both bathed and dressed in our Sunday best, usually reserved for visits to Ouma. Mother rouged her cheeks and applied waxy red lipstick, something I hardly ever saw her do. When the grandfather clock in the sitting room chimed eleven, we went to sit on the swing chair by the front door to wait for Papa. We waited in silence, squinting against the glare, trying to catch a glimpse of Papa's dust cloud. We broke our vigil only to use the toilet.

Lunchtime came and went and Mother gave me a sandwich. It sat on the plate, becoming crusty in the sun, the one bite I had managed a gaping wound in its side. The day dragged on and boredom replaced my earlier apprehension. I kicked at the ground, wishing I could take off my white, lacy socks and black church shoes. My feet were hot, and I thought my toes might catch fire if I was forced to wear them for much longer. I looked to Mother for a sign that we could give up this endless waiting and go change into something less stifling, but she just sat there, hardly moving, staring at the drive. Black marks formed under her eyes where her lashes bled their waxy coating on to her skin. Her rouged cheeks were smudged. Mother looked like she was melting in the heat.

At three o'clock she decided to drive into town to Tannie

Marie's house. Tannie Marie Bezuitenhoud was a thin bony woman who operated the telephone exchange switchboard at the post office. Our phone on the farm had not worked since the pole was struck by lightning the month before, and we were still waiting for the telephone men to come and fix it. Mother was hoping Papa had phoned and left her a message at the post office. If he had, Tannie Marie would know.

Mother said Tannie Marie was all sweet smiles to your face but was the biggest gossip in town. She listened in on everybody's conversations and was only too happy to be the first to spread a bit of bad news, even if it was nothing to do with her. As Mother parked the car in front of Tannie Marie's house, I wondered if she would give us bad news about Papa, and I imagined her smile that was all teeth and false sympathy.

Tannie Marie opened the door and looked surprised to see us. Mother faltered, and Tannie Marie didn't hesitate to invite us in. Since we were there, we couldn't refuse, and had to follow her down the dark hallway into the sitting room. Tannie Hettie sat in an olive-green velveteen armchair, opposite Tannie Hannah, who sat on the matching settee, taking up as much of it as Tannie Hettie did the armchair. Between them was a coffee table upon which was a pack of cards and two quart bottles of Lion lager. Half a milk tart wobbled in a silver pie dish. Tannie Hettie raised an eyebrow and nodded at Mother. Tannie Hannah called me to her side and I went willingly, expecting I would win a slice of milk tart for my effort, but she just pinched my cheeks, wiggling them back and forth between her meaty thumb and forefinger.

'Bella, the child has grown so much since I last saw her. Where have you been hiding?' she asked me without releasing my reddening cheek. I eyed my captor, taking in her polyester dress and noting that it matched her flushed cheeks. The dress was elasticized under her breasts, accentuating their magnificent proportions, but it left the rest of her disguised as a huge, satin-pink circus tent. Every exposed part of her fleshy skin was covered in tiny beads of sweat.

'Well, we've not seen you at the market recently,' replied Mother, giving her a look that conveyed her dislike of the huge woman. Tannie Hannah withdrew her smile and hand simultaneously.

'I've not got out much since the accident.' Tannie Hannah gestured to the bandage on her foot.

Mother eyed the bandage, but made no comment. Instead she turned to Tannie Marie. 'We can't stay long; I just dropped by to ask Hettie if she needed a lift to the market on Monday.'

Tannie Hettie shook her head slowly. 'No, my car is back from the panel beaters. Thank you for thinking of me.'

Tannie Hettie knew better than to pry for the true reason for Mother's visit, but Tannie Marie, with her sharp nose for scandal, was not going to let gossip pass her by that easily.

'I see you came in the van,' she said. 'One would think Marius would bring you in his fancy car, considering.'

Mother shot her a look that would have made a lesser woman wither, but Tannie Marie went on.

'Just last night I was watching TV. The President was on the news again, as if he doesn't have enough to do without having to make statements for the television. Running a country can't be easy.'

Tannie Hannah clucked her agreement.

'Seems there's been some trouble with the blacks in the townships again,' she went on, 'and more rioting in those independent homelands. There is talk of a state of emergency if this nonsense continues.'

Tannie Hannah shook her head and muttered something about the world and what was it coming to.

'I've always said that letting the blacks govern themselves was a bad idea. I'm only glad Mr Bezuitenhoud is not alive to see this country go to the dogs.'

Tannie Hannah nodded.

'And what has this to do with Marius's car?' Mother sighed.

'Well,' said Tannie Marie, 'a woman alone with a child should not be driving around too late, in this unstable climate.'

'Yes, so we must be going before it gets too late.' Mother took me by the hand and thanked Tannie Marie for her hospitality. Tannie Marie smiled woodenly and gestured towards the door. I was pleased to leave even though I had not had any milk tart.

Mother drove half the way home in silence. Then, as if she was talking to herself more than to me, she said, 'When we first came here I could tell those old bats would be trouble. They didn't like me from the beginning. I'm not from their precious little town. Worse, I'm not even an Afrikaner.'

I closed my eyes to the passing landscape and wondered about the state of emergency. What was the emergency and what did 'govern' mean? I thought about the blacks and about Moses. I thought of the whistles he had made me from the stems of pumpkin plants and I hoped he was not one of the blacks who were making trouble. I thought I might ask Papa if he knew the President, next time I saw him.

Chapter Four

A MONTH WENT BY, bringing autumn's cooler nights, and Papa still didn't come home. The day of my seventh birthday drew close and Mother said she would take me to the roadhouse in the next town for a Coke and ice-cream. I looked forward to it until I ran into Sannie du Toit. Sannie was two years older than me and a lot bigger. She had a mottled brown face covered in freckles with an upturned nose and she looked as if she would wrinkle like an old woman before she was twelve. The skin of her left arm was like melted pink plastic and she couldn't bend it at the elbow. Once, when I had tried to take a boiling pot of water off the stove, Mother had screamed and pulled me away, crying that I would end up like Sannie du Toit if I ever did anything so stupid again.

Now, as I deposited a letter in the postbox for Mother, listening to its hollow landing inside, she sneaked up behind me.

'Your daddy's got a fancy-woman,' she teased. I stood quietly for a while, pretending to ignore her, but she said it again, this time leaning in close over my shoulder so I could smell the meatiness of her breath.

'I said, your daddy's got a fancy-woman.' Tears bubbled up inside me, even though I wasn't sure what a fancy-woman was. I squirmed around, trying to escape her, but she blocked my way, pinning me against the postbox with her unbending arm.

'Look at the cry-baby,' she taunted, and I saw that she was not alone. A group of girls in their checked green school dresses lined up behind her. Sannie pushed up against me, bending slightly so her face was level with mine, our noses almost touching.

'Your daddy's run off and left you.'

'No.' I tried to push her away.

'Oh yes.' She grinned. 'Met some fancy-woman at the roadhouse, prettier than your ugly mother.'

'No,' I repeated, blinking back angry tears. As if I could make her words disappear just by saying no.

The other girls were laughing now, mimicking me:

'No, no, no.'

I looked from Sannie's scrunched-up face to the jeering faces of the other girls. Some girls I didn't know but a few I recognized from the market, all taunting me with the words 'fancy-woman' and 'cry-baby' and 'no, no, no'. Hatred boiled inside me and I reached out and grabbed one of Sannie's tightly bound plaits and jerked it as hard as I could. She screamed and pulled away, clutching her head, giving me enough space to slip under her grotesque arm. I ran down Kerk Street towards the market without looking back to see if they were following me. I didn't stop until I was safely hidden under our trestle table.

On the day of my seventh birthday I sat alone in the red booth, sucking on the dregs of my Coke. The roadhouse was quiet; nobody noticed me. The blonde cashier sat behind her till reading a women's magazine and blowing chewing-gum bubbles. They burst with a popping sound, leaving a transparent film around her waxy pink lips, which she cleaned away deftly with her tongue. Once in a while she adjusted the banana clip that held her frizzy hair away from her face. Peering over the booth I could just see her pink leatherette skirt. My Coke was finished and I sucked up the stale meltwater from between the shrinking ice cubes with a gurgling slurp.

Mother had gone to the toilet, and I waited impatiently for her to come back. She had been gone a while, it seemed like hours, and I was beginning to worry that she might be feeling ill. She had told me not to go anywhere and to be good while she was gone, kissing me on the forehead. I was becoming restless. I edged closer to the window and got up on to my knees so I could see out. There were a few cars in the parking lot, a white car like Papa's and a smaller blue car which we had parked next to, but Mother's van wasn't there. I strained my neck to try look further around the side of the parking lot. Maybe the blue car had moved or there was another blue car. Panic began to beat a drum inside me. I sat back down in the booth and looked at the front desk. The blonde cashier still had her head buried inside the magazine. I looked at the back wall of the roadhouse. There were three doors. One swung open and a uniformed waitress emerged, carrying a tray and the sizzle of fat out with her. The door on the far left had a black sign with the picture of a white stick man on it, and the one on the right had a similar figure that had a triangle instead of thighs.

I slipped out of the booth and made my way to the right

door. It was heavy and it took some effort for me to push it open. I went in and the door closed slowly behind me, held in check by a metal arm. The roadhouse toilet was cool and tiled to the ceiling in white. Three stalls with doors that didn't reach the ground faced three white basins and a large mirror. All three doors were closed. 'Ma,' I whispered. There was no reply. The only sound was my ragged breathing, amplified by the sterile tiles. Taking a huge gulp of air I bent down to look under the doors. I didn't see any feet so I pushed them open one by one, just to make sure. Maybe she'd gone back to the booth and I had missed her because I was in the toilet. This idea brought some relief, until I discovered that it was easier to push the door open from the outside than it was to pull it from the inside. The handle was round and slippery, too big for me to grasp properly. I couldn't turn it with both hands and pull the door at the same time. I was trapped. I stood staring at the door, willing it to open. It didn't.

The Coke had worked its way through me and I needed to pee. I sat on one of the toilets and, as soon as my hot stream of pee stopped, tears started. I'd been abandoned and now I was a prisoner in the toilet. With my pants around my ankles I sobbed until I hiccuped. Crying made me tired so, still sitting on the toilet, I leaned against the partition and closed my eyes.

A toilet flushed. As quick as I could I pulled up my pants, and was out of the stall in time to catch the closing door with my hands and a foot before it sealed me in again. I was free, but the roadhouse was almost empty and Mother wasn't there. My glass had been cleared away and a man with greasy hair sat in the booth where we had been. I looked around.

There were booths at the back of the restaurant and I could wait there without being seen. I climbed into a corner booth, hunching down into it to make sure nobody tried to serve me. At once I felt invisible and this made me a little less afraid. I didn't want to believe Mother had left me for good.

I looked into the yellow beams of afternoon sun that shone through the window, warming the vinyl seat. I closed my eyes and the light made coloured patterns on the backs of my eyelids. Swirling reds swimming in black waters. Keeping my eyes closed, I latched my fingers on to the underside of the table. It felt rough and splintered and pulpy. I stretched out and dragged my fingertips gently along the table's underbelly, gliding over the hard lumps of chewing gum that lined the joints, some smoothed by fingers pressing them in, others jagged with teeth marks. I drifted on the sounds of the roadhouse. Snatches of muffled conversation, the clatter of falling cutlery, the sizzle of burgers on the grill. The thought that I might be here for ever no longer seemed so bad. I contemplated a secret life in the back of the roadhouse kitchen, eating leftover burgers and having unlimited access to the Coke machine. I'd pretend to be a normal customer by day and always sit in the same booth. Then one day, when I was old enough, I would apply for a job in the kitchen.

My dreaming was interrupted by a firm shake. I opened my eyes and realized my face was stuck to the red plastic. It sucked on to my skin as I turned my head, leaving my cheek smarting from the separation.

'Little girl, it's closing time.'

I looked up into the cold blue eyes of the blonde cashier. I stared at her, confused.

'Where's your ma?' she asked, shaking me a little as if I hadn't heard her. I opened my mouth to answer but my tongue stuck to the top of my mouth. Nothing came out.

'Hey, what's wrong with you? Cat got your tongue? You deaf or something?' She sucked air through her teeth. 'Ag, for God's sake, come.' She pulled me by the arm, her long pink nails digging into my skin.

She dragged me to the cashier's desk and picked up the phone. 'Wait there,' she said, 'an' don' touch anything.'

I stood in front of the desk, rocking back and forth. It seemed to take for ever for her to dial the number. Her long pink nails rotated the dial one way and then let it revolve all the way back with a whirr and a click. Once dialled she hooked the black receiver between her ear and shoulder and examined her hands. When she finally spoke her voice was high and agitated. My ears rang and my arm smarted where her nails had dug into me, leaving bright red half-moons. After a while she replaced the receiver and came out from behind the desk. Taking hold of my arm again, she steered me towards the door.

'Listen,' she said in a loud voice as she manoeuvred me out of the door into the biting night air, 'my boyfriend's coming to fetch me, then we'll take you to the police station. Maybe you'll talk to the police, hmm?'

When I didn't respond she shook her head and let go of my arm to lock the door.

'Fuck.' She held up her hand, revealing a dismembered nail. She looked over at me and I realized it was stuck in my arm. Disgusted, I brushed it off.

'You stupid brat.' Pushing me aside, she bent to pick it

up. She wrapped the pink talon in a tissue and put it in her bag.

'Look what you did.' She held out her hand for me to see. I couldn't believe that she blamed me as I looked at the thick yellowed claw that tipped her middle finger. It looked like the nail on Ouma's big toe. I wrinkled my nose.

'Why you little . . .' she said and she swatted me. At that moment I would rather be caught by Tit Tit Tay than stick around with this crazy woman. I ran. Ducking underneath her flying pink nails, I escaped into the parking lot. I didn't get far before I felt the strong jerk of her hand on my collar, snapping me back so hard that her knuckles bruised the back of my head.

At that moment a car pulled into the parking lot, blinding me with its headlights. I was terrified and trapped. I couldn't escape the pink witch and now someone new had arrived to torment me. I burst into tears, hoping this would make her feel bad enough to stop hurting me, but she just shook me. Then I remembered Sannie du Toit. Three weeks earlier she had tried to steal a packet of sugared fruit from Tannie Hettie's stall. Tannie Hettie had grabbed her by the collar and given her a good shake, at which point Sannie let out a scream so loud the entire market turned around to look. Tannie Hettie let go and Sannie had run off clutching the fruit.

I screamed. A wailing scream that would have made a banshee proud. She let go and I bolted, straight into a man's arms. Without looking up I kicked at my new attacker as hard as I could, squirming round to try to loosen his grip. But he just pulled me closer until his arms surrounded me and my face was pushed up against his chest. He smelled of day-old sweat and stale Van Dijk cigarillos, a smell so familiar it shocked the fight out of me.

'Just like your mother,' he murmured.

I STARED OUT of the window of Papa's green Ford Cortina, watching the cats' eyes as they lit up the curves of the road. My mind was full of questions. Who was the woman? Was she a witch? Had she cast a spell on Papa? Was a fancy-woman the same thing as a witch? Papa said nothing. He just sighed and looked at me with sad eyes.

Finally, as we drove up the dark dirt road to the farm, he said, 'Don't believe everything your mother tells you, Faith. You're too young to understand what's going on, just don't believe her.'

Chapter Five

THE HOUSE WAS dark when we arrived. A black silhouette against a black night lit only by the sliver of a new moon. The cacophony of bush insects fell silent as we picked our way carefully past them towards the stoep, resuming in the darkness behind us when we reached the front door.

It was locked. Papa rapped his knuckles sharply against its worn wooden surface. Our front door was sturdy, made from old railway sleepers, thick and capable of absorbing bullets. Often I'd run my fingers over the two embedded in its surface, trying to re-enact in my imagination just what had caused them to be there. I'd once overheard Papa telling Oom Piet that the previous farmer had gone mad on the day his wife gave birth to their first child, a child so dark it might well have been a kaffir. The farmer had gone on a rampage, shooting all his labourers before turning the gun on his wife and then, finally, himself. The baby was the sole survivor. Papa said it was thanks to that kaffir baby that he got the farm for next to nothing. Oom Piet laughed and said it was probably nothing more than a touch of the tar brush.

I spent hours running my fingers over the weather-worn wood, imagining kaffir babies. Pitch-black babies with sticky treacle skin and hot breath that stank of tar. Babies with small protuberant tails or puff-adder scales instead of hair. Babies so hideous they could drive you mad just to look at them.

'Dammit.' Papa rubbed his knuckles in the palm of his hand. The thick door absorbed his rapping and left his knuckles red. He kicked the door with the tip of his shoe. Nothing. His nostrils flared and he turned and rapped sharply on the nearest window.

'Bella!'

A distant jackal barked in reply, a yipping howl that made my breath catch. Dark nights were mischief nights on the farm. Fairies would be out and I imagined them moving towards us. Dark figures shifting in the shadows of the trees, disguising themselves as gnarled growths against the trunks until the wind rustled the leaves. I pressed myself closer to Papa's leg, kneading the fabric of his trousers in my clammy palms.

'Bella!' Louder this time. A shout. Papa banged on the window pane with his fist. It rattled in anger. The insects stopped singing. The vibrating glass whined and then nothing.

Papa exhaled sharply through his nose. 'Wait here, Faith,' he muttered, pulling my hands away from his leg. I looked up at him with wide eyes and shook my head. I did not want to be left in the dark alone. I opened my mouth to protest but he cut me short. 'I'll only be a minute.'

I watched him make his way along the front of the house and disappear around the side. I was alone. The sound of millions of beetles rubbing their legs together had stopped as he moved through them and had still not resumed. I stood staring at the dark surface of the front door, feeling the hot prickle of eyes from the darkness behind me. My ears buzzed with the effort of reaching for sounds of movement. I knew they were there, hiding in the shadows, coming ever closer. Dark fairies. Dead Rex. A chill trickled down the back of my neck like the winter breath of a water spirit.

'Please open, please open, please open,' I whispered.

Something crashed from the side of the house where Papa had gone, making the hair all over my body stand up. Panic heaved up from the pit of my stomach. The fairies. They'd got Papa. Leaves crunched behind me. I tried to force myself to turn around, but I was stiff with fright. They were coming. Only my eyes listened to my desperate signals to turn around; they felt like they were about to pop with the effort to see around my immobile head.

The click of the front-door latch brought my eyes swinging forward. Papa stood in the doorway, his white shirt the only point of light in the dark pit of the hallway.

'There's broken glass,' he explained, stooping down. I latched my arms around his neck and clung to him in relief. He turned into the house and as he did so I looked over his shoulder out into the night. Nothing moved.

Slowly we picked our way down the passage towards the kitchen. Holding me in one arm, Papa patted a way along the wall with his free hand. At the first doorway he felt for the round brass light switch and flicked it. It didn't work.

'Bella,' he shouted, 'for God's sake, this isn't funny.'

No reply.

'Stupid fucking bitch,' he muttered.

Papa made his way through the dark farmhouse, flicking light switches. None worked. Progress was slow, it was impossible to tell how far we'd gone in the dark and only a bump told us we'd reached the end of the passage and the kitchen door was closed. It was never closed.

Papa kicked the door. It swung open and suddenly I felt like I was balanced on the edge of a precipice. 'The step,' I whispered, almost to myself and a moment too late. We twisted into the dark kitchen, unbalanced by the short drop. Papa clutched me tightly with both arms, protecting my head in one hand. We bumped against the kitchen table, sending objects crashing to the floor. Almost instantly the kitchen came alive; it was as if we had woken the devil by the banging of pots and pans. A shape unfolded from underneath Papa's feet, squealing and yelping, and then, with a wet snarl, it lunged. Papa roared and kicked at it, but that only seemed to aggravate it more. We fell backwards into the range, and my elbow connected with the cold metal, making it zing. I screamed and Papa shouted words that he'd only ever muttered under his breath. Panic pushed up and out of me in a piercing shriek.

A crack as loud as thunder silenced us. I clamped my hands over my ears to hold out the noise. The monster that was attacking Papa jerked against us and then dropped, its snarling snatched away in the noiseless vacuum that followed. For a moment we stood, frozen against each other, then Papa fell to the floor and pushed me under the table.

'Lie still,' he rasped in my ear, clamping his hand over my mouth. I twitched, overcome by terror. The stink of sulphur and the tang of copper mixed in my nostrils in a darkness so black I couldn't make out which way I was facing.

Someone moved in the kitchen. I heard an uneven scrape which I recognized as the kitchen drawer opening. Something clicked and the bright beam of a torch arced round the kitchen, stopping on where Papa and I lay huddled under the table. I blinked, my eyes watering at the sudden light. For a long moment it held us in its gaze. Papa lay beside me, his body stiff.

'Are you bitten?' The tremulous voice belonged to Mother. 'This rabies outbreak . . .' She trailed off as if waiting for someone else to speak. 'I hoped it was Billary, should've known when he wouldn't drink.' She stood for a moment, swinging the torch from Papa to me. Neither of us moved.

'I need to fix the generator, you've probably noticed the power's out,' she said finally before she turned and left through the open back door.

I followed the path of the torch through the kitchen window as she made her way to the generator shed. After a while Papa got up, hitting his head on the kitchen table as he tried to stand. He walked to door and stood there awhile, reaching out with both hands to steady himself against the lintel. He cut a dark hole in the brighter darkness of the outside night. Standing there with his head lowered, the shape he made reminded me of the picture of Jesus carrying a cross I'd seen at Ouma's church. Then Papa stepped into the yard and was gone.

I lay on the kitchen floor, letting the cold seep into me until my ragged breathing stopped and I couldn't hear my heartbeat in my head any more. Careful not to hit my head on the table, I picked my way across the kitchen and sat down on the step at the back door. The light of a paraffin lamp filtered through the joins in the corrugated-iron walls of the generator shed. I could just make out the hushed tones of my parents.

I sat on the step, stretching my jersey over my knees.

'Boesman,' I whispered, hoping he would come and I wouldn't have to be alone in the dark. I thought I heard a whine behind me and I looked over my shoulder into the kitchen, thinking of the monster that had attacked us. Nothing moved.

Their voices became louder.

I tugged at my jersey, listening to their angry words intermingling with metallic noises. 'Lousy fucking mother,' and then the clang of a hammer. My fingers found a knot in the rough wool and I picked at it. 'Stupid to break in' was cut short by a coughing splutter as the generator kicked briefly into life and then died again to 'You fucking left her.' I rocked on the step, worrying the knot with the fingers of both hands.

'She's your bloody child!' Mother's voice shrieked. 'Your whore no good with kids?' The knot came undone and my busy fingers pulled at the two threads, separating them. The generator coughed and roared into life, drowning out their voices and throwing dull yellow light into the yard. I took a deep shuddering breath and tugged the threads.

My father's voice rose above the din of the generator, sharp and accusatory. 'That's it. I can't fucking do this any more. You fired a gun at your own child.' The stitches that held my jersey together began to unravel.

They screamed at each other, yelling at the same time. I clamped my hands over my ears, trying to block out the din until suddenly, it stopped. The quiet echoed, making me feel hollow and cold inside.

Finally, when it seemed a black hole would swallow me, Papa said, 'I'll send money.'

'Fuck you, Marius,' came Mother's reply a second before

Papa stumbled backwards out of the shed, doubled over and holding his temple. I didn't notice Mother, standing in the doorway holding a large spanner, until Papa stood upright.

His face contorted with rage, he walked towards her, one hand reaching out, as if trying to placate her. Mother didn't move and for a long time they stood, a foot apart, staring at each other, saying nothing. I could see a bright red trickle tracing its way down Papa's face, dripping off his chin on to his shirt, where red flowers bloomed on the white cotton. Finally he placed one hand on her shoulder and, leaning into her, he whispered in her ear. Then he pulled back and with one quick flow he punched her squarely in the face.

Chapter Six

I NOTICED THE LARGE grey lizard on the bottom step as I perched outside the kitchen door. It lay sunning itself, mouth open exposing a fat tongue, lazy in the morning sun. Now that I had joined it, it was alert, poised to dart away. I sat still, pretending I hadn't seen it. Catching lizards was a game that took patience. If I moved too soon, it would be away before I could reach it and quickly disappear into a hole or run up the wall out of reach. I waited, watching it out of the corner of my eye. Neither of us moved. Slowly my stillness and the warm sun began to lull the lizard. Almost imperceptibly it relaxed, and that was the moment. Before it had time to remember me, my hand shot out and closed over it. I felt a wriggle as the lizard fled awkwardly. Turning my closed hand upwards, I unclasped my fingers and watched the lizard's thick grey tail jerk on my grubby palm. As its life waned my eyes flicked to the generator shed. I couldn't help thinking of Papa and the way he had left us.

The sound of his fist connecting with her face was hard and soft, like chopping watermelon. She flew into the door of the shed, making the whole building shake. He lunged for her.

'No, Papa!' I shrieked.

He spun round, the snarl on his face drained to pale disbelief.

'Oh God.' The words choked him, and he took a few steps towards me, shaking his head. 'No, Faith, please God, no.'

I screamed and the sound hit him in the chest and when I stopped screaming Papa looked empty. He backed away from me, pulling at his hand as if trying to rid himself of some constricting cuff. Finally he jerked free and flung his hand forward, throwing something away. Then he disappeared into the dark.

I shook the memory off and blinked into the sun, my eyes tracing the arced trajectory imagined by my mind and settling on a sharp glint that made my eyes water. I stared at it for a while before I pocketed the lizard's tail and picked my way across the yard towards it.

A ring lay in the dirt close to the generator shed, like some pirate's forgotten treasure. I sat down on my haunches, hovering over it, and cleared a circle in the dirt around it with the side of my hand. It was a thick silver ring, with a raised wavy pattern. I perched over it for a short time. I thought of Papa, of the many evenings we had sat on the swing chair, watching the sun go down, Papa showing me birds, or stars as it got darker, the ring part of his hand as he pointed out constellations. I reached out and stroked it, it glowed with sun-warmth. I picked it up and held it in my open palm, feeling its weight, moving my hand up and down, testing its power. I traced my finger along the rim, and then the pattern. Some sort of magic intertwined in the pattern, I thought. I held it up to look through it, thinking the world on the other side might be one of fairies, but it looked the same. There was writing inside, tiny numbers. I closed my hand around the ring and, squeezing it tightly, I looked inside the shed.

I was not allowed near the generator by myself and usually the door was shut and padlocked. After Papa had gone I had sat on the steps, shivering and crying and tugging fitfully at my jersey.

'Ma.' I was so afraid she was dead. Eventually I got up and approached the shed on wobbly legs. I stood at the door and peered on tiptoes over the hulking generator. From behind it came a snuffling noise and I crept round to see what it was. Mother lay, propped up against the back wall, her body twisted away from me. Her chest heaved, sending little shudders through her. Mother was crying. I had never seen her cry before. She didn't cry when they phoned to say Grandma English was dead, or when Papa dropped the cake we baked for the competition in the church hall, or even when Papa left to go on the road. Seeing her cry made my stomach twist. I stared at her, unsure of myself. I considered reaching out and ruffling her hair and saying 'Don't be a cry-baby,' the way she did to me, but it didn't seem right. I chewed my bottom lip and started to back away slowly, my eyes glued to her. Mother turned and looked up at me through puffy eyes. Her face looked soft and slack. One side of her face was swollen, and blood mixed with snot on her upper lip. I felt sick. Black dots swam in from the edges of my vision, landing on my face with prickly legs, then went up my nostrils and filled my mouth. Mother's broken face bobbed between the dots and I slid downwards. Everything went black. I struggled to breathe; it felt like there was a heavy weight on my chest. Someone lifted me up and I felt myself moving. The smell of sulphur and copper stung my nose. I forced my eyelids apart, my vision rolled, a congealing red pool, sharp yellow teeth, a lolling tongue. Eyes, gelatinous and murky, stared up at me. I pulled away from the ghoulish sight and slipped into darkness.

The memories from the previous night filled the generator shed and I didn't want to be there any more. The ring had begun to feel heavy and sad and I didn't want to hold it now. I dropped it in my pocket with the lizard's tail and went to find Mother.

I found her at the bottom of the garden, up to her waist in a hole. The dust from her digging formed a film over the world, tingeing it red. I cut sideways glances at her, taking in her damaged face. Sweat trickled down her cheeks, leaving gleaming pathways like snail trails.

Her face was now divided into two sides, her profiles different people. One side was smooth and flawless, her tanned skin offset by her thick white hair. One eye, cold and blue, looked out at the world, alert as ever. Even her nose, bruised by the punch, seemed sharper on that side. On the other side, her face was so swollen that her eye was forced almost completely shut. That would have been better, I thought, than the seeping slit between the blackened eyelids. Her usual glowing skin was now an array of turgid hues. A blood-blister black fading to a stormy purple in the most swollen parts, making the rest of her tanned skin look liver-yellow. Her upper lip was like an overripe plum, its skin split by pecking birds.

Behind Mother a large lumpen shape lay wrapped in a faded blue mattress blanket. A dark patch seeped through the rough fibres. My fingers moved across the blanket, over the patch, towards the fold, my curiosity itching to expose whatever lay inside.

'Leave it,' Mother barked. I snatched my hand back.

'It's ugly, you don't want to look,' she said more gently, 'come away, come sit here.' She lifted the gardening fork with both hands and pointed to the other side of the grave, away from the dead monster wrapped in blue.

Watching her was boring so I wandered back to the house, to the kitchen, hoping to gather clues on what devil lay wrapped in the blanket. When I'd woken up that morning everything was normal. There was no sign that anything had happened the night before. The pots and pans sat innocently on the shelf, the kitchen table was planted squarely in the middle of the room. The floor was clean, freshly scrubbed, uncluttered.

I dragged a chair up to the wall and climbed up to get a closer look at the pots. Picking up each heavy pot with effort and balancing precariously, I turned it slowly around in my hands. One had a dent in the side, but it was an old pot, scuffed, its silver surface beaten back to a leaden dullness. I remembered that Mother had dropped it on her foot once, making her so angry she had cursed it and thrown it into the back yard where it spun noisily in protest before settling stubbornly just outside the door, heavy and handleless and no longer perfectly round.

I climbed down and went to the old range. Mother cooked on the newer gas oven and I couldn't remember it ever being used. Papa had wanted to throw it out, but Mother had said that it gave the kitchen some old-world charm and, though Papa scoffed, the range stayed. It squatted, black and angry, ready to leap out and crush me. A witches' oven. I edged towards it. When I was certain it wasn't about to move, I grabbed the handle and with an effort that strained every muscle in my arm, I pulled it down. The door swung open with a dull *clunk*, revealing a dark cavern that echoed ominously. I peered inside, my heart pounding. Fear crawled up my neck and on to my skull. The inky blackness swelled and shrank towards me. Quickly I shut the door and forced the latch back down. The devil that lay dead at the bottom of the garden had come from the range, of that I was sure.

By the time I returned to the dig, Mother stood staring at a fresh mound. She'd placed a rock at the head of the grave, I presumed to keep the ghoul inside from escaping. On it, in white paint, she had painted symbols, a magic I could not understand, but I traced them with my fingers just the same, to reinforce the magic.

Chapter Seven

'WHERE IS BOESMAN?' I asked Mother that night over a supper of toast and rooibos tea.

She looked at me with a furrowed brow for a while. 'What do you mean?' she asked, shaking her head. Eventually she sighed, 'He's gone, Faith. God's taken him. Do you understand?'

I nodded slowly, absorbing this new information. Boesman was gone, like Papa was gone. Taken by God. I had formed a vague idea about God from the limited religious education I had received from visits to Ouma's church, which was the house of God, according to Ouma. It was quite an ugly house, I thought, with its A-frame steeple, thick, frosted orange glass windows and new brick facade. I remembered it as cold and smelling of old books. What God wanted with our dog I couldn't fathom, but I was sure it must be something to do with God's will. Whenever I asked Ouma why something was so, she said it was God's will. I'd learned the hard way that you weren't to question God's will.

I was still pondering God's will when Mother said it was time for bed and went, leaving me sitting alone at the kitchen table with my unfinished toast. She always told me it was rude to leave the table before everyone finished eating, but I didn't take her up on it. I took another bite of cold toast and chewed slowly until it became spongy and stuck to the top of my mouth in a saliva-glued lump. It made a sucking sound as I dislodged it with my tongue. I swallowed slowly, willing it to go down without feeling its texture. I didn't want to see what it would look like if it came back up.

I tipped the rest of the toast into the bin and tiptoed down the passage, stopping outside Mother's door. A slice of light escaped through the bottom. I could just make out snuffling noises, the same ones she had made in the generator shed. They made me feel uneasy, so I slipped into my room and shut the door behind me.

Once I was sure Mother wasn't going to come in, or make me open the door, I took Papa's ring out of my pocket. I sat on the bed, rolling it between my thumb and forefinger, wondering why he had tossed it in the sand. I had only ever seen Papa with this ring, and when I pictured him without it, he no longer seemed to belong to us. His long tanned fingers, with patches of golden blond hair, stained yellow from the Van Dijks, were a stranger's without the ring.

I looked around my room for somewhere to hide it. My room was sparse. The bed had a sprung base of interconnecting metal links on which the mattress rested. The ring would fall through them if I hid it under there. Other than a small dresser and wooden rocking chair, passed down from Grandma English when I was born, upon which King Elvis, my worn bear, sat, there was only a wooden tomato box for my toys, and a brown corrugated-board suitcase Papa had bought me when I turned six. He had meant for me to carry my schoolbooks in it, but I had not gone to school that year – we couldn't afford the school uniform and Mother was too proud to ask the school for a second-hand charity one, so I had to wait until the following year when we had more money. I wondered, now that I was seven, when I would be enrolled.

The suitcase contained an assortment of treasures I'd gathered over the year. Half a sheep's jaw, most of the teeth intact, which I had found in the park opposite the town hall; a tiny, speckled brown bird's egg, unhatched, fallen from a nest; a collection of bottle tops from every soda I'd drunk that year, Coca-Cola, Fanta, Cream Soda and some Pine Nut, not my favourite; two Van Dijk cigarillos, with lighter, which I had stolen off the kitchen table when Papa wasn't looking; a discarded weaver's nest, not good enough for the mother bird but good enough for me; and an assortment of pebbles, feathers and acorns with hat, some of which I had dug three holes into with a nail to represent eyes and an exclaiming mouth.

I placed the ring in the suitcase and closed it. Then I opened it again. The ring seemed conspicuous so I rearranged everything to cover it up. Still it seemed to stand out from my other treasures. Someone would surely find it if they opened the suitcase. I picked up the weaver's nest, and gently, like I was putting a baby bird to sleep, I placed the ring inside. Hovering over the suitcase I examined the contents, adjusting the angle of the nest three times before I was satisfied the ring wouldn't be found. Then I closed the lid and fastened the metal latches before I slid it carefully under the bed.

Three weeks later, as I tried to light up one of my treasured Van Dijks for the first time, Tannie Hettie arrived in her

Morris. I knew that Mother was not going to come out of her room and I'd hidden around the side of the house. I was so focused on the process of rolling the wheel of the lighter back with enough force for the flame to catch that I didn't notice her presence until she smacked me on the back of the head, sending the cigarillo that was clutched between my pursed lips flying. It landed in the dirt and lay there for a few seconds, guilty, before she crushed it, grinding it into the ground with the ball of her foot.

'And what do you think you're doing?'

I stared at her thick ankles, my face burning with shame. I couldn't think of a single excuse; there was nothing I could say to make myself seem innocent. I braced myself for the hiding I knew was coming, so it caught me off guard when she sighed and pulled me close to her, enveloping my head in a tight embrace. I had never touched Tannie Hettie before, other than an accidental brushing against her, and I was surprised at how soft she felt. I'd always thought that she would be hard to touch, like wood.

'Where's your ma?' she asked, suddenly letting me go and looking away.

'I don't know,' I mumbled in reply. 'I think she's in her room.'

Mother had taken to spending afternoons in her room with the door shut. All the daily farm chores that had been our routine went undone. Even the vegetable garden had been set upon by birds, something I pointed out to her one morning as she sat on the swing chair. She had looked at me as if from some faraway place. 'What's that, Faith?' she asked me and I repeated myself. 'Vegetable garden,' she echoed and nodded. I thought then she had understood, but now as I led Tannie Hettie past the neglected patch it was obvious she hadn't. The thick plastic sheeting she'd so carefully secured had blown off, leaving her seedlings exposed. What the birds hadn't pillaged, the sun had destroyed. Older plants wilted and drooped, their fruit overripe. It was like Mother had gone to bed the night after Papa left and never properly woken up.

A wave of shame ran through me as I opened the kitchen door and the stink of unwashed dishes and rancid milk rushed out to greet us. Tannie Hettie's face wrinkled in distaste and I hesitated, thinking I should've told her Mother was out. Mother wouldn't want anybody to see the house like this and I was sure she'd be angry at me for letting Tannie Hettie in. Guests on the farm were rare, but when they were expected Mother rushed around, beating cushions and arranging flowers. As if she had read my mind, Tannie Hettie gestured with the tilt of her head that I should stay outside and went in alone. She didn't come out until the sun had set.

Chapter Eight

THE NEXT MORNING as I watched the dust trail Tannie Hettie's Morris kicked up, I thought about her fearful words from the night before.

'Your ma's sick.'

I'd felt like I was on a swing, grasping for a handhold while I flew back and forth, about to fall off. Papa and Boesman had gone and now Mother was sick. She didn't look sick. She wasn't covered in spots like I had been when I'd had chickenpox, she wasn't scratching, sneezing or blowing her nose. Her illness was mysterious and the thought of it made my hands clammy. Mother didn't get sick.

'She needs somebody to take care of you.'

Usually, this meant Ouma, and the thought of spending a long period of time in Ouma's care brought me to the edge of a tearful protest. I always had to be clean at Ouma's house in case I dirtied the furniture, and I wasn't allowed to touch anything. She would make me bathe every night and wash my hair and, unlike Mother, she always got soap in my eyes, leaving me steaming and blind. She read to me from the Bible and made me recite passages from it after her, and she lost patience when I couldn't remember the names of

Bible people. Even though I was a little afraid of Tannie Hettie, I was prepared to kick up a fuss to prevent being sent to Ouma.

Sensing my distress, Tannie Hettie placed a hand on my shoulder.

'Ag, it's not so bad my child, you'll like Nomsa.'

THE HUM OF the Morris's cooling fan kicking to life brought me back from my thoughts. I peered out of the sitting-room window, my breath leaving mist circles on the glass as I exhaled. A sharp white blade of light reflected off the car window, obscuring my view of the passenger in the back seat. The driver's door swung open and Tannie Hettie heaved herself out. She stopped to smooth her rumpled skirt before looking up at the house. Her eyes scanned the front stoep and stopped at the window I thought concealed me in a web of reflective lace. She nodded, a gesture of greeting I knew all to well and one that made me shrink back, startled at being caught out in my game of peek-a-boo. I'd waited at the window since I'd woken up and planned not to answer the door when she came. I wanted to watch them from the safety of the sitting room and I hoped that they would think we weren't home and leave. Then there was a chance things could go back to the way they were.

I took a deep breath and slid down off the back of the couch. My heart knocked in my chest as I undid the latch on the front door and opened it slightly. I stood, for a moment undecided, then retreated down the passage and into the kitchen. I looked around, my eyes scanning the mess before settling on a cup. I filled it with water and sat down at the kitchen table, hoping they would think I had been occupied in the kitchen and if asked I could deny being at the window, I could blame one of the fairies. At the sound of the front door being pushed open I lifted the cup to my mouth and took a small sip. I held it at my lips until Tannie Hettie stood in the kitchen doorway looking at me, then I drained it and turned towards them.

A young black woman stood just to the side of Tannie Hettie, and although she bent her head downwards, her eyes looked up and she was smiling. Her teeth were luminous in the shadowy passageway, floating in the depth of her dark face. I stared, so absorbed by their whiteness that I forgot Tannie Hettie even though she partly obscured my view of the strange woman.

'Faith, Tannie Hannah needs me to drive her to the doctor so I can't stay. Show Nomsa to her room, I must go.'

I blinked at Tannie Hettie as she turned and left, watching the space where she had been until I heard the front-door latch click shut. We were alone. Nomsa stepped out into the kitchen and placed the worn bag she was carrying on the floor. On top of the bag, between the brown plastic handles, was a short straw broom, bound by coloured plastic wire. I eyed her from my seat, taking in her faded brown skirt, gathered at the side and pinned with a large safety pin, and her T-shirt, greyed from too many washes. In contrast her brown skin glowed with an oily sheen and her eyes were like a bird's, the irises so dark I couldn't see her pupils. Her hair was tightly plaited against her head and the plaits made circular patterns on her scalp. She held out her hand to me.

I'd seen Papa and Oom Piet greet each other with a handshake whenever they saw each other, but it was not something I'd seen anyone other than men do. I put the cup down and stood up, wiping my hand on my shirt. I imagined I was Papa and stuck my hand out stiffly. She clasped it in her cool dry palm, then swiftly moved to make a fist around my thumb. I looked up at her, surprised. Papa had never done that.

'It is an African handshake, mosetsana. Like this. Shake, fist, shake.' We shook again.

'You are Faith?' I nodded, still unable to take my eyes off our hands. 'It is a lucky name.'

She let go, and without our hands to focus on, I looked at her shoes. They were closed black shoes, the kind Sannie wore with her school uniform, but Nomsa's were dusty and scuffed and she had no white socks to roll down into sausages around her ankles.

'You must show me my room, mosetsana,' she said. I looked at her blankly, unsure of which room I was meant to show her. We only had two rooms in the house, mine and Mother's. I decided that my room was probably the best option because once, when Ouma had come to visit, she had slept in my room and I had slept with Mother and Papa in their bed. I wasn't keen to give up my room to Nomsa but I didn't see any other option. I sighed and nodded.

'You can have my room,' I mumbled.

She smiled. 'Thank you, mosetsana, that is very kind of you, but where do the servants sleep?'

I shrugged. We didn't have any servants.

'Is there a room outside?' she prompted.

I nodded. 'Moses' room,' I said, brightened by the idea that she would sleep outside. 'He's not here any more, the Tokoloshe took him away.'

Nomsa's face creased into a frown, and suddenly I relished the idea of showing her the room from which Moses had disappeared.

I opened the decrepit door of Moses' old room and took a sniff of its musty interior. The dank room sucked the yellow out of the light and turned it into a milky grey in which the sparse furnishings seemed to float. I stepped aside, allowing Nomsa a look at the old metal bed which was raised off the floor on rusty paint tins. The mattress sagged in the middle where it remembered Moses. She stepped inside, business-like, taking the straw broom and leaving her bag at the door. She pushed the short curtains aside to reveal a small window, which she opened. Then she brought the broom down sharply on to the bed, sending up a dust storm that tickled my sinuses and made my eyes water. I left her to it.

Soon Nomsa had removed the contents of the room, with the exception of the metal bed frame, and they stood sunning themselves in the back yard. The mattress was propped up against the wall, an offcut of carpet that served as a rug hung over the washing line ready for a beating, and the bedside cupboard seemed poised to run off on short legs. A pale green tin stove held my attention for a moment as I twiddled the only knob, releasing fumes that made me dizzy.

Bored by the contents of the room, I sat on the kitchen step. The *shup-shup* sound of straw on concrete floated out of the room, mixing with a rhythmic singing Nomsa had struck up. The warmth of the sun and the hypnotic noises made my eyelids heavy. I felt my blood buzzing in my veins, throbbing a sleepy rhythm as the world blurred into hazy shapes. My mouth went slack, letting a spit-string escape, which I couldn't be bothered to wipe away. Then my head dropped, jerking me out of my trance, and I scrambled to regain my balance as I rolled sideways off the step. Nomsa laughed. I wasn't sure how long I had been drifting, but she had finished sweeping out the room was now standing in the doorway. She heaved, laughing so hard she could do little more than point at me with her straw broom. I wiped the drool off my chin with the back of my hand and attempted to regain some of my dignity. I'd never seen anyone laugh so much, especially not at me, and I didn't like it. I tried to stare her down, the way Mother would when she disapproved of someone. Keeping my face as stiff as I could, I sucked in my cheeks. Nomsa laughed more, tears ran down her cheeks. I found it difficult to keep my face together. Suddenly, everything seemed very funny and I began to laugh. I heaved until my ribs hurt and my face itched with the salt of my leaking eyes. Finally I couldn't laugh any more. Nomsa came over and sat down next to me. She draped her arm over my shoulders and we sat quietly for a while, allowing our cramped stomach muscles to unknot. Then she said, 'You remind me of an old woman, your face is so serious, like my koko. Too serious for six years.'

'Seven,' I answered solemnly, wondering what Koko meant but too shy to ask.

That evening I sat eating the first hot supper I'd seen in three weeks while Nomsa washed dishes and tidied the kitchen. All day I had spent with her while she cleaned the house, breathing in her smell of Sunlight soap, paraffin and Zambuk. I had decided that of all the woman I knew, Nomsa was the most beautiful. I liked her plaits, they accentuated the perfect roundness of her head. I liked the way her head curved inwards at the base to meet her long neck in opposing balance to her chin. And she laughed a lot, making jokes I didn't understand but that sounded so funny they made me laugh too.

I was so busy admiring Nomsa that I didn't notice Mother come in until she cleared her throat. Nomsa stopped singing and turned around to look and when their eyes met, Nomsa seemed to get smaller.

'Evening, madam,' she said quietly to Mother. 'Can I get you some supper?'

Mother stared at Nomsa. She said nothing, but I knew that stare and I had never managed to hold it. Nomsa looked at the floor.

'Who are you?' Mother asked, her voice thin.

I looked down at my plate. My stew was getting cold and the piece of yellow fat I had pulled off my meat swam in congealing gravy. What had seemed so appetizing a few minutes ago now made my stomach twist. Carefully I put down my knife and fork, trying not to let them clink.

'Nomsa, madam. Madam Hettie brought me this morning.'

I twisted around so that I could see Mother. She was shaking her head slowly, mouthing Nomsa's name. Eventually she looked up. 'Hettie,' she muttered to no one in particular, before retreating back into the darkness of the passage. Nomsa turned back to the dishes and continued washing them in silence. I sat in my chair, unsure of myself. I noticed for the first time how hard the wood was and how the slat of the back-rest pushed against my shoulderblades.

The silence between us lasted until Nomsa pulled the plug and the soapy water was sucked down the pipes.

'It's time for bed, Koko.'

I went without objection.

Chapter Nine

THE NEXT MORNING, after a breakfast of gritty milk porridge eaten with two spoons out of a shared pot as we sat on the kitchen step, Nomsa and I set off to explore the farm. She'd said we, meaning me and her, were responsible for the running of the farm until Mother was better, and my first job was to show her everything on it. I showed her the flat-topped outbuildings that housed the generator and essential implements first, because they were closest to the house. I pointed out where Mother kept the diesel to run the generator and the small tractor that we hardly ever used, mainly because it was always breaking down and there was no one left to repair it. I didn't know how to work the generator. Nomsa bent over it, examining it and running her hands over its mysterious bulk like it was some kind of animal that needed to be soothed. 'It's a good generator,' she said and sent me to fetch a jerry-can of diesel from the garage, which she emptied into a hole she'd uncapped. She resecured the cap and tugged the starter cord. The generator kicked into life.

'I remember the day they delivered the first generator to the farm when I was a little girl. It came on the back of a lorry and it took six strong men to carry it. One man, his arms were tired, he couldn't hold it.' Nomsa sighed and shook her head, clicking her tongue against the roof of her mouth. I looked up at her, waiting for her to go on. She hit a switch and the generator died.

I followed her out of the shed. She pointed to the path that led away from the back of the house.

'The path, where does it go?'

As we wound our way up the rise that led to the reservoir I thought about Nomsa's story. I wondered about the farm she'd grown up on and asked her if her parents' farm was like ours. At first she looked puzzled, then she threw back her head and laughed.

'No, Koko, it wasn't the same. My father and mother worked on the farm, they weren't rich, not like you.'

I looked down on the house from our elevated viewpoint. The roof had seen better days, the red paint peeled and flaked and cracked to reveal the lead-dull tin. Further off I could see the hulking mechanical monster that rusted on the border of our farm. It was surrounded by old tyres, sprouting long brown grass from their centres, and bits of corroded corrugated sheeting. A dumping ground that we never added to, but that had always been there and seemed to grow and shrink inexplicably. The monster – Papa once told me it was an old harvester – reminded me of a winged dragon the way it reached out on both sides. Then again it also looked like a stretched mouth full of teeth. I shook off the picture of teeth and thought about dragons. Once I had heard a story of a princess who was rescued from a dragon. Her father, a king, had rewarded her rescuer with treasure and the princess had lived happily ever after with her rescuer in a castle with turrets and red and gold flags. I looked back at the fading red of our roof and wondered how Nomsa could think we were rich.

Nomsa tugged at my T-shirt, robbing me of my thoughts. We continued up the rise in a silence. I focused on the way Nomsa's skirt moved up and down as she walked in front of me and on how the dry air rasping in and out of my nostrils felt. After a few minutes of walking we came across the old borehole. Wanting to show off, I pumped the lever, using my entire body-weight to force it down, and was rewarded with a thin trickle of brackish water. Nomsa stood, hand on her hip, trying not to laugh. 'You're very strong, Koko.'

The land surrounding the farm was flat and, from the rise, we could see the vast expanse of uncultivated veldt, scrubby grasses and dull shrubs that belonged to the neighbouring farm. In the distance an outcropping of low mountains bordered the horizon, painted in the pinks and purples of rock and shadow. Papa had told me that our farm was once part of a bigger farm. The farmer's favourite daughter refused to marry and chose to stay on the farm and take care of her father. As a reward he split a few acres off and built her a small house so she could live there when he died. In those days girls weren't allowed to inherit farms or houses, so he gave it to her when he was alive.

'That's how the farm got its name,' I told Nomsa sagely: 'My Daughter's Home.'

We stood looking out over the grazing land for a time, squinting at the black dots of cows peppering the yellow scrub. We had no grazing animals any more, though the most we'd ever had was a bad-tempered goat and three sheep. Papa had called them living lawnmowers. One day Oom Piet had come to collect the sheep; he loaded them into his pick-up truck and I never saw them again. Mother said they had gone off to heaven, but I knew that wasn't true. A few days later we were invited to Oom Piet's house and I smelled the stink of sheep fat sizzling over hot coals and I couldn't eat. The goat disappeared around the same time as Moses. I think the Tokoloshe got the goat too.

Surrounded by a few thirsty trees, we came across the reservoir. The water was dark and thick, the level low. The rain had come to nothing, being too late in the summer to last. Filaments of luminous algae spread through the water, exuding a hot stagnant smell of rotting potatoes and squashed earthworms. Tiny air bubbles clung to the green strands like glass beads and the strands clung to the edge of the reservoir, matting where the water receded into a knot of dirty emerald.

'Ssh,' I whispered to Nomsa, 'that's Sillstream's hair. If we're quiet she might stand up and we'll see her.'

Nomsa frowned, but kept quiet. We stood in silence, the only sound a bloated fly buzzing in the ochre heat. After a few minutes Nomsa cleared her throat.

I shrugged. 'She always knows I'm here, doesn't matter how quiet I am.'

'Who, Koko?'

I shook my head, hadn't she been listening?

'Sillstream.'

She still looked puzzled so I explained further.

'You know, the water fairy; the one that brings rain.'

Nomsa threw back her head and laughed.

'No, Koko, a fairy? Who told you this?'

I looked at my feet, a little confused. Surely Nomsa knew about the fairies; everybody knew about the fairies. My cheeks felt hot. I shrugged my shoulders, I didn't want Nomsa to laugh at me.

'It's not funny,' I said and turned away. Nomsa stopped laughing. She squatted down on her haunches and took me gently by the shoulders. I refused to look at her.

'I'm sorry for laughing at you. I would like to hear about your fairy.'

I shrugged again, I didn't want to tell her any more.

'I also know of someone special who brings rain. If you tell me about your fairy I will tell you about my queen.'

I looked at her, curious, but still a little angry. She smiled, showing all her teeth, and stood up.

'But first a cup of tea. Let's see who can run the fastest.' She turned and began to run down towards the house, shouting that I was a snail.

I SIPPED AT MY tea, my cheeks still flushed from the race and pleased Nomsa couldn't call me a snail because I'd beaten her to the kitchen door easily. I listened to her story as she cut thick slices of bread and smeared them with butter and jam.

'My mother comes from Lobedu,' she told me, 'and there, high up in the mountains, lives Modjadji.' She folded a slice of bread into a triangle and dipped it in her tea. She chewed it slowly.

'Every year there is a feast and Modjadji pours her magic water to appease the ancestors and bring the rain.'

'Is she a fairy?'

Nomsa shook her head. 'She is the Rain Queen.'

I pondered this, imagining a queen made of rain.

'What does she look like?'

Nomsa shrugged. 'Nobody knows, Koko, only her induanas can see her, she is so special she cannot be seen by anybody's eyes.'

'Maybe Sillstream is one of the ancestors,' I said. 'Ma says she makes the rain.'

'Faith!'

I swung round. Mother hovered in the passage, her eyes bright. She beckoned me, her face white and frantic. Nomsa opened her mouth to speak but Mother backed away down the passage. I shrugged my shoulders and followed her.

I found Mother at the other end of the passage, looking at the painting of Sillstream. She leaned towards it, whispering. Her hands worked at her nightgown, clenching and unclenching the fabric.

'Ma,' I whispered. I felt like I was intruding and wanted to shrink back into the kitchen. She let go of her nightgown and gestured with her hand that I should come closer, never taking her eyes off Sillstream. I edged up to her until I was standing right next to her. She placed her hand on my shoulder and began to knead it.

'Listen.' She exhaled the word through her teeth. I cocked my head. I couldn't hear anything but Mother's shallow breathing. Sillstream looked at me with watery eyes, she wanted me to know something and I thought she might be holding back tears because I couldn't hear her. I closed my eyes and tried harder, tried to open my ears to the magical sounds Mother could hear.

'That woman doesn't belong here.' My eyes snapped open. Mother was looking at me now, she looked angry. 'She'll make the fairies leave.' Mother leaned down until her face was level with mine. She took my face in her hand and turned it slowly like she was examining me for dirt. I looked at Mother and something clutched at my insides.

'Don't tell her about them. They'll hear you and they'll leave.'

I shook my head. I wanted to tell her Nomsa was good, that she was my friend and the fairies wouldn't mind. 'Ma,' was all I managed to squeak.

Mother narrowed her eyes into slits. She took me firmly by the shoulders.

'Don't tell her.' It was an order. I recognized the tone. I nodded. She softened and kissed me on the forehead.

'I don't want us to be alone, Faith,' she said.

Chapter Ten

I DREAMED OF FAIRIES that night. They looked at me with accusing eyes; they were taking Mother away. I ran after them. I ran in the grazing land. Mother sat on a bench in the middle of the field. I ran towards her but she seemed to be getting further away. Suddenly I was right in front of her and she looked up at me with empty eye sockets.

'Wake up, lazy snail.' Nomsa shook me awake. I blinked the remnants of dream away. The smell of porridge drifted from the kitchen.

While I ate my porridge Nomsa made three cups of tea and placed one with a slice of toast and a jar of fancy marmalade that we saved for guests on to Grandma English's Five Roses tray. Then she disappeared down the passage. I listened to her gentle knocks, which became more insistent as the seconds ticked away on the kitchen clock. Eventually she returned with the tray and poured the tea down the sink. The cup had just drained when Mother's door opened and she came into the kitchen. She stood stiffly in the doorway for a moment, surveying us, before she stepped down, flaring her nostrils, and put the kettle on.

'Good morning, Faith,' she said, sitting down at the table

with me and turning her back to Nomsa. I mumbled what I thought could pass for a greeting through a spoonful of porridge. Behind Mother I saw Nomsa pick up the sheets she had stripped from my bed and disappear out of the back door. Mother looked down at the table, as if absorbed by the grain of the wood. She cocked her head sideways and stroked the wood, like she was smoothing the creases in some invisible tablecloth.

'Yes, that's right,' she whispered to the table, tapping it twice with a dirty fingernail. For a moment she remained frozen in that pose, like she was listening to someone on the other end of a telephone. I leaned forward, hoping to catch snatches of the voice on the other end. Suddenly she looked up at me. Her eyes were wide and bright blue, two topaz jewels in sunlight. With a sudden movement she snatched my hand and leaned closer to me. Her musty hair brushed against my face; it smelled like the wet feathers of a dead chicken.

'Who let her in?' she whispered. I felt her breath staccato against my cheek, hot and acidic. I swallowed the bile that burned at the back of my throat.

'I didn't mean to.' I struggled to keep the sick down.

'They made you, forced you, forced my little girl.' Mother's face twisted into a feverish hatred. 'Cunts.'

She stood up, sending her chair crashing backwards. Her grip on my hand tightened and she lurched forward, dragging me with her. My elbow banged the kitchen table, and pain, sharp and intense, sent an electric pulse down my arm, numbing my hand and blinding me with tears. I stumbled, but Mother didn't stop; she just jerked my hand up, pulling me back on to my feet, and lunged down the passage.

Suddenly we were in front of her bedroom door. She kicked it open, pulled me round so that I was in front of her, and shoved me into the room, slamming the door behind her.

My eyes took a moment to adjust to the dimness of the room. The curtains were drawn, blocking out the light. It smelled of old ashtrays and her unwashed body. Mother stood with her back to the door. Her breathing was sharp and ragged, each breath expelled violently through flared nostrils. I looked from her to the room. Pages from my parents' wedding album that I had spent hours poring over, dreaming of princes and three-tier cakes, littered the floor, torn from their red and gold leather cover. The shoebox in which Mother kept all her other photographs was empty. Every picture in it had been systematically ripped to separate Papa. A pile of tiny smiling Papas looked up from the floor, divorced from a pile of smiling others, Mother, me, Ouma, friends. One Papa was wearing an army uniform and waving at the camera. I felt like he was waving at me, a goodbye caught in fading Polaroid hues.

Mother pushed away from the door and walked over to the curtain, stepping on the Papas and scattering them with her foot. She didn't notice them as she peered out of the curtain.

'Look' – her voice was shrill and excited – 'they're waiting for me.'

Even though I couldn't see them, I knew who she meant. Dark fairies, the really bad ones, like Dead Rex. I could feel them closing in on the house, surrounding us until there was no escape. Mother's room was hot and stuffy; I was finding it difficult to breathe. Heat flushed up my neck and into my head, my ears rang with an electric hum. My head felt like it was underwater. All I could hear was a loud buzzing but I knew Mother was talking because her lips were moving. I focused on her face, struggling to make out what she was telling me. Everything around her disappeared into darkness until her face was the only light left in the surrounding black, then the dots swarmed in and covered her up.

Damp seeped through the dark nothing, wet against my skin. It must be raining. In the periphery of my vision I could see the heads of the bad fairies that crowded into the room through holes they had gnawed in the floorboards. They bowed down, ducking their jaundiced heads under the fragmented edges of the wooden boards. I heard Mother's voice, soothing them: 'Come back, come back to me.'

No, I wanted to cry out, but my tongue felt too thick to speak, swollen by their poison. No, Ma, don't call them. All around I saw them, nesting in their holes under the house, little tar-black babies clutched to turmeric breasts, swarming, like wasps in a hive, crawling over each other in their eagerness to get closer to Mother.

'No, Ma.'

My body jerked, forcing my vision to a brighter place. Mother's blue eyes hovered over me, her hand pressed down on my forehead. She smiled, 'No what, Faith? Were you dreaming?'

She stroked my hair, turning over the facecloth she had pressed against my head to the cool side. Was I dreaming? I blinked, taking in the brightness of the room, my room. King Elvis sat in Grandma English's rocking chair, mocking me. Sunlight streamed into the room through the open window. Nomsa stood at the door, arms folded across her breasts, shaking her head.

'Koko, why didn't you say you felt sick?'

Mother's face hardened; she leaned in so close to me that her eyes merged into one. 'You must get her out,' she whispered, 'or the fairies won't come.' Then she leaned back and smiled again, as if nothing had happened. She stroked my head one more time before she left, passing Nomsa with a smile and a nod that left me cold.

LATER THAT DAY Nomsa pronounced me fit to leave my bed and help her in the vegetable garden. She repaired the makeshift greenhouses while I collected red tomatoes that had fallen off the vine and placed them in a basket. I'd arrived with my spade and bucket, planning to make mud cakes, but Nomsa said I should do something of value and had given me the task of picking up tomatoes. I felt very important as I carefully examined each one for worms, lifting it off the ground and brushing dirt off the ones I deemed satisfactory. The rest I placed in a plastic supermarket bag for use in our kitchen.

'Koko,' she said to me as I arranged all the tomatoes in the top of the basket according to which I thought looked the most appetizing, 'it's good that you have time to play with the tomatoes. One day you will say, "Nomsa, the only tomatoes I want to play with are boys' tomatoes."' Laughter rumbled from her gut. I didn't know what was so funny, but I laughed anyway.

When Nomsa decided that we had done enough work for the afternoon, she went back into the house to begin preparing dinner. She picked up the bag of rotting tomatoes and slipped off her muddy shoes at the kitchen door. I stood in the cold afternoon shade of the generator shed, contemplating whether I should join her. My elongated shadow clutched itself, gooseflesh prickling purple along my bare arms. The idea of sitting at the table while the stove heated the kitchen was tempting, but after an afternoon spent working Mother's vegetable garden, I missed her. Shamed by the tears that spilled on to my cheeks, I turned away from the kitchen door. I looked towards Mother's window, hoping to catch a glimpse of her through the drawn curtains. Maybe she would peer out, watching for fairies, and see me. Maybe she would be Mother again.

I stared at the window for a long time, until the silky reds of dusk drew the last light from the sun. Twilight, the fairy time.

I turned, stepping out from behind the shed, until I could see the silhouettes of citrus trees, cut-outs against the burning sky. They called to me, in the way I imagined the fairies called to Mother. The orchard was where Dead Rex reigned and somewhere in that orchard, perhaps inside trees, the souls of his victims were trapped. Suddenly everything made sense. Dead Rex had stolen Mother's soul: perhaps she'd accidentally looked him in the eyes. The cold fist of fear tightened around my guts, squeezing until I thought I might vomit my stomach up. I swallowed hard, and forced my feet, one step at a time, towards the orchard gate.

The rusty bolt gave way with a screech that set my teeth on edge. The gate swung open, squealing back and forth on its hinges in a diminishing arc before coming to rest. Dusk sat heavily in the orchard, dark trees floating in haze, blurred at the edges. The smell of dry sticks and hard ground mingled with a faint smell of rotten oranges. Soundless, except for the determined stridulation of crickets and the distant banging of a pot from the kitchen.

'Boesman.' I whispered his name as if, somehow, it would offer some protection, and stepped over the threshold. I crept slowly forward, trying to peer into the haze, eyes wide, listening for any sound hidden below the buzzing hum of insects. What did souls look like? I imagined something wispy and vaporous, like steam breath on winter mornings. Ouma once told me that when you sneezed your soul could blow out, that's why you should always put your hand in front of your mouth, to catch it. Mother said that was just an old wives' tale, that I shouldn't believe her. But Ouma is an old wife, she even holds her nose when she sneezes, so I always put my hand up. My soul never came out though, perhaps it was something you only needed to worry about when you got old.

I picked my way between the rows of trees, looking carefully at each one for signs of souls. I tried squinting through half-closed eyes; sometimes you can see things, shapes and colours, through squinty eyes that you can't see when looking at things normally. I could see nothing that resembled a soul. Then, at the far end of the orchard, a flickering light caught my eye. Two tiny greenish glows, luminous, disappearing, then reappearing, then disappearing. Blinking on and off like a twitching eye, they wound their way through the trees towards me.

'Fairies,' I whispered in hushed awe.

I tried to remember what sort of fairies they were. They were flying, but they were too small to be Night Scares, besides, Night Scares had blue-black skin with blue-black wings and they didn't glow. The thought of Night Scares made me peer up into the trees to make sure there weren't any there. I shrugged the fear-prickle off. When I was little Mother used to sing me a fairy song at bedtime. The tune was in my head now, but the words evaded me. I looked towards the fairies and, as if by magic, the words came.

Little fairy glowing bright,
Lead lost children to the light.
Home to bed they safely go,
Following your golden glow.

That was it, these were guiding lights, they would lead me to Mother's soul. Feeling braver, I walked towards them. They had veered off to the right now, dancing around each other, weaving light traces. I began to whisper the little song to myself, comforted by it. The glowing had become more intense, flickering faster and faster, until they came to rest on a tree. Mother's soul tree. The fairies moved close together, glowing green, until they seemed to join. Under my breath I muttered the song, remembering the second verse.

Warning comes when glowing red,
Follow then and you'll be dead.

I faltered; something came after. The fairies were flashing madly now, as if they wanted me to hurry up. The tree was only a few metres away. I just need to pass between two other trees and I would be there.

Green signals a dangerous path

I froze. These fairies were green, not golden. It was almost completely dark, the sky had turned deep purple. The glow now resembled a luminous green eye.

Green signals a dangerous path,
For soon you'll meet Dead Rex's wrath.

I turned and ran, stumbling on jelly legs. Trees loomed towards me, closing in on all sides. I couldn't remember the way out. I veered left, then ran straight until a metal twang hit me in the face. I clutched my nose, disorientated, tears obscuring my vision. I reached out for something to steady me, and closed my hand around cold wire.

'Nomsa!' I screamed.

I PRESSED THE wad of Dettol-soaked cotton wool against my nose, inhaling its orange disinfectant sting. It was comforting somehow, reminding me of scraped knees and banged heads, of being led firmly by Mother into the kitchen, where she would run water into a bowl and pour in the Dettol, watching the water turn cloudy and then metallic orange. The unbearable sting of it that made me pull away, Mother's insistent hand, pressing firmly down until the sting subsided. The stain that remained, marking out the wound, fading away as I healed. Dettol was a cure for every gash, cut and scrape I had ever sustained, and it was still here even though Mother wasn't.

Nomsa sat next to me, saying nothing. The slow, steady drip of the kitchen tap counted time until eventually she spoke.

'Koko, nobody has stolen your mother. She is sick.'

I shook my head. The lump in my throat strangled my voice. I so wanted Nomsa to believe me, to help me find Mother's soul.

'One day soon she will be better, and then you will laugh at yourself, running around in the dark chasing these fairies.'

As much as I wanted to believe her, I couldn't. I had been into the darkness of the orchard and seen what was there. Mother would not be coming back, not unless I helped her, and I didn't know how.

Nomsa cupped her hands around my chin, tilting my head upwards so I was forced to look directly at her.

'Everything will be fine, Koko, you wait and see. Besides, Madam Hettie is coming to take you and Madam to the market, then you will see for yourself.'

I went to bed hopeful that night. We would be going to the market, Mother and me, like we used to. As I clutched King Elvis I whispered a mantra into the night:

'Everything will be fine. Everything will be fine.'

Chapter Eleven

Tannie Hettie arrived at six a.m. My basket of tomatoes was waiting by the kitchen door, ready to be loaded into the car. Next to the tomatoes, in brown cardboard boxes, were carrots, onions and some white mielies Nomsa had picked.

'That's not very much,' said Tannie Hettie, perusing the meagre offerings.

Nomsa shook her head. 'It's all there is, madam.'

The three of us stood over the vegetables, each of us sighing and shaking our heads. I felt a little disappointed that all my hard work had amounted to these few boxes, so I took deep breaths and expelled them as forcefully as I could.

'Where is the madam, Nomsa?' Tannie Hettie asked, cutting her eyes at me after an especially loud sigh.

'In her room, madam.'

Tannie Hettie was quiet for a moment.

'Make me some coffee and bring it out on to the veranda, and some for her too if she doesn't already have it.'

I watched Tannie Hettie walk down the passage to Mother's door while cold apprehension slid down my spine. She stopped and gathered herself, lengthening her neck and pursing her lips, before rapping her knuckles against the door and letting herself in. Nomsa and I looked at each other and she gave me a half-smile, but we couldn't hold the gaze and both of us turned away. We waited for Tannie Hettie to come out, half expecting she would be alone. But a few minutes later the door opened and they came out, Tannie Hettie dwarfed by Mother who seemed taller than usual. Mother looked over to where I hovered in the kitchen doorway and narrowed her eyes. She flashed me a look that contained traces of her old pride, the shell she drew around herself whenever she left the farm. It was the look that always accompanied the lesson 'One thing you must learn, my girl, is never to cry in front of other people.' It was a lesson Mother had drummed into me from as far back as I could remember. Every time I cried she mocked me – 'Cry-baby!' – but still I could never stem the flow of tears that made me feel like I was, at those times, not her daughter. In that look I recognized the part of Mother I didn't like, the woman who stood in the centre of the market and surveyed it like it belonged to her. This time, though, she looked brittle.

I slid from her line of sight and out of the back door. I wanted to know what Mother and Tannie Hettie would talk about, so I sneaked round the side of the house. I thought about hiding by the stairs, pressing my back against the cold brick of the veranda wall, but if they caught me I would be in trouble. There was a patch of grass a little way off from the veranda. I knew from listening in on my parents' conversations that I could sit there and if they didn't swing on the chair, its squeak wouldn't drown out their voices. I couldn't imagine Tannie Hettie to be the swinging type.

I sat down and stared at the grass, pretending to be

preoccupied with some important lawn excavation. I dug a small hole with a twig, wondering what was taking them so long. I looked up when the door finally opened, then quickly down again when Tannie Hettie caught my eye. I looked at the hole and it blurred as my focus went to my ears.

The swing chair squealed with their weight. I heard Nomsa come out with the coffee and Tannie Hettie's mumbled thanks as she stirred in some sugar. I heard Nomsa retreat and, for a while, the only sound was the slurping of hot coffee. Finally, when I thought my straining for sounds would make my head explode, Tannie Hettie cleared her throat.

'They want to give your stall away.'

I looked up.

'I tried to talk them out of it, but Cyril said you hadn't been there for a month and he's been losing revenue.'

Mother smiled, a thin twisted smile. 'Have people been talking?'

Tannie Hettie didn't respond. After a long a pause she said, 'I've paid for the stall for today, but I can't afford to keep an empty stall.'

Mother looked down into her coffee.

'Nomsa tells me that you spend most of your time in bed. You have a child, Bella, responsibilities.'

Mother looked up, her face expressionless and slack. 'I didn't ask you to bring Nomsa here, you brought her because you feel guilty. We don't want her.'

Tannie Hettie sighed and tried to take Mother's hand. 'You can't blame me for the way Marius behaved, I'm just trying to help.'

'You could have warned me. You knew.' The accusation

hovered in the air, like static before a storm, but the storm never came. Mother stood up, walked to the edge of the veranda and looked directly at me.

'Take Nomsa to the market.'

THAT NOMSA WOULD be taking Mother's place at the market was both exciting and disappointing. I was eager to show off my new friend, the only one I had ever had who was human, and was sure that with Nomsa my tomatoes would sell quickly.

While Nomsa unpacked the car, Tannie Hettie took up her usual seat in the next stall and opened a newspaper. Only her beige-stocking-clad legs and Green Cross shoes were visible behind the black and white face of a mean-looking bald man with his podgy finger in the air. I didn't know who he was, but he seemed to be threatening me, and his beady eyes followed me around from behind thick square glasses.

I inhaled the crisp morning air and looked up at the blue sky. In a few weeks the market would move to the newly constructed indoor site on the outskirts of the town. I hadn't seen the new market, but I had overheard the traders' talk. Market fees had gone up in order to fund the building, and there were many complaints, but everyone seemed to agree that an indoor market would be better. I wasn't quite sure how being indoors could be better. I loved the buzz of the morning market: traders unloading their goods, crates of oranges, butternuts, potatoes, lettuce, carried on the shoulders of black men in blue boiler suits; the different stalls; Tannie Saarjie's home-made jams and preserves, pyramids of tomato chutney, her top seller, good with hamburgers but best at a braai, in between jamjars of marmalade catching light like orange jewels, each jar carefully labelled by hand and the lid covered with mauve material held in place by green ribbon; Oom Jan's home-made cheese, rounds of cheddar or gouda inside waxy red or black skins, creamy white cheese that crumbled in your fingers, processed cheese that was almost orange and speckled with cumin seeds; Oom Piet cooking boerewors next to his stall, where all the different varieties of sausage waited, coiled and marinating, for the buyers to stream in; Tannie Hettie's dried and sugared fruits; Tannie Hannah's crocheted tea cosies and doilies, lace creations so delicate they seemed unlikely to have sprung from her meaty hands. The market was a flood of colour, sounds and smells under a canopy of blue sky and sunshine.

That morning the market was quiet, absent of the greetings and gossip the stallholders exchanged over cups of steaming coffee. I looked round to check where everyone was and saw a small gathering a little way off. Tannie Hannah, who seemed to be at least half of the gathering, stood slowly shaking her head. Everyone was looking at me. I suddenly felt exposed, like I was in the dream where I had come to the market naked and only realized it when I stood in the middle of the stalls with everyone laughing at me. I glanced downwards and was relieved to see my clothing still intact.

Tannie Hannah broke away from the group and lumbered off towards the town hall. I watched her progress. It gave me something to focus on other than the group staring at me. She seemed to be moving in slow motion though her chest moved up and down in double time. She disappeared through the door and seconds later Cyril Nel, the market manager, emerged with his clipboard clutched tightly to his chest. Every Monday he walked up and down through the stalls with his clipboard, collecting money and ticking off payments with a black pen. Mother would often not pay until the end of the day, which caused his nicotine-stained moustache to twitch and resulted in a red mark being made next to her name. I found the mark embarrassing, but Mother seemed to relish it. Now he walked rapidly towards me, stiff as an ironing board. I considered running to Tannie Hettie, but she was gone, heading off towards the toilets with the newspaper under her arm. He stopped directly in front of me and cleared his throat.

'Ja, nee, look who's back,' he said with a slight leer, puffing on a cigarette, 'and where is your mother?'

I looked around, wishing the ground would swallow me up. Oom Cyril had never addressed me directly before and now that Mother wasn't around, here he was, asking about her. I looked back up at him and shrugged my shoulders.

'Well,' he said looking down his sharp nose at me, 'I want to talk to her.'

I shrugged again. Mother hated Oom Cyril and I was sure that even if she were here, she wouldn't want to talk to him.

Oom Cyril rolled his eyes at the crowd of onlookers, who'd moved closer.

'Is – your – mother – here?' Each word dragged out in a nasal whine.

I shook my head. Oom Cyril pointed his clipboard over my head. 'Who is that girl?'

I looked over my shoulder to see who he was pointing at and caught sight of Sannie du Toit, marching across the square in her green checked uniform, schoolbag slung across her shoulder.

'Sannie du Toit,' I mumbled, looking at his shoes. They gleamed, two shiny crocodile snouts poking out of the bottom of his trouser legs. Oom Cyril sucked his lips.

'Are you trying to be funny?' He took hold of my shoulders and swung me round until I was facing Nomsa. 'Who is that?'

The acrid smoke from his cigarette stung my eyes and burned in my nostrils. He squeezed the tendons at the base of my neck, his bony fingers seeking purchase deep in my flesh between the muscles. Out of the corner of my eye I could see the crowd, their faces hostile. Even Tannie Hannah, who had always been friendly to me, pinching my cheeks and sharing her chocolates, stood arms folded, glaring. The only person whose attention was focused elsewhere was Samson, the old man who swept the market and emptied the bins. The sound of his broom against the concrete filled the world. I took a deep shuddering breath. 'Nomsa,' I managed.

Oom Cyril relaxed his vice grip. 'I suppose this stall now belongs to Nomsa?' He spat out her name.

I shrugged, unsure of who owned the stall now that Mother wasn't here.

'Your mother is always trying to break the rules. She thinks that laws do not apply to her.' Oom Cyril was slowly turning the colour of the overcooked aubergines Ouma force-fed me. He continued, 'This person,' he gestured towards Nomsa with his clipboard, 'cannot, under any circumstances, own a stall here. If she wishes to sell her kaffir mielies, I suggest she does what the rest of her kind do and—'

Tannie Hettie cleared her throat sharply behind him, cutting him off. He swung round, pivoting on his skinny legs to face her.

'Is there a problem, Cyril?' she enquired. She looked formidable even though she had to look up at him, barely reaching his shoulder. It was a relief to no longer be the focus of his attention, and I considered retreating to the safety underneath the trestle table, but any sudden movement might cause him to swing back round and grab me, so I stayed put.

'Mrs Els, with all due respect, this is market business and no concern of yours.'

A murmur rippled through the crowd. Tannie Hettie faced Oom Cyril, arms folded across her chest. He towered over her, thin and weedy, a snake ready to strike.

She shook her head slowly, her lips a thin line of disapproval.

'Any business concerning this stall is my business, since this stall,' she pointed at the stall, 'is my stall.' Her words were slow and clipped, in the way Mother addressed Papa when he came home drunk.

Oom Cyril opened and closed his mouth, a fish gasping for air. I wondered if he was drunk. Tannie Hettie didn't give him time to reply. She pointed at Nomsa.

'That person is in my employ and will be selling my mielies for me.' Tannie Hettie stood facing Oom Cyril as if she dared him to contradict her. His eyes bulged as if they were about to pop out of his head, but, after what seemed like a lifetime, he handed her the clipboard and she signed it.

For the rest of the day I felt invisible even though I didn't hide under the table. I sat next to Nomsa watching as people walked past our stall, some of them looking at us with a disgust I could not comprehend, some commenting on how shameful we were, or how they would never stoop to buy from a kaffir, but most just walked by and bought nothing. It was the longest day I ever spent at the market. The tomatoes baked in the sun, their shiny red skins attracting no attention. By the afternoon, as the shadows grew long and cold, I began to realize that it was Nomsa that people didn't like. Even people I had always thought were nice, the ones who stopped to chat with Mother every week, enquiring about our health and other news, gave us a wide berth.

By closing time I realized that Tannie Hettie hadn't sold much either: though she had done better than we had, her table looked like it had just been laid out. Her face blank, her lips a thin set line, she proceeded to pack up without uttering a word, and we did the same. In the close confines of her Morris on the way home I waited for one of them to break the silence, wishing someone would explain what had happened, why people had behaved the way they had. I thought of asking, but what could I ask?, and deep down I knew that neither of them wanted to talk about it.

I sat in the back of the Morris, focused on the road ahead, not wanting to look at the back of either woman's head and see the stiff way she held it up, like it was an effort. I felt as though the world was somehow different, like I had been exposed to something that made no sense, that had no reason to be the way it was. It was an unfathomable thing, made up of tenuous strands that had to fit together, if only I knew how to place them. Yet, even as I grappled with the threads of it, trying to weave them together into a solid idea, I knew that what I would find when I finally managed was something rotten.

Chapter Twelve

THE PHONE WAS ringing. It hadn't rung since the day Papa left and now it was, breaking the early-morning silence with its shrill insistence on being answered. I pulled my blankets up around my head, waiting for Mother to answer, but the ringing went on and on. Eventually it stopped, only to start again a minute later.

I wasn't allowed to use the phone. The phone was Mother's and I only answered it if she told me to, and she only told me to if she was washing dishes and wouldn't be able to dry off in time. She was afraid if she answered the phone with wet hands she would get a shock. Papa laughed at this, saying the phone was well insulated and it could never happen, but she still wouldn't pick it up with wet hands.

Sometimes when Papa was away Mother would let me say hello to him when he called, but if I spoke too long she would get agitated and gesture wildly, meaning I should get off. Mother didn't like to say too much on the phone either; she was sure Tannie Marie listened in, and she didn't like Tannie Marie knowing our business.

The phone had now started ringing for the third time. I wanted to answer it; it might be Papa and if it was I could ask him to come and get me, tell him about how Mother was sick. Even if Tannie Marie was listening, I didn't care. I threw my blankets off and scrambled off the end of the bed, running down the passage, eager to pick up the phone that was normally forbidden.

The phone sat on the little round table like a black toad, unmoving although I'd expected it to be jumping with every shrill ring. I grabbed it, feeling the weight of the receiver in my hand before I put it to my ear.

'Hello.'

There was a click and then a long, low, repetitive tone. I was too late. I put the receiver back and waited for it to begin ringing again. Surely they would phone back. My hand hovered, ready to snatch it up. The phone squatted, silent, mocking. I was willing Papa to phone now, wishing him into existence with such determination that I could smell his cigarette smoke. I closed my eyes, breathing in the smell and letting it envelope me, hoping that when I opened my eyes he would be there. The smell was becoming stronger now, permeating the air. I opened my eyes and saw white tendrils hovering in the early-dawn light, smoke fingers playing against the first blades of winter sun that sliced through the window. I felt that somehow I was working a magic, bringing Papa to me just by thinking about him. I closed my eyes again, trying to picture his face. It seemed just out of my reach. The most I could manage to conjure was shape and hair.

How long had it been since I had last seen him? It didn't feel as long as a year; it was only just turning to winter now. Summer would need to come again before I turned eight, but I couldn't remember his face. If I couldn't remember his face, how could I expect him to phone? If I couldn't remember him, perhaps he had forgotten me.

The faintest sound of a scratch and a hiss reminded me that I had been hovering over the phone for quite some time, my back to the painting of Dead Rex. I jerked round, knocking over the table and sending the phone crashing to the floor. Dead Rex was above the fireplace. He stood, frozen in his frame, menacing. I tried to remember if he was in that position the last time I saw him, so close to that tree he was almost part of it, like some grotesque leafless branch. Was he trying to climb it to get out? Were his hands always poised on the edge of the frame like he was about to lever himself out, knuckles straining at the effort it took to keep still?

A movement from below the painting shifted my focus. Sitting on the floor beneath the mantel was Mother. She must have been there all the time, watching me as I waited for the phone to ring, and before, just watching the phone.

I stared at her, taking in her sallow skin, her limp ropy hair, the stick-like arms that protruded from her filthy nightgown. What I knew of the bad things in life, I knew from her. All the stories she'd ever told me about the bad things Dead Rex or Tit Tit Tay could do, of the awful things that Night Scares do, of the Tokoloshe's tricks or the Burrowing Blood's digging tunnels from the dark centre of the earth, she now seemed capable of herself. The way her eyes sank into their sockets yet glowed a brighter blue than they'd ever been. The way she walked, the strange shuffle like she never lifted her feet suddenly erupting into what seemed like flight, hardly touching the floor. Mother was becoming one of them, crossing over into the realm of fairies. Hadn't she said they were coming to get us?

She's just sick, I told myself, remembering what Nomsa had said. I took a step towards her. She watched me, head cocked to the side like she was waiting for me to get close enough to her so she could reach out and grab me. I stopped. Dead Rex might be able to take the form of Mother to trick me. I looked up at the painting. He was still there, poised above her head. He couldn't be in two places at once, even if they were so close together. I shook the fear off and took another step. 'Be brave.' That's what Grandma English would say, and Grandma English was Mother's mother. She would want me to be brave now and help Mother. I took another step. Mother smiled at me, and brought her hand up to her mouth. She took a long drag of a cigarette. I stopped. I hadn't noticed the cigarette before. It was the same brand that Papa smoked, Van Dijks, that same smell. It was the first time in my life I had ever seen Mother smoke. It looked unnatural, so staged that I wondered for a second time if this shrunken figure sitting on the floor next to the fireplace was my mother.

'Are you afraid of me, Faith?' Her voice was like a deep bell, so much my mother's voice that if I closed my eyes I would be able conjure her on that sound alone. I looked at the woman who sat in front of me now and asked myself the same question. Was I afraid of her? There had been times in my life when I had done things that made Mother angry, times when her blue eyes flashed with fury, times when she had put me over her knee and spanked me with a slipper, threatening to make sure I wouldn't sit down for a week.

She'd scared me then, but that was different. I'd known who she was then. But now, looking at this person in front of me, this person who was supposed to be my mother but didn't feel like her, I was gripped with deep penetrating fear, the same fear I felt when looking into a dark cupboard at night.

'I found them, they remind me of him.' She held up the cigarillo. I knew what she meant. Their smell, I had been fooled into believing he might be coming back just a few short moments ago by that smell.

'Your new friend is afraid of me. She thinks I'm possessed by evil spirits.' Mother laughed, a hollow sound that could have been a cough. 'Are you afraid of me, Faith?'

I nodded. Mother had always been able to see through lies.

'Nomsa says you're sick, but that one day you'll be better and we'll laugh . . .' I trailed off, realizing I had just got Nomsa into trouble. Mother opened her mouth to say something, but closed it again. Then she leaned forward and whispered, just loud enough for me to hear from where I was standing:

'I see them, Faith, the other world, the real one. It's perfect there, no one will bother us. Make up lies about me. I belong there, Faith, you belong there, with me, with us.'

She sat back and turned her head to the side, pressing her ear to the wall.

I didn't want to belong there. I loved the farm, it was all I had ever known. Tears spilled on to my cheeks. If Mother was one of them, it meant that I was one too. I would have to go with her, unless Papa came to get me. As if she plucked him from my mind, Mother leaned forward again.

'That's where he's gone, you know. I can hear him

sometimes, talking to me. He's the one who told me where to find this.' She held out her closed fist, taking the final drag of the cigarillo with her other hand before stubbing it out in the fireplace. I looked at her fist, curious to know what she held. She smiled, gesturing for me to come closer. I swallowed hard and went to her. As afraid as I was of her, she was still my mother and I couldn't disobey her. Slowly she turned her fist around until her palm faced the ceiling and, with a flick of her fingers, she opened her hand. Papa's silver ring glinted in her palm.

I gasped and, without thinking, tried to snatch it from her. 'That's mine,' I yelled.

Mother snapped her hand shut, her face dark. I grabbed her fist, digging my nails into her fingers, trying to force them open.

'Give it back.'

Hot tears dropped on to our hands. Mother had destroyed everything that was Papa, all his pictures, and now she had stolen the only thing I had left of him. The cigarillo she had just stubbed out was mine too, the last one I had. I clung to her hand, trying to force it open, screaming, 'Give it back, it's mine.'

Through my tears I could see the shock of Mother's face. In all the time I had been her daughter I'd been quiet and obedient, looking up to her like she was the Fairy Queen. I'd had my moments, times when I'd pushed to see what I could get away with, but I'd never attacked her, never been one of those children who threw tantrums, never screamed in temper.

Mother clenched her hand, the tendons along her arms taut with effort. My fingers scrabbled and scratched, my nails left red welts in her flesh. No matter how hard I dug my nails in, she didn't react. She was waiting until I ran out of steam. I lunged forward and bit her. The moment my teeth sank into the fleshy mound left exposed on her upturned palm, I knew I had gone too far. Her fingers opened and the ring fell. It bounced on the wooden floorboards, making a sound no more special than a dropped coin. My hands gripped hers, they were the same hands, long-fingered with squared-off nails, twin hands though hers were wider, longer, older. Now her upturned palm displayed the violence of my teeth. The ring spun and rolled and settled, silent. Then she slapped me.

I didn't feel her palm connect, I was already halfway to the floor, the prickly heat of unconsciousness closing in. The last thing I saw was Papa's ring, lying against the wall, dull and lifeless, like all the magic had leaked out.

I SURFACED TO the sound, familiar, a song, something I hadn't heard for a long time and couldn't remember where I knew it from. It was comforting somehow, that song. It made me want to stay buried in my dark space, but I couldn't. I felt constricted, something was wrapped around me, a tight grip held me in a place that reeked, pungent, yeasty, stale, bitter. Light slipped between my lids. My eyes watered. I squeezed them shut, blocking out the light, but the smell, it was making me sick. I opened my eyes. Mother held me in a tight embrace; she was gently crooning the familiar melody. I wriggled, wanting to escape from her. She let go, the tune trailed off. I pulled free and stood up. The world spun and settled. I closed my eyes until the ground hardened under my feet. Then I looked at Mother. Something in her face had changed. Some of the intensity had gone and there was a glimmer of the person who had once been my mother. She gave me a watery smile.

'I'll get us out of here soon, Faith, I promise.'

They were words I didn't want to hear. I knew what she meant now, and I didn't want to go. I looked at her, feeling for the first time that I'd finally learned the lesson about not crying.

'I hate you,' I muttered through gritted teeth as I backed out of the room and left her at the mercy of Dead Rex.

BACK IN MY room I dragged the corrugated-board case out from underneath my bed. I snapped the locks open and looked inside, thinking that it looked untouched from the outside. It wasn't. I was confronted with a jumble of bottle tops, acorns and grass; my carefully arranged treasures looked like litter. My precious weaver's nest had been shredded, reduced to a matted tangle, like witch hair. The lighter and cigarillo were gone, as was the ring, and strangely, the speckled bird's egg and sheep's jaw were also missing. I cried for everything I loved and had lost. I cried for Boesman and Papa, for the market and my treasure box. When I stopped crying I decided that I would no longer love Mother. I would never again care about what happened to her. Even if she went to join the fairies I wouldn't go with her. I would rather spend the rest of my life going to Ouma's stuffy church than follow her.

Chapter Thirteen

WINTER SETTLED IN, covering the farm in the early mornings with a white crust of frost. The house embraced the cold, drawing it in like some forgotten cousin, and once inside it refused to leave. Even when we collected wood to light a fire in the evening, the cold hovered around us, chilling our backs as we warmed our hands. I spent my afternoons chasing pools of winter sun from window to window, sitting in their ever-shrinking warmth until they completely disappeared.

Mother did not welcome the cold; she had never liked winter, complaining bitterly of chilblains and stiff fingers. In that respect, this winter was no different. The cold forced her into our company and, although she never spoke to Nomsa, she began accepting cups of tea and hot soup from her. Mother would sniff at the cups, then dip her smallest finger into the hot liquid and lick it with the tip of her tongue. In the end she drank them, though never while Nomsa was there.

Mostly she sat on the swing chair, wrapped in an old shawl, talking to herself or just staring at the sky. Once I sat next to her; she didn't seem to mind, but she started to speak about the fairies and I didn't stay.

One afternoon she watched from the door as Nomsa bathed me. When we were done, Nomsa refilled the bath almost to the top with hot water. She took some of Mother's special soaps and creams from the cupboard and arranged them along the side of the bath. Without looking at Mother, she ushered me out, wrapped in a towel. For a while we sat on my bed in silence, not wanting to move in case we missed a sound. Then we heard the click of the door and the swirling of water.

Nomsa smiled.

'Dress quickly, Koko,' she said, 'then we can clean Mommy's room for her.' My heart almost stopped. I started to shake my head. I wanted to tell her that I didn't think we should go in there, but Nomsa was already out of the door. She worked quickly. By the time I was dressed she had changed all Mother's bedding and opened the curtains. I stood at the door, wondering if I should go in and help.

'Nomsa,' I hissed. Nomsa turned to me and frowned; a tiny bead of sweat trickled down her forehead. She cocked her head to one side and gestured to her ear.

'You watch,' she whispered. 'If you hear Madam coming out, tell me.' She turned her attention back to the cleaning. I looked at the bathroom door, then into the room. Nomsa was sweeping up all the shredded photos into a shoebox. I looked at the bathroom door again, it was still closed. Nomsa touched my shoulder, making me jump. She held out the shoebox. I took it from her shaking hands, noticing the wet circles that had formed under her arms. She wiped her forehead. Nomsa looked like she had been running; she was a little out of breath and smelled sweaty.

'One last thing,' she smiled at me. I clutched the box to

me and watched her, listening all the time for sounds above the hammering in my chest. She went to Mother's cupboard and opened it carefully, stopping when the door creaked. We stood stiff, listening, but when we heard nothing she opened it a little further. Dresses hung on the rail, next to skirts and some jeans. Nomsa reached out and picked out a blue dress, one Ouma had made for Mother. I hadn't seen it since the day Mother unwrapped it and held it up against her. 'Look,' she had said to Papa, 'your mother sent me a tent for my birthday.' I wondered if I should tell Nomsa, but thought that it would take longer for her to choose another one, so I didn't.

Nomsa laid the dress out on the freshly made bed.

'Let's go,' I hissed at her. I couldn't imagine Mother would be in the bath for much longer. It felt like we had been here for hours. Nomsa nodded and closed the cupboard. She scanned the room one last time, and then scooted me out with both hands. We stumbled into my room, arms full of soiled sheets and the photo box. Nomsa opened my wardrobe and stuffed the bundles into the cupboard.

'We'll wash them tomorrow,' she said, and she collapsed on the bed. We lay side by side for a second, hearts hammering, then Nomsa sat up. 'Let's go make dinner,' she said.

I sat at the kitchen table, wishing I could be anywhere else. Nomsa busied herself chopping carrots and potatoes, the carrots into thick rounds, the potatoes into chunky squares. I wished I was old enough to hold a knife, then I could distract myself with vegetables. My stomach was in knots. I found myself glancing down the passage, waiting for the bathroom door to open, wishing it never would.

The pile of vegetables grew and grew. I watched Nomsa's back, her elbow moving up and down with the slicing motion. Up and down, it went, like the seesaw in the park, up and down. Then the bathroom door opened and her elbow stopped. I bent my head towards the table and looked sideways down the passage with my eyes. Mother emerged from the bathroom in a billow of lilac-scented steam, a pale yellow towel wrapped around her middle, a towel-turban on her head. Her legs stuck out at the bottom like sticks; a trickle of blood ran down one shin. She held her head high as she turned down the passage towards her room. My heart thudded in my chest, it thudded in my neck, my wrists, my fingertips. I felt dizzy. Mother stopped at her door and opened it. I wanted to vomit. I couldn't see her face and I didn't want to imagine how it looked at that moment, but the pictures came. Mother, teeth bared like Boesman would do at strangers, Mother, the snarling monster. I cringed where I sat, expecting her to come rushing down the passage at me. I closed my eyes, bracing myself for a blow. None came. My ears picked out the sound of a door closing, then seconds later the chop-chopping of Nomsa's knife. I opened my eyes, Mother was gone, Nomsa's elbow moved up and down, up and down.

Slowly, as the evening progressed, the waiting feeling began to go away. Maybe Mother wouldn't come out, maybe she would stay in her room a very long time and when she came out she would have forgotten what we had done. I began to believe these things. Nomsa started to sing one of her songs. It started to feel like just another evening, preparing supper. But Mother did come out, she closed her door so quietly I didn't hear it, and she appeared at the kitchen door and stood framed by it, one step higher than us. Her face looked like a stone carving, her lips set in a line. I looked up at her, my breath snatched from me. Mother wore a long brown woollen skirt with a winding pattern of big red roses, a woollen top that I remembered had once been tight on her, and her shawl. She waited until Nomsa noticed her too, then she raised her eyebrows and tilted her head slightly. Nomsa opened her mouth to speak, but before she could say anything, Mother turned around and left.

Nomsa took a deep breath, I sighed, the pot of soup simmered and steamed on the stove. Soup was all we ate, but the stock of vegetables that Nomsa topped it up with every week was dwindling. She'd kept the garden going right up until the first frost, when the hardiest plants succumbed. She picked even the meanest and most bitter marrows to add to the store in the cellar. I was grateful for Tannie Hettie's visits, when the monotony of soup might be broken for a few meals by a leftover stew or pie. I wondered why she called them leftovers, when the piecrust was unbroken and the pot of stew still warm. Hardly like the funny-smelling remnants of meals Papa used to scoff out of plastic containers when he was around.

She also brought us tins of coffee. She and Mother sat on the swing chair blowing into hot mugs of it. She spoke about the market if she spoke at all and Mother hardly said a word. They seemed satisfied somehow, just to sit in the mild winter sun, like this was the way things had always been and would always remain.

That week when Tannie Hettie came her face was grim and set, her eyes red. She sat on the swing chair with Mother, but she didn't lean back and she didn't speak. After a while she reached out and took Mother's hand. I felt like that hand clamped around my throat and squeezed the breath out of me. Her words didn't carry to where I sat underneath the umbrella thorn, but I could see her lips moving as she stared ahead. She wasn't looking at Mother when she spoke. Then her lips stopped and she turned to Mother, as if expecting something. Mother's reaction was not immediate, but it was no less shocking for its delay. Her face crumpled and her mouth opened, letting out a low keening noise that built into a wail.

The sound of Mother's wailing went on and on. At first I stared, unable to understand what was happening, but her crying burrowed into my head and travelled through my body until it seemed that it would split me open. I couldn't sit and listen to it, so I stood on shaky legs and began to walk away. The sound followed me around the side of the house, allowing me seconds of respite where it seemed less penetrating, but soon it became the only sound I could hear. I walked until I began to crack open, the keening scissoring through me, trying to find a way out. It pushed between my hips, into my gut, boiling upwards until it reached my throat. I couldn't breathe. My legs gave up their march. I crumpled to the ground, mouth open to let it out.

It was Nomsa who found me, on a mound in the vegetable garden, rocking back and forth, my hands clamped over my ears. I let her carry me down to the house, wrapping my arms and legs around her. She felt like the only solid thing in the world. For a long time we sat in the kitchen and she rocked me on her lap, but the noise went on and I couldn't let go. She asked Tannie Hettie to take me away, at least for the night. I didn't want to go, but Nomsa bundled me up and eased me into the back of the Morris, unlatching my hands and placing them on King Elvis. When she closed the door the world seemed far away. I was in a small space where the outside was muffled and it made me feel safe.

I stared out of the back window at Nomsa as we drove off. She stood on the veranda, arms folded across her chest, she didn't smile or wave. When she went inside I continued to stare at the diminishing place she had been. Even when the farmhouse was completely obscured, I stared. Then we turned off the dirt road on to tarmac, and the farm was gone.

'WAKE UP, MY child.' I opened my eyes slowly, unwilling to let go of the safety of sleep. Tannie Hettie leaned over me. I felt stiff and cold and miserable. I sat up, straightening my neck. Dusk had settled over the world, making Tannie Hettie's house look hazy. I pushed the car door open and got out, stretching and yawning. A slick black torpedo shot towards me on stiletto legs, snarling, yapping, barking, strings of saliva stretched across its spiky teeth. I backed away.

'Pinkie, no!' Tannie Hettie took me by the shoulder and propelled me forward. 'She won't bite,' she reassured me as she steered me towards the front door. She fished a large bunch of keys from her bag and slotted one into the lock. Pinkie scuttled between my legs into the house before the door was completely open. I followed Tannie Hettie into the shadowy hallway. The house seeped cold. Tannie Hettie put her bags down.

'It's late, best get some supper on the go.' I followed her into the kitchen. It was much smaller than ours. Orange and brown linoleum covered the floor, curling back on to itself where it met the wall. A faint whiff of rotting fruit seemed to be coming from the cupboard under the sink. There was a table with metal legs and a yellow Formica worktop against one wall, hemmed in by three matching chairs and a fridge. It was the kind of fridge Mother told me never to climb inside; the kind that clicked shut when you closed it; the kind where no one outside could hear your calls for help; the kind that sealed you in and all the air out. I sat down on one of the Formica chairs and watched as Tannie Hettie lit the gas under a tin kettle the colour of wet concrete.

'There's a TV in the sitting room, I'll put it on if you like.' I nodded. We didn't have a TV on the farm. Mother wouldn't have one in the house, she said it rotted the brain. I followed Tannie Hettie into the living room. A standard lamp in the corner cast a gloomy light. Pinkie lay curled on an armchair, watching us with beady eyes. Tannie Hettie went over to the television and switched it on. It flashed and popped before the screen lit up. I stared in fascination as the head and torso of a monochrome man addressed me directly. I sat down opposite the television, on the settee. Pinkie growled and farted, filling the air with a rotten-cabbage stink. I pinched my nostrils shut and glared at her. She sneered, baring a row of crooked teeth, shifted in the chair and closed her eyes.

I stared at the man on the TV. The sound was very low and I didn't know how to turn it up. The picture changed to show a building in ruins. Policemen wandered around rubble with dogs. Then another man came on; he stood in front of a burnt-out car. He spoke into a microphone and gestured at the blackened car. It wasn't very exciting. I looked around the room. Heavy brown curtains blocked out the night. A painting of a familiar landscape hung on the wall above an anthracite heater. Framed photos hung on another wall. I went over to get a closer look. Some of the photos were yellowing. One was of a man in a uniform, khaki shorts and shirt, holding a rifle similar to the one we had at the farm. He smiled at the camera, looking very proud, his black hair combed to one side. Next to that one, in an oval frame, the same man wore a suit and stood next to a young bride.

'Can you believe, that was me.' I swung round. Tannie Hettie stood in the doorway. I turned back to the picture. Now that she had told me, I could see it might have been her. It seemed strange that she had once been young, like Mother.

'Twenty-five years we were married, but God took him early.' I looked at her, unsure of what to say.

'God took Boesman too,' I volunteered, hoping to show I understood.

She sighed. 'Yes, child, so He did.'

I looked back at the wall again. A young woman smiled out of a square frame. It was the only colour photo on the wall. The woman had blonde hair and looked similar to the young Tannie Hettie. The picture made me feel uncomfortable; fear prickled down the back of my neck. I peered at the photo. I was sure I'd seen her before. I wondered who she was.

'Who's that?' I asked, pointing at the woman.

'My daughter. Come and eat.' Tannie Hettie turned abruptly and left the room. I glanced at the woman one last time before following her into the kitchen.

A boiled egg sat in an eggcup, hot and uncracked. I sat

down at the table in front of it while Tannie Hettie scooped a second egg out of a pot into a matching eggcup. She sat down next to me and I watched as she buttered some toast and then, with her butter knife, she sliced the top of the egg off. She scooped the runny egg out of the shell with a teaspoon and mashed it onto the toast.

I picked up my knife and swung at my egg. It flew off the table, landing on the floor with a wet splat. I looked at the mess of egg on the floor, and the yolk dripping off the table leg. My cheeks burned.

'Ag, child. There's a cloth by the sink.' Tannie Hettie heaved herself up. 'Clean it up and I'll put another one on.' I stared at the Formica table-top, unable to look at her. I wished I was at home with Nomsa.

'It's not the end of the world, my child.' I pushed my chair back and got the cloth. I wiped at the egg, feeling miserable. Shell crunched under my hand. My efforts just smeared it.

'Pinkie,' Tannie Hettie called out. I heard the patter of Pinkie's nails against the floor. 'Pinkie will help you clean it.' Pinkie nosed at my hand, pushing it out of her way in her eagerness to get at the egg. I stood up and watched her snuffle against the linoleum, licking the egg away.

Tannie Hettie pushed her plate towards me, instructing me to eat hers while she waited for the next egg. It was cold and sticky, but I didn't want to seem ungrateful. I ate it with long teeth.

I WOKE ON the settee, covered by a heavy suffocating blanket. Pinkie lay curled at my feet. I blinked as Tannie Hettie drew the curtains.

'Morning, Faith, time to get up.' I untangled myself from the blanket, making Pinkie growl, and followed Tannie Hettie into the kitchen.

A sweet, fruity smell hung in the air. It wafted from the oven into my nostrils and made my mouth water. Large trays of dried fruit covered just about every surface in the kitchen. A mincing machine was attached to the table. I knew it was a mincing machine because Mother had one. Mother used hers to make hamburgers, feeding chunks of raw meat and bunches of fresh parsley into the top, then slowly turning the handle until long red worms speckled with green wriggled out at the other end into a big bowl. Sometimes she would let me turn the handle, I loved doing it even though it made my arms ache. Tannie Hettie was feeding handfuls of dried fruit into her mincing machine.

'There's Weet-bix in the cupboard and milk in the fridge,' she said. I hated Weet-bix, it tasted like cardboard, so I sat down at the table and offered to turn the handle. She frowned, saying it might be too difficult for me and instead gave me a palette knife and placed a bowl of fruit mince in front of me. She spooned the mixture into a baking tray and showed me how to spread it out evenly using the knife. The mixture fascinated me; it was smooth and sticky and slightly elastic, deep red, the colour of blood.

The phone rang. Tannie Hettie wiped her hands on her apron.

'That'll be Dr Fourie,' she muttered and went to answer it.

I flattened the mixture as best I could. I was satisfied that it was as even as it was ever going to be and wondered what I should do with it. I slipped off my chair and went to find Tannie Hettie. She would know. I found her in the hallway, speaking on the phone.

'She's not been well since he left,' she said. There was a slight pause. 'Yes, I understand, but she won't leave. If she would, I would have brought her in before.' Tannie Hettie nodded and made 'um huh' sounds.

'That's very kind of you, doctor. I will see you tomorrow morning. Six.' She hung up and turned around. She raised her eyebrows when she saw me, but made no comment and ushered me back into the kitchen, where she popped my tray into the oven.

Chapter Fourteen

MIST HUNG OVER the road like wet smoke, tainting my view of the passing landscape with a speckled lace of moisture. The windscreen wipers dragged over the glass, their rhythm broken by the air that whistled in and out of Dr Fourie's nostrils. I watched the back of his head, so much higher than Tannie Hettie's I could see where his slick grey hair stopped and his neck began. I wished he would snort or sniff away whatever was blocking his nostril, or even stick one of his fingers up his nose and pick it out, but his big hands stayed on his knees, not budging, no matter how many thought waves I sent their way. I remembered Dr Fourie from the times I had been to his surgery. He gave me injections, no matter what was wrong with me, sometimes when there was nothing wrong with me. After each visit he'd given me a lollipop, for being a good girl and not crying. The lollipops were always sticky and had no wrappers. Sometimes there were small bits of fluff or tiny hairs stuck to them. I think he sucked them himself before giving them away. I took them home and ran them under the tap before putting them in my mouth.

Tannie Hettie edged her Morris slowly up the drive.

Stones and frost cracked under the tyres. The house loomed over the opaque curtain of mist, its bottom half obscured. Tannie Hettie stopped the car and we got out. The world seemed hushed. A dove cooed mournfully, lonely for company. Fairies whispered to me as I walked through the mist, reaching out with icy fingers to caress my skin. The farm seemed to hover halfway between our world and theirs. I wondered if they had come to get Mother while I was gone. I slipped my hand into Dr Fourie's as we ascended the three steps that led to the front door. He was big and could offer some protection. He looked down, slightly surprised, but squeezed my small hand gently.

Tannie Hettie knocked and pushed the door open. The smell of fresh coffee followed Nomsa out of the kitchen. She stopped when she saw we were already in.

'Môre, baas, madam. Faith,' she smiled at me. I let go of the doctor's hand and wiped my hand against my trousers. We followed Nomsa into the kitchen, where she poured coffee. Tannie Hettie told me to go play outside, that they needed to talk about grown-up things. I went into the yard. The door clicked shut behind me. I sat on the kitchen step. I knew the doctor had come because of Mother, and she was my mother, I didn't want to be excluded. I wanted to hear what was wrong with her, why she was sick, if the fairies were making her ill. I wanted to know if she would ever get better. I pressed my ear to the kitchen door. I could hear the doctor's deep voice clearly through the wood. He asked Nomsa questions about Mother. How had the madam behaved? Did she cry a lot? How was she feeling? He cleared his throat before each question.

She was a little better, had stopped crying, but had stayed

in bed all yesterday. She wouldn't come out of her room. I had to strain to hear Nomsa's answers. Then it was quiet. I stood on tiptoes on the top step and peered through the window. Dr Fourie sat at the table making notes on a white pad. If I held my breath I could just hear the pen nib scratching against the paper. Finally he stood and asked to see the patient.

I sat back down on the step and let the cold seep into me. Patient, the word sounded ominous. It was like a stain on Mother, something that might never come off. When I was four, Oupa got sick and everyone called him 'the patient'. Papa took me to go and see him in the hospital. He was in bed. I'd never seen Oupa in bed before. Nurses in stiff white uniforms and polished shoes marched up and down the ward, stopping at his bedside every so often. They held his wrist and looked at their watches, they tugged his blankets and made them straight.

'How is the patient today?' they asked, as they plumped his pillows and made him swallow small blue pills. 'How is the patient feeling?'

Then Oupa died and I never saw him again.

We went to his funeral and there was a long black box with brass handles. It was covered in flowers and I thought that it was one of those window boxes that people who lived in flats have instead of gardens. I wondered why people were wheeling a window box into the church. Mother had smiled even though she was crying. She told me it was a coffin, that Oupa's body was inside and they would bury it in the cemetery. People in Ouma's church said that when you died, if you were good and believed in Jesus, you went to heaven. I'd wondered why Oupa wasn't going. When we got to the cemetery there were lots of stones. Papa said they marked the places where people were buried, so that when the families visited they could find them easily. I had bad dreams thinking about all those people who didn't get into heaven, buried in the dark in boxes. So many stones, so many bad people. It made it worse that Oupa went to church and prayed to Jesus. I couldn't think what he had done that was so bad he never got into heaven. He was always nice to me. It didn't seem fair. Now I know that only their soul goes to heaven.

Oupa's was the only funeral I'd ever been to. No one else I knew had ever got so sick as to become a patient, until Mother. I wondered if Mother's soul would go to heaven. She didn't believe in Jesus. Mother didn't believe in things she couldn't see. I felt sick thinking of Mother dead.

Dr Fourie's voice brought me out of my head. I stood up and peered in through the window again. Dr Fourie was talking to Tannie Hettie and Nomsa.

'It's a typical nervous breakdown, she's depressed,' he said. I could see the back of Tannie Hettie's head as she sat at the table; she looked like she was nodding. Nomsa stood by the oven. From where I was she seemed to be stroking it. It took me a moment before I realized she was cleaning. Dr Fourie stroked his chin and smiled, then he patted Tannie Hettie on the shoulder. I held my breath.

'Not to worry,' his deep voice seemed to boom in the early-morning quiet, 'it's happened before, lots of women around here come to me with these sorts of problems.' I thought I saw him wink at Tannie Hettie, before he went on, 'It's because Marius left. For some women, this is like death.' He placed his hand on Tannie Hettie's shoulder and gave it a squeeze. 'At least she's not drinking.' Tannie Hettie seemed to stiffen when he said this, but the doctor didn't notice.

'I'm not too concerned. She will get over it, given time. My main concern is she's not been eating properly.' He turned to Nomsa and said something I couldn't quite hear, and she stopped what she was doing and came over to fill the kettle. I ducked down, hoping she hadn't seen me. I waited for the tap to run, crouching on the top step, praying she wouldn't open the door and send me away. I strained to make out words from the murmurs through the door, but I couldn't hear anything. After a while I thought it was safe and resumed my spying.

Dr Fourie was sitting at the table. He had his notepad out and was reaching into his shirt pocket for his pen. He clicked it on with his thumb.

'Yes, Mrs Els, you're right, we can do something. I'm going to prescribe a sedative. It will calm her, help her sleep. Women think to much, don't get on with things. People underestimate the value of a good night's rest on health. Half the world's problems could be solved with a good sleep. When you're overtired, there's stress on the body, and when there's stress, you can't sleep. Vicious circle.'

He wrote something on his pad, tore it off and folded it in half. He held it up between two fingers, making it look important.

'After a good night's rest, I can assure you, she will be right as rain. Early to bed, early to rise, et-cet-ter-ra.' He pronounced each syllable of the last word like it was the most important thing he'd said. Then he handed the paper to Tannie Hettie.

'That' – he nodded at the paper Tannie Hettie held in her

hand – 'will rid her of the anxiety. She'll sleep, I guarantee it.'

I sat down on the step again. I tried to make myself believe that all Mother needed was sleep. I was grumpy when I was tired, but Mother wasn't grumpy. She was more than that. I didn't believe Dr Fourie. Not sleeping didn't make you go away, it didn't make you not you.

TANNIE HETTIE TOOK the doctor away and returned later that afternoon with a small paper bag. She put it on the kitchen table and went to use the bathroom. While she was gone, I sneaked a peek into the bag. It contained a brown glass bottle with a sticker on it. I opened the bottle and carefully tipped the contents into my hand. It contained pills, the size of dried peas. Blue pills. The same colour as the pills Oupa had been given before he died. The toilet flushed. I put the pills back, closed the lid and slipped the bottle into the bag.

It was Nomsa's job to make sure Mother took her pills, Tannie Hettie said. Three times a day, with food. That evening Nomsa took Mother a bowl of hot soup and one blue pill. I tried to talk her out of it. I told her about Oupa, but she wouldn't listen.

'The doctor knows what's good,' she said. 'Don't you want Madam to get better?'

I did want Mother to get better, but I wasn't sure about the pills. Mother didn't trust them either. She ate her soup and left the pill. The next morning Nomsa tried again. She made Mother some toast from the bread Tannie Hettie had brought, and placed the toast with a cup of tea and the same blue pill on Grandma English's Five Roses tray. Mother drank the tea.

Before lunch Nomsa called Tannie Hettie on the phone. I hid in the passage just outside the sitting-room door to listen to what she said. She told Tannie Hettie about supper and breakfast. Then she listened.

'Yes, madam, I'll try,' she said before she replaced the receiver. I hung back in the shadows so she wouldn't see me then I followed her to the kitchen. She sat at the table with a bowl of soup in front of her, two spoons and a blue pill. She placed the pill on one of the spoons, then put the other spoon on top. She pushed down on the top spoon and mashed them together. When she took the top spoon away, the pill was gone and a fine powder covered the spoon. She tipped the powder into the soup and stirred it, then she tasted it. She wrinkled her nose.

'It's bitter,' she said, 'needs some salt and pepper to hide the taste.' I looked at her, angry. I couldn't believe she would deceive Mother that way, just when Mother was beginning to accept her. I knew she wanted me to fetch the salt for her, but I wasn't going to. I wasn't going to be part of giving Mother blue pills, especially from Dr Fourie. I left her to her nasty trick.

Out in the yard I watched the chickens pecking the ground. We had run out of chicken feed, now the chickens were left to find their own food. All they got from us were vegetable peelings Nomsa chopped up finely so they could pick them up with their beaks. We didn't get much from them either. They didn't lay many eggs, maybe one a week, if any. Nomsa threatened them every morning when we went to collect eggs. She waved her hand at them, shouting how she would pluck their feathers and eat them if they didn't start laying. She said she would boil their feet and suck them, make gravy from them for her pap. I'd laughed at the time, thinking about Nomsa eating chicken feet.

It wasn't so funny now. Maybe she hadn't been joking, maybe she was really going to kill the chickens.

I nursed my anger with Nomsa. Every time I watched her crush a pill into Mother's tea or soup, it grew. I avoided her and began to spend more time outside alone. I ignored her when she called me from the kitchen door. I hid from her when she tried to find me. I tried to rally the chickens against her, but they just looked at me, black eyes glinting, heads bobbing. They circled me. I thought they were listening, but one tried to peck my foot and I realized they only wanted food.

Once I walked up to the reservoir. It was cold and windy, my ears ached inside. I wanted to tell Sillstream what Nomsa was doing. Sillsteam was Mother's favourite, I was sure she would help. But the reservoir was low and Sillstream wasn't there. Only a few strands of dead hair clung to the sides, brown, lifeless. I sat there for a while, spoke to the air, hoping she would hear me and come back. I even closed my eyes so I wouldn't see her step back into the water, but she never came.

When I went back down the sun was setting. Nomsa was waiting for me.

'Where have you been?' she asked, her expression dark. It was the first time I had ever seen Nomsa angry. I folded my arms and refused to tell her.

'I've been worried, it's getting dark, I looked everywhere. Ai, Koko, it's not like you to go off like that.'

I stared at her, my own anger fuelled by hers.

'Why are you angry with me?' Her voice wobbled.

I shook my head, tears stung my eyes. I wouldn't speak to her, I didn't trust her any more.

'Tell me, why are you so angry?' She reached out and shook my arm, as if she could shake my thoughts out of me.

'Why won't you just go away and leave us alone!' The words flew out of my mouth before I could catch them. In the silence that followed, I wished I could take them back. Without Nomsa I would be alone. I wanted her to hug me, not be cross with me. I wanted her to stay and save Mother from dying.

'Go to bed.' She let go of my arm.

For a moment I didn't move. I could feel her anger, it buzzed in my cold ears.

'Go,' she said.

I went.

That night in bed was the coldest I'd ever been. My feet felt like ice-blocks. I huddled under the blankets, clinging to King Elvis, but even he couldn't keep me warm.

Chapter Fifteen

IN THE DAY that followed, Nomsa punished me. She gave me breakfast in silence. She ignored me as I sat on the step, watching her hang out wet sheets on the washing line. The sheets whipped and cracked in the wind; even they seemed angry. I followed Nomsa on her chores, keeping a safe distance in case she told me to go away. Her face was like stone, her lips turned slightly down. She fed the chickens, collected what eggs there were, cleaned out their coop, without uttering a threat or encouraging cluck. At lunch she made us sandwiches and tea, but she sat in her room with the door closed and ate, leaving me alone at the kitchen table. I thought about apologizing to her, but then a surge of indignation would overcome me, and I'd think about everything she had done and not said sorry for. I'd go away and think nasty thoughts about her, but soon I'd feel lonely again and resume following her around. Afternoon came and the sheets were dry. Nomsa took them inside and ironed them. I loved the smell of ironing, the hot scent of clean cotton and fabric softener that filled the room, but I didn't feel comfortable sitting in the kitchen so close to Nomsa's anger, and I couldn't sit out on the kitchen step to catch the wafting smells, it was too windy. I ended up sitting in my room, playing with King Elvis.

At first I just sat there, looking at him, him looking at me. He looked so dejected, so unhappy, that I decided to play an old game to cheer him up. I took my pillowcase off my pillow and tied it round my neck. I dug in my cupboard until I found an old scarf I'd stolen from Ouma. At the time I didn't think she would notice. She had so many scarves that she wore around her neck and secured with a little brooch, I didn't think she'd ever know one was gone. But she did see, and I'd spent the whole day pretending to help her look for it. When I got home I'd stuffed it in the bottom of the drawer where Mother put all my fancy clothes. I didn't have reason to wear fancy clothes very often, so I knew it would be safe. I hadn't thought of it until now, but it seemed the perfect thing to make a cloak for King Elvis. Then I was Supergirl and King Elvis was Superman. I tucked King Elvis under my arm and climbed on to the bed. I turned his arm until it faced up, and stretched my arm out, clenched my fist and braced myself, ready to save the world. I was about to fly off into the air when Mother's door opened.

Mother stopped when she saw me. She looked as surprised to see me in my room as I was to see her out of hers. We looked at each other for a moment and I began to feel embarrassed. I lowered my arm and a hot blush rose up my neck.

'What are you doing?' Mother asked. Her voice seemed like her old voice, calm and steady. I looked at the person in front of me, trying to see the old Mother that was hidden inside, the one who had just spoken.

I shrugged my shoulders. 'Nothing, just playing,' I said.

'You look a little bit silly,' she said, still in her old voice.

I nodded; now that she said it, I knew I looked silly. I looked nothing like Supergirl. I wished I had a mirror in my room so next time I could make sure I looked like I did in my head before anyone else saw me.

I tugged at the knot around my neck, trying to rid myself of the pillowcase. I didn't want to look silly in Mother's eyes, even if she was sick. Suddenly Mother was in my room. She wrapped her arms around me and King Elvis and she squeezed me tight.

'I'm sorry,' she whispered. Sorry, I thought, why? Mother had never been sorry for saying things to me before; now that she was sorry, I was confused. I tried to shrug, to show her that it didn't matter, it was only a game, I wasn't very upset that she'd said I looked silly, but I couldn't, she was holding me so tight I couldn't move.

Then she began to cry, clutching me as she did, so all three of us shook with her sobs. She kept whispering she was sorry. I felt embarrassed, I kept thinking it wasn't a big deal, she'd called me silly lots of times before, but then I got scared. I got scared that this was Mother's sickness, that her crying was part of her sickness, because my real mother didn't cry, the Mother that was sick cried, the fairy-sick Mother cried, but not my mother.

I stiffened, too afraid to pull away. I wanted to, but I felt wary of this Mother-person and I didn't want her to touch me. I turned my face away from her, scared to breathe the air that came from her mouth. I didn't even want her tears to touch me, maybe I thought they would burn me.

Eventually she stopped crying and let me go. I didn't move from where I was standing on the end of the bed, I was scared she'd get angry if she saw I didn't want to be near her.

Mother turned away from me and wiped her face with the hem of her dressing gown, bending slightly to angle her face so she could reach it with the gown. I caught a glimpse of her leg, pale yellowy skin pulled taut over her shinbone, strangely hairy. She straightened up and turned to me again; she smiled a little, like she was unsure of herself, like she didn't know who she was or who I was. For a moment she looked confused, then she sighed.

'I've been selfish,' she said. I didn't really know what she meant. I nodded slowly, wary of upsetting her further. 'Things will be better from now on,' she said, 'you'll see.'

'Are you better?' I whispered. I looked down at the floor, it seemed so far away. I realized the floor must always be that far away for Mother.

'I'm feeling a little better.' Mother sat down on the bed. I looked down at the top of her head. I could see pink skin in the middle of her head where her hair separated into two sides. I sat down next to her. My feet didn't reach the ground, Mother's were flat on the floor, but somehow I still felt that I was more on the ground than she was.

'Did the fairies leave you alone?' I asked, hoping that they'd gone and this was real.

Mother smiled at me. She reached out with her hand and stroked my hair.

'You have such soft hair,' she said, 'sometimes I wonder where it came from. Your father—' she faltered, and swallowed. 'He's got such coarse hair.'

'Like a lion,' I said.

She nodded. 'My hair's so thick, yours so delicate, fine, like silk threads.'

I felt a warmth suffuse me. Mother never used to say such

nice things to me, even before she was sick. She wrapped my hair around her fingers.

'I think the fairies gave you your hair, Faith, you're a child of the fairies.'

I froze; the warmth emptied out of me and the space it left was filled with a sick feeling.

Mother's voice was dreamy now, like she was drifting off somewhere.

'I think the day I conceived, the fairies came and put you inside me. I used to wonder about that; your father wasn't even there, I think.'

The sick feeling was rising. I thought I might vomit.

Mother turned to me and smiled. I don't think she even saw me when she looked at me. I think she was looking at somebody behind me.

'The fairies will never leave me, don't worry about that, not as long as you're here.'

Mother stood up. She wobbled a bit and she touched her hand to the wall to steady herself.

'I'm going to bath now, but we'll eat dinner together later, OK?'

I nodded.

When she'd left, I ran outside and threw up.

Chapter Sixteen

I SNEAKED INTO Mother's room while she was in the bath. I'd heard the water run and then waited for the gentle lapping as she lowered herself in, before I pushed her bedroom door open. The curtains were open and the sky, clotted with dark clouds, cast a grey light into the room that made it seem cold. Mother's bed was a tangle of sheets and blankets, and there was a dirty coffee cup on her bedside table, but the room was still fairly clean and tidy. I wondered if she'd been letting Nomsa clean it when she brought in trays of food. I didn't want to think of Nomsa being in the room and what that meant, so I shook the thought out of my head and focused on what I wanted to do.

I went over to Mother's dressing table. Its mirrors reflected me back at me, it made it look like there were three of me in the room, one in the wide centre mirror and one in each of the thinner side mirrors. I touched the varnished wood of the table-top. My finger left a clean line in the dust that covered everything, revealing the dull veneer of the wood underneath. I thought about how Mother used to polish the wood with beeswax, carefully moving her things – the jewellery box, her gold powder-puff box, the purple glass bud-vase that looked like an alien flower – and make the surface shine. It didn't look polished now.

Mother used to keep her make-up bag in the middle drawer. I knew this because I'd seen her use it every Saturday after our bath. I suspected it was still there; she hadn't worn any make-up since Papa left, there was no reason for it not to be there.

The drawer slid open silently, letting out a faint smell of perfume and talc and revealing the flower-dotted fabric of the make-up bag, just as I remembered it. I lifted it out, careful not to disturb anything else, and opened it. It didn't contain very many things: a lipstick I knew was red, because it was the only one and Mother only wore red lipstick, when she wore lipstick at all, a tub of Vaseline, a small flat plastic box and a tarnished silver compact. I took out the compact and closed the bag. I opened the drawer a little more so I could slide the bag back in without difficulty, and as I did so I saw an envelope. It had been opened and I could see it contained a letter and two photos. My curiosity burned. I slipped the envelope out and put the bag back in. I briefly contemplated taking the envelope with me, but I was afraid Mother would notice and get angry, so I looked at the photos there. The first photo was of a house. It wasn't a particularly interesting house, white with a red roof and a lawn in the front. The lawn looked brown and patchy, like nobody cared about it. The next photo stopped my breath. It was a very close-up picture of Papa. He was smiling and waving at the camera, but his smile was strange because it didn't touch his eyes. The picture was distorted because it was so close. His hand seemed very big, but I could tell it wasn't very old. He looked the same as when I'd last seen him.

I looked at the photo for a while. I wanted to cry but something in me couldn't cry for him any more. I put the photos into the envelope and put it back in the drawer.

THE HOUSE FELT empty even though I knew Mother was inside. Nomsa was in her room and it seemed that all the background noise had gone with her. Nothing bubbled on the stove, no plates clinked together in the sink, the hum of her singing that had woven its way through all the rooms until it seemed to me the very house was singing, was gone. I couldn't even hear my own breathing.

I sat in the lounge and looked at the painting of Dead Rex. At first I was a little afraid, but after a short while, when he didn't move, I felt more confident. Dead Rex didn't seem as menacing this time. He didn't look like he was trying to climb out, today he was just leaning against the frame. He seemed amused, like he was mocking me. I took a deep breath and clicked the compact open. The small round mirror was coated in powder. I blew it away, but it still seemed slightly foggy, so I wiped it with the sleeve of my jersey until I could almost see myself clearly. Then I held it up to examine my face.

Blue eyes stared intently back out at me. Where did they come from? I wondered. Mother's eyes were a deeper blue, more intense, nothing like the pale eyes that looked out at me. And Papa's? Papa had brown eyes. I looked from the mirror to the painting and back again. Dead Rex had slimy green eyes, but there was something about the way he looked at me, something in the expression, that seemed to me to be the same eye looking out at me from the compact. I snapped the compact shut and tried to clear my head of the crowding thoughts. I must have imagined it, I told myself. Dead Rex looked nothing like me. His face was horrible, twisted and evil. I opened the compact again and pulled my face into what I thought was an expression like his. I scrunched up my nose, creased my brow and narrowed my eyes. See, I told myself, I look nothing like him. I closed the compact, feeling slightly better. For a moment I looked at the dull metal object in my hand, then my focus shifted. There was a knob that stuck out on my wrist – everyone had it, I knew, but mine had always protruded more than other people's. Like my knees were knobbly, so was my wristbone. I got up and walked closer to the painting, not too close though, not close enough for him to grab me, but close enough to get a better view of his hands. I held my hand up and looked at his hand. The certainty I'd felt moments before that I looked nothing like Dead Rex disappeared. There, in the painting, were the same long fingers, the same knuckles, the same knobbly wristbone. Even the tiny freckle between the knuckle of my little finger and my ring finger was mimicked on his hand, on the hand of the most terrible fairy.

I backed away slowly, not willing to believe what my eyes were telling me. My whole life was a lie. I wasn't even a person like other people were. I was something else, a halfling, a changeling. I knew from the fairy stories Mother read to me that people hated halflings, left them in the woods to die. That was probably why Papa had left, because he knew and he hated me, why everyone in the market looked at us funny, why Sannie du Toit and her friends always bullied me. They all knew. And if they knew, then Tannie Hettie knew. Tannie Hettie pretended she was my friend, but in all the time she'd known me, she'd only ever touched me once. Now, I knew why.

I looked up at the mocking face of Dead Rex and rage flooded me. I clutched the compact so hard it dug into my palm, then I clutched it harder still, wanting to feel the metal bite deep into my flesh, a pain to match the anger inside me. Still Dead Rex mocked me. I screamed and threw the compact at the painting. It bounced off, flying back and hitting me on the forehead. Tears streamed down my face, but I didn't care about the pain, they were angry tears, raging tears. I picked up the compact from where it had landed, open, on the floor. I wanted to throw it at him again, but as I lifted it up I saw my face, contorted with rage, in the round glass. It was the same nasty expression that Dead Rex wore. I felt dizzy, sick. The walls of the room suddenly seemed much closer. I closed my eyes, feeling a stifling flush of heat rush up my neck into my head. I opened my eyes but the room was gone, replaced by millions of tiny points of light.

Chapter Seventeen

COLD SEEPED INTO my dark world, trying to wake me up. I held out, keeping my eyes closed, wanting to escape back into sleep. But my mind reached out to my stiff limbs until I could focus on nothing else but my body's discomfort. I blinked to adjust to the fading light. I was on the floor. My head felt stuffy, my nose was blocked and I was breathing through my mouth. I lay for a moment, trying to remember where I was and how I had got there. Something dug into my hand, something hard and round. I moved my hand until I could see it. Mother's dull silver compact. Everything came back to me. I sat up and looked around. I felt uneasy, unsettled because I remembered everything but not lying down on the floor. The room was darker than it had been when I came in, not yet night, but late afternoon, shadowy. Not remembering was scarier than all the things I did remember about earlier.

I stood up. My legs felt a bit wobbly, but I didn't feel sick. My head throbbed, and I reached up and touched my forehead, feeling a bump. I wondered for a moment if Dead Rex had hit me on the head, knocking me out, but then I remembered throwing the compact and how it had bounced back at me. I blamed him anyway, feeling sure that he had somehow been responsible for making the compact bounce. My legs, numb as they were, were colder than the rest of me. I rubbed them with my hands to try and revive them, and noticed that my jeans were wet. For a moment I felt confused, then disgusted as I put my damp fingers to my nose to sniff them. I had wet myself, like a baby. If Mother or Nomsa were to see me, what would they think? I made my way quietly to the door where I listened for sounds, but the house was still. I crept up the passage to my room and closed the door.

After I had changed out of my wet jeans, I sat on my bed and thought for a while. Everyone knew I wasn't a person and nobody had liked me until Nomsa. She must have known because Tannie Hettie knew and Tannie Hettie would have told her, probably, because grown-ups always spoke about other people's business, especially if the business was something horrible. But Nomsa had still been my friend. I felt bad now, thinking about how mean I'd been to her, about the ugly thing I'd said. I wanted to make it better, so I tried to think about ways to make things better. Papa had always brought Mother flowers when she was cross with him, but it was winter and there were no flowers. Still, I thought, I could give her a present to say sorry, but I didn't have anything. The only important things I'd owned were in my treasure case, and Mother had destroyed all of those. I picked up King Elvis and held him tight. He still had Ouma's scarf tied round his neck. I thought about giving her my spade and bucket, but I'd never seen Nomsa make mud-cakes so she probably wouldn't have any use for them; besides, they were old and scratched, not very nice. The only thing I had that

Nomsa might like was King Elvis, and I couldn't part with him. But, the more I thought about it, the more it seemed he was the only thing I could give to her. I didn't want to lose Nomsa more than I wanted to keep King Elvis. I was sure he would understand, and Nomsa would look after him. I looked at King Elvis. He seemed so sad, but I knew he understood.

Outside the wind whipped up dust and dead leaves and a plastic packet. The chickens had taken refuge in their coop, and all other living things seemed to have been blown away. All that remained were the trees, leafless and grey.

I stood in the yard, holding my cardigan tightly closed, and stared at Nomsa's room. I imagined I could see her looking back at me through the small window, but it was impossible to tell if she was really there, it was so dark inside. I took a deep breath and walked across the yard. I put up my hand to knock on the door, but at the last moment, my courage failed. I didn't know what to say. I hadn't thought about anything. And what if she was angry when she opened the door? And what if she was sleeping and didn't want to be woken up? And what if she didn't want to see me and chased me away? I didn't think I was brave enough, after everything that I had discovered, to face Nomsa's anger. I knelt down in front of the door and placed King Elvis against it on the ground. I made him sit and wrapped Ouma's scarf tightly around him, to protect him from the cold. I didn't look back as I closed the kitchen door behind me.

Chapter Eighteen

THE FIRST THING I noticed was the light, morning light, the second, I was fully dressed on top of my bed, but someone had covered me with a blanket, and the third, I was holding on to King Elvis. I blinked, dispelling any residual sleepiness, and waited for my mind to remember. Once it did, I wanted to go back to sleep and not face the world, but my curiosity as to how King Elvis had come to be in my bed kept me awake. I held him up, unsure whether I should be happy or sad. What did it mean? Slowly the sounds of the house filtered through to me, and I realized that Nomsa must be back. I could hear water running in the kitchen, and a low melody interspersed with clicks that I was certain was Nomsa's voice, because only she sang songs with clicky words, and the clinking of a spoon against porcelain.

I got out of bed and stretched. I didn't need to get dressed, I thought, because I had slept in my clothes. I decided that I would never wear pyjamas to bed again and save myself the bother of getting dressed every morning.

I was eager to see Nomsa, so I hurried to the kitchen, forgetting for the time being about my recent discoveries. I didn't even think about Mother. But when I got to the kitchen I saw her, sitting at the kitchen table, drinking a cup of coffee. Half a slice of buttered toast with one bite taken out of it was on a plate in front of her. She was dressed, a bit oddly I thought, with a large straw hat on her head, but at least she wasn't in her dressing gown.

Nomsa stood with her back to me at the sink. She was singing, something she had never done in front of Mother before. And, she had Ouma's scarf tied around her head.

Mother looked up at me. It seemed for a moment that she wasn't focusing on me but at some point just to my left, but then she blinked and her eyes seemed to readjust.

'Would you like some toast?' she asked, pushing her plate towards me. I looked down at the slice of toast, at the missing tooth-marked round. She didn't wait for my reply. 'Come sit,' she said, and began to smear jam on the toast from a jar on the table in front of her.

'Tannie Hettie brought this by early this morning' – she gestured at the jam with her knife – 'and that' – she pointed at a round of yellow cheese – 'and some other things. They're from the people at the market.'

I sat down and looked at the array of goods scattered round the kitchen. I should have felt pleased at having such treats in the house, but instead I felt like I had swallowed something heavy. Why had the people at the market sent us all these things? It wasn't as if any of them were our friends, most of them disliked us. Of course they had always been civil, greeting Mother whenever she went to the market, but it was obvious by the way they never stopped for a chat, like they did with other stallholders, that we weren't very popular. They hadn't bothered with us in months, why now?

I looked at Mother, hoping she might fill me in, but she was busy applying layer upon layer of jam to the half-eaten toast. She pushed it towards me. The jam formed a thick red misshapen pyramid on the toast. I looked at it, feeling a little repulsed. I liked a scraping of jam on my toast, so I could taste the butter. Mother should have known this. I looked up at Nomsa, unsure of what to do. She was watching us over her shoulder, her back towards me. She gave me a half-smile and turned back to the dishes, humming to herself.

I sat down at the table and looked at the plate in front of me. I didn't think I could eat the toast. The more I examined it, the more I didn't want to eat it. One of Mother's long hairs had worked its way into the jam, disappearing into its gloopy depths and re-emerging at the crust side, where it snaked across the plate and twisted around the knife. Almost the entire hair was coated in jam. Mother stared at me from across the table. She was smiling, a lopsided grin that wasn't her smile. It looked like someone had cut a smile out of a magazine and stuck it on her face. She was waiting for me to eat. I picked up the toast, wondering how I could get the hair off without her seeing me. The toast sagged with the weight of the jam as I tried to lift it. I put it back down and looked at it. I briefly considered picking it up with both hands, but it was enough effort just to touch it, I couldn't bear the thought of my other hand getting sticky as well. I looked up at Mother, who smiled her funny smile. I realized all I could do was eat it as quickly as possible. Filled with stomach-churning determination, I took hold of the soggy toast firmly on one side and lifted it towards my mouth. For a moment it seemed the toast would hold, but then it flopped towards the plate like its back had been broken, and the mess of jam slid off, landing on the plate with a polite *plop*.

I looked up at Mother, wondering how she would react, but she didn't seem to have noticed. She continued to look at me, the grin that wasn't hers stuck to her face.

'Sorry,' I mumbled, not knowing what else to do. She looked down at the plate and her grin disappeared. For a moment we sat, both staring at the blob. There was no point in me continuing to try and eat the toast, I thought, so I placed it gently back on to the plate. I couldn't bring myself to lick my sticky fingers.

Mother reached out and picked up the plate. She took it over to the kitchen door and flung it into the yard. For a moment she stood there, watching its flight path, then she followed it out. I looked up at Nomsa. She'd stopped singing and was standing on her toes, watching Mother out of the window. She shook her head and clicked her tongue against her teeth: 'Ntsk.'

Mother returned with the plate a few seconds later. She sat down and placed it on the table. It was covered in a layer of dirt, thicker where the jam had been.

'Would you like another piece of toast?' she asked, looking at me. I shook my head. Mother frowned and blinked. 'She ate half the toast, didn't she, at least? ' she faltered. I wondered who she was asking.

'Yes, madam,' Nomsa replied. Mother looked at Nomsa and narrowed her eyes, then she turned to me and leaned across the table.

'I'm going to the orchard,' she whispered. 'Do you want to come with me?' I shrank back. I knew what lived in the orchard, and I didn't want to go there. If she had asked me that a year ago, I wouldn't have hesitated, I would have led the way, but not now. If I went with her, they might take me, they might take us.

'Why don't you go with your mommy?' Nomsa smiled. 'It's not so windy today.'

Fear crawled over me. How could I explain why I didn't want to go? Mother would get angry if I told Nomsa about the fairies, and Nomsa wouldn't believe me. I nodded, it felt like I was far away.

I FOLLOWED MOTHER out of the house and down the veranda steps. I watched her feet, they half shuffled, half walked. She was talking, saying something about the fairies; every now and again my mind snagged on a familiar name, but I couldn't focus on her words. At the kitchen table I had grasped for ways to escape, but now, forced as I was into this situation, I felt far away, like some small distant bird, sitting in a tree above myself, watching. I was lost, surrounded by a cold sky that had no colour. Inside I was shrinking down, disappearing.

I walked through the world I knew so well, but it seemed unfamiliar, an alien landscape. The clumps of dry grass were sharp and spiky, small spears that would pierce the thin soles of my shoes as I walked over them. The air seemed tainted, like the wind had blown up all the dust in the world and, when it died down, the dust had refused to settle. After a while I felt like every breath I took was dusty, and each breath felt dustier than the last. The inside of my nose was caked with it, my throat constricted. I was sure I would soon choke.

I put one foot in front of the other, taking one step for every step Mother took. She walked slowly, and I was in no hurry.

As we got closer to the orchard, I could see the rusty gate and the branches of the trees reaching into the bleached sky. They looked like arms, very old, bony arms, straining with the effort to hold themselves up. Orange trees are not as big as some trees, but somehow, even with their leafy round heads that looked like old ladies' set curls, they seemed alien, and now that alienness made them seem bad. Under all those leaves they were skinny deformed people with lots of arms and lots of fingers. But all trees sort of looked like people, I told myself, all trees look like they have somebody trapped inside. So why did these ones bother me? I looked at them as we walked closer and closer, and I realized they all looked the same. Rows and rows of the same tree. It was as if someone had planted a lot of identical twins in the ground.

The transition from Mother's babble to her silence was so subtle that it took some time for my distant mind to notice that she wasn't talking any more. She'd stopped walking and looked towards the road. I followed her gaze and saw what it was she was looking at. A dust cloud sped down the road towards us. I don't know why, perhaps because we had been so isolated, but at first I thought it was a small distant whirlwind. As it drew closer though, I realized it was a car, or rather a pick-up truck.

We stood on the side of the road and watched its arrival. It slowed down as it neared us, and finally stopped in front of us.

Mother stood and looked at it for a while, like it was some

foreign thing she had never seen before, then she walked slowly round to the driver's side.

I followed her, trying to see who it was through the dust-coated windscreen. The pick-up was familiar. I remembered seeing it before, but my distant mind wouldn't come close enough to put a name on the owner.

As we rounded the car, the driver wound his window down and leaned out.

'Morning, ladies, out for a walk?' he boomed, his bushy moustache wriggling around on his top lip. It was Oom Piet. Mother stared at him and said nothing. I looked up at her, not knowing what to expect. He was not her favourite person, that much I knew, but the look on her face was not the usual disdain she displayed whenever she saw him, but the confusion she seemed to have whenever something or somebody who hadn't been there a moment before appeared.

Oom Piet squirmed slightly under her silent examination, and some part of me felt a little sympathy for him. I knew how that felt. Another part of me was embarrassed: no outsider had seen Mother since she got sick, and I wanted to hide her illness from the world. I reached out and touched her sleeve.

'Ma,' I said. This seemed to break her stare and she turned and looked at me. The look on her face brought out an overwhelming urge in me to protect her, but I was the child and I didn't know how.

It was a long time before anyone said anything. Mother and I stood, looking at each other, both at a loss, not knowing what to do or how to save ourselves. In the end it was Oom Piet who broke the silence.

'Dr Fourie told me you were sick.' Mother didn't say

anything so he went on, 'Ja, I saw him at the bar last night. He said he'd been round to see you, and you weren't doing very well.'

Mother looked up and furrowed her brow. 'Did he?' she almost whispered. I knew she meant had he come to see her, but Oom Piet seemed to take it differently.

'Of course, he didn't tell me what was wrong, he wouldn't do a thing like that, he's professional, but being a friend, of course, I thought I would come around and see if there was something I could do, ja?

'I brought some meat,' he added as if to explain himself further.

Mother looked at him, like she was seeing him for the first time ever. She inclined her head slightly forward, like someone would if they were trying to get a closer look at some strange animal hiding at the back of its cage at the zoo.

'Piet?' she said. I nodded and, taking my cue, Oom Piet nodded as well. 'Marius isn't . . .' she trailed off.

'Ja, I know,' he said, in a quieter voice. Oom Piet looked, at that moment, like he wished he hadn't come.

'Have you seen him?' Mother asked.

Oom Piet's face reddened, he shrugged. 'Maybe once or twice.'

My heart skipped a beat. Had Papa been around town and seen other people? I hadn't thought about that before, that Papa might be somewhere close. Since he had left I had just thought of him as gone, like he didn't exist any more. I used to think a lot about what happened to people when I didn't see them, that maybe they were like clothes I wasn't wearing, hanging around in cupboards, waiting for me. I would imagine them frozen in position, moving only when I was close enough to see them. I had never once wondered where Papa had gone to, or what he was doing, or how far away he was. He could have been right around the corner all this time, living another life that had nothing to do with me, and I hadn't even considered it. He could be so close and yet, he hadn't come to see me.

The little bird that was me flew further away.

Things became hazy, like they weren't real. Mother and Oom Piet spoke for a while, but I couldn't make out the words. They were underwater and I was at the surface, except there wasn't a bottom or a top, just two sides, and their side was filled with water. Their words bubbled out of their mouths with no meaning or form, all I could do was stare at their unreal shapes. Eventually the shape of Oom Piet unfolded from his cab door, and he went to stand next to the shape of Mother. The two shapes became one and some distant part of me realized that he had his arms around her and that the bubbling coming out of her was crying. I looked away and up at the sky. I felt myself lifting into it, like a lost helium balloon, going up and up until I was nothing more than a tiny speck, irretrievable and far away.

The cab door slammed and my balloon burst, dropping me back down to earth. Mother and Oom Piet were gone. A moment went by before I realized they were in the pick-up. Oom Piet was looking at me.

'Hop in,' he said, his words clear. I climbed on to the rear tyre and hoisted myself into the back. I looked around for somewhere to sit. Some plastic shopping bags lay in the far corner. The plastic was wet, clinging to its meaty contents like taut skin, oozing a brown-red liquid goo. I sat on a large toolbox that had been securely tied down, and knocked on the cab window to signal I was ready.

The shopping bags bounced in the corner on the short ride back to the house. With each bump they lifted up and landed with a wet slap, spattering the truck bed with blood freckles and sending a thin trickle of fluid down the metal ridges. It looked like the shopping bags were being battered to death.

Chapter Nineteen

GRANDMA ENGLISH ONCE told me that crying was good for you. She said that crying let out the hurt that you were feeling inside, that if you didn't let it out it would grow until it made you sick. Crying was like medicine.

Mother said Grandma English cried too much. Mother didn't cry when Grandma English died.

Chapter Twenty

OOM PIET LEANED over and took a small red tub from the glove compartment, opened it and scooped out some white gloopy stuff with his fingers. He rubbed the goo between his hands before slicking it over his head. Then, leaning down, so he looked like he was trying to squash himself between the steering wheel and seat, he pulled out the comb he kept in his sock. For a moment he studied himself in the rear-view mirror, then he raked the comb over his head. I adjusted the knob on Papa's binoculars and magnified his head until I could only see slick, evenly spaced grooves.

I'd been playing this game of spy for three days now, ever since I'd found the key to the secret cabinet. The secret cabinet was the only place in the house I'd never been able to explore. It was a no-go area, a wooden cabinet with ball-and-claw feet and straight sides that arched at the top, and it stood, a grim-faced sentry, against the wall in the sitting room. To me it was like the doors in *Alice in Wonderland*, doors that led to who knew where. It was a door that wouldn't let me in. It had never been opened in my presence, and if I happened to be in the room when someone wanted to open it, I was told to go and play somewhere else.

I'd long since given up on finding the key. I'd spent hours looking for it, and I'm sure if I added up all those hours over my life it would amount to days, months even. Finding it had been a complete accident. I was helping Nomsa with the dusting when I'd knocked a small wooden block off the mantelpiece. The block was nothing special, just a plain block of wood, one of those things that people keep for no reason, like pens that don't write or china cups with no handles. The block fell to the floor, and when I bent to pick it up, I noticed a small rectangular bit had popped out at the side. It was a tiny drawer that slid open to reveal a dull, silver key.

I didn't even need to think about what the key was for, I knew. Excitement coursed through my veins. I pocketed the key, slid the drawer closed and placed the block back on the mantelpiece. Finally I could open the cabinet, finally I would have access to all the secrets it contained. I fantasized about what might be inside, maybe a magic wand, maybe it was full of treasure, or a map that would lead to buried treasure, or even a doorway to a secret tunnel. It could be anything; my imagination ran wild. I was startled back to reality by Nomsa popping her head round the door. Mother was ready for lunch and Nomsa wanted me to wash. I looked at her, guilty feelings crawling out of my stomach. I hadn't thought about Mother when I took the key. What if she wanted to go into the cabinet? What if she caught me with the key? She'd go mad, she'd shout and scream, I'd be in big trouble.

'Is something wrong?' Nomsa asked, creasing her brow.

I shook my head.

'I'm coming,' I squeaked.

Nomsa looked at me for a moment longer, then her head disappeared.

I felt in my pocket for the key. I wanted to put it back now. I examined the wooden block, looking for anything that would tell me how to open it, but the surface was smooth. I couldn't even feel a difference in the grain when I ran my fingers over where I thought the drawer was. I dropped it on to the floor again, hoping it would pop open, but it remained tightly sealed. I looked up at the painting of Dead Rex; Nomsa had covered it with a sheet so I wouldn't have to see him. I wondered if I should lift the sheet and ask him for help, he must have seen Mother open it a thousand times. In the end I decided against it, he wouldn't help me, he'd probably relish the idea of me getting into trouble, even if we were related, I didn't think that would matter to him.

I tried rubbing the box, tapping the box; I even blew on it, but nothing I did would budge the drawer. I was beginning to wonder whether I had imagined the whole thing, but a dip into my pocket reassured me that the key was real, and I was in big trouble.

I could hear Nomsa speaking to Mother in the kitchen; they were wondering what I was doing. It wouldn't be long before Nomsa would be back looking for me. I squeezed the block tightly in my hands, ready to pray to Jesus to help me, when I felt something push against my palm. I opened my hands and looked at the block: the small drawer stuck out slightly.

'Faith!' Mother's voice called out to me, and she sounded annoyed. I heard a chair scrape on the kitchen floor. Panic was making my hands shake, making it difficult to put the key back. Finally I managed to slip it back in and close the drawer, putting the block back on to the mantelpiece just as Mother came through the door.

She looked at me, the question What are you doing? written all over her face. Before she could open her mouth I said, 'I was just finishing the dusting.' My voice sounded strangled and guilty.

'You can finish that later,' she said, 'we're waiting for you.'

FOR THE REST of the day I could think about nothing but the cabinet. I had come so close to being able to see what secrets it held that my curiosity, reawakened, burned like a veldt fire. It swept across my mind, eating up all my other thoughts in its flames, until even my earlier fright at nearly being caught was pale and smoky in comparison.

I felt like the cabinet was teasing me and I brooded upon it. I brooded upon the key and upon the block that held it. I was so wrapped up in my brooding that I didn't hear Nomsa when she spoke to me and she eventually gave up trying, saying that talking to me was like talking to a deaf donkey. I brooded until my brooding turned into determination to see inside the cabinet, and determination turned into a plan.

That night I gobbled my stew, swallowing chunks of lamb and potatoes before they were properly chewed, some so large they had to squeeze their way down my middle, but even that didn't slow me down. I wanted dinner to be over and everyone to go to bed. I was too excited to think about anything but my plan. Mother had slipped into one of her quiet moods. She didn't say anything all the way through dinner, and I was glad of it. When she was talkative, the meal could go on for ever.

I lay in my bed, waiting for Nomsa to leave the kitchen and go to her room. Mother had gone straight to bed and I'd followed her shortly after. It was just Nomsa I had to wait for. I listened to the sounds of her washing the dishes. She seemed to be taking a long time. The stew was heavy in my stomach and the warmth of my blankets was making me sleepy. I blinked and took deep breaths, trying to shake off the urge to sleep, but my eyelids felt heavy and I couldn't keep them from dropping down. I closed my eyes, just for a little while, just until Nomsa was gone, just for one moment.

THE NEXT NIGHT I was determined not to make the same mistake. I sat upright in Grandma English's rocking chair in the cold, waiting for Nomsa to go to bed. My eyes felt dry and scratchy; they wanted to close, but this time I was determined I wasn't going to fall asleep. Every few minutes I gave myself a hard pinch to make sure I was awake. I didn't trust the darkness; it played tricks with my eyes and I found it difficult to tell if they were open or closed. After what seemed like a very long time I was jolted into wakefulness. The house was quiet and dark and my body felt stiff and cold. I sat in the chair, listening for any noise. The floorboards creaked, but they did that every night. Mother once told me it was the fairies walking around, but the thought of Dead Rex wandering round the house while we were all asleep had given me nightmares and, eventually, Papa had told me that it was just the wood losing heat that made the boards creak. It's contraction, he'd said. I still didn't know who to believe. I'd never heard of contraction but I also hadn't come across any fairies wandering down the passage.

I stretched and made my way to the open door. I checked for a crack of light under Mother's door that would signal she was still awake, before stepping out into the passage. There wasn't one, the house was dark. I guided myself down the passage, keeping one hand on the wall, low enough so I wouldn't touch any of the fairy paintings. If they were asleep, I didn't want to risk waking them up by bumping the frames. I kept my eyes wide, trying to make out any unusual shapes that might move. I didn't know what I would do if I did come across a fairy, so I hoped that Papa had been right. Finally I felt the sitting room's painted door frame. I edged around it slowly and felt for the door. At first my hand touched nothing as it reached into the darkness, but after a few blind reaches I finally grasped it and pulled it towards me. Trying not to make any noise or bump anything, I moved into the room and clicked the door shut. Still grasping the handle, I ran my free hand up the wall until I felt the light switch and clicked it on.

Bright light flooded the room, making my eyes tear. I blinked until the light was bearable, then I looked around. The painting of Dead Rex was still covered up, and I wondered if he was behind it or if he'd come out and was hiding somewhere in the room. The hairs on my neck stood up; should I pull the cloth off to check? – but that seemed worse. He might be asleep and that would wake him up. I didn't relish the idea of waking Dead Rex up in the middle of the night when everyone else was asleep. I looked around the room, checking anywhere where he could hide. I looked under the coffee table and behind the couch, but found only dustballs. When I was sure he wasn't anywhere in the room, I switched on the table lamp and turned the overhead light off. The lamp gave off a hushed glow, like gentle yellow twilight, less noticeable if Mother woke up.

Excitement and nerves buzzed inside me. I hurried over to the box and took it in my hands. I took a deep breath and squeezed the box. The drawer popped open.

I slid the key into the cabinet's lock, held my breath and turned it. It turned halfway and then caught. I tried to twist it further, but the key wouldn't budge. Perhaps I'd been mistaken, this was the wrong key. I tried to turn it back, but the key was stuck. Panic surged through me. I couldn't leave the key in the lock, Mother would definitely find it. She'd know. I was in big trouble. I had to find a way to get the key out. I took a deep breath and tried again. It refused to move, even when I used both my hands, twisting until my fingers hurt. I scrunched up my face and stared at the hateful cabinet. I felt tricked, it was laughing at me, I could almost hear its jeers. I grabbed the key and pulled it in frustration, determined to get it out any way I could. The cabinet door came slightly forward and I felt the key give a little. I looked at the door, surprised, my anger subsiding as quickly as it had arrived. I took hold of the little latch handle and pulled it towards me, twisting the key at the same time. The key turned easily and the door swung open.

I faced the open cabinet, breathing in its dusty unused-air smells. It smelled like the cupboard in Ouma's spare room, the cupboard where she kept old clothes that she didn't have the heart to throw away: her long wedding dress, decorated with yellowing lace and wrapped in plastic; a fox-fur stole with two shrivelled heads, dull glass eyes and two limp tails; sequined evening dresses that each had a story about dancing which Ouma told in a dreamy voice; dusty hatboxes containing hats made out of thick felt and lace and feathers; all things she no longer wore and I couldn't imagine her ever having worn.

The secret cabinet, though, contained fewer things. Far from being a doorway into a secret place, the back of the cabinet was nothing more than unvarnished wood, against which Papa's rifle leaned. The rifle was nothing new to me. I'd seen it before, I'd even been allowed to hold it once, aiming it at a tin can Papa had placed on the fence. I'd never fired it though. I had to wait until I was bigger before being allowed to do that. I reached out and ran my finger down its cold barrel, but I knew better than to try and take it out. The day I'd been allowed to hold the gun, Papa had told me that if I dropped it, it might go off, and I didn't want to risk that happening now.

I turned my focus to the other things. At the bottom of the cabinet were two hard leather cases, stacked one on top of the other, a pair of brown army boots, and a neatly folded army uniform. Papa had to go and be a reserve soldier sometimes, and this was the uniform he dressed in before leaving to report for duty.

'I'm off to report for duty,' he would say in a stern voice, 'off to defend my women.' He would then stamp his foot and salute me, and I would stamp and salute him back.

I touched the rough material of the uniform and thought about the times he came home after his service was up. Sometimes he'd come back a different person, quiet and moody, other times he would be the same, just not laugh as much as usual. Always, he was glad to be home.

I let go of the rough fabric and turned to the two leather cases. One was bulky and brown and reminded me of an animal's head, maybe a cow without ears or horns. It was Papa's camera case, I wasn't supposed to touch it. I lifted it up and quickly placed it down on top of Papa's uniform. The case was heavy and awkward to hold in my hands, I was afraid I'd drop it. There would be hell to pay if I dropped the camera.

I was beginning to feel cheated. There was no hidden mystery in this cabinet, everything in it I'd seen before. There was only one thing left to look at, the other case. It was shaped like two cylinders and not as big as the camera case. I opened it and looked at the binoculars inside. Papa had often let me look through them as he pointed out different birds; they made birds that were far away seem like they were right in front of my eyes. Papa liked to look at birds, he had a book with pictures of all the birds in the world. Whenever we saw a strange bird on the farm, we would look through the book when we got home and see if we could name it.

I took the binoculars out, uncapped the lenses and held them up to my eyes. Everything looked blurred. I rolled the knob with my finger, the way Papa had shown me, but the blur just shifted; nothing was far away enough.

I hung the strap around my neck and went to the window. Looking out, I could see the bright moon and stars, lighting up the night sky. I put the binoculars to my eyes and looked up at the moon. It glowed, big and bright and blue-white. I could see its features carved out on its surface. The man in the moon was clearer than he'd ever looked before.

I stayed at the window for a long time, focusing on different parts of the sky, patches of twinkling stars against the velvety purple-black of the night, but always I came back to the man in the moon.

I FOLLOWED OOM PIET'S path to the front door through the binoculars, and watched as he knocked and waited. He tugged at his trousers, pulling them up, and readjusted his belt. I was pleased with the strength of the binoculars: I could sit far away, almost all the way to the orchard, and still watch what went on at the house. It was like I was right up close. The only thing was that I couldn't hear what anyone said, but I wasn't really interested in anything Oom Piet had to say, and besides, he didn't like me being around when he came to visit Mother.

Oom Piet had been visiting the farm every day since the day he'd first come by and saved me from having to go into the orchard. After he'd driven us back to the house, he had sat with Mother for several hours, talking about Papa and how she didn't deserve to be treated so badly. Mother had cried and Oom Piet had put his arm around her shoulder and drawn her close, so that her head was resting against him. I thought I saw Oom Piet smile a little that day, as Mother cried on his shoulder. The horrible things Oom Piet said about Papa made me feel uncomfortable – they were supposed to be friends, and I didn't think that friends should say ugly things about each other. It made me think that Oom Piet wasn't really Papa's friend.

I focused on the bunch of flowers Oom Piet held out as

Mother answered the door. He hadn't brought flowers before, today was the first time.

After Oom Piet had left the first day, I went and sat next to Mother. We sat for a long time, staring at the sky's changing red and orange hues as the sun set. As dusk settled over the farm, Mother said, 'He's not coming back, you know.'

I cried a little when she said that because I knew she meant Papa. Papa would never come back. Mother put her arm around my shoulder and drew me close, the same way Oom Piet had drawn her close.

After I'd stopped crying, Mother told me that we'd have to find a way to look after ourselves, that she'd hoped that Papa would come back or that the fairies would help us, but that now, seeing Oom Piet, she'd realized that no one would help us.

'We're alone, Faith,' she said, 'all alone in the world.'

BUT SOMEONE DID come to help us, and I watched him hand Mother the flowers through Papa's binoculars. Spying on them through Papa's binoculars made me feel I had a little hope left. I knew it was stupid, but I hoped that somehow, because the binoculars were like eyes and these eyes belonged to Papa, Papa would see what Oom Piet was doing and come back to stop it.

Mother and Oom Piet went inside, the door closed behind them and I was left lying in the long dry grass with nothing to look at. I turned over and stared at the sky. It was completely cloudless and endless. The sun was high and gave off a bright glare that made my eyes water if I looked up through the binoculars, so I just lay there and felt its heat on my face.

I closed my eyes and listened to the stillness of the day. In the distance I could hear Nomsa singing. I rolled over and focused on the back yard. I could see the edge of a white sheet on the washing line, but the angle was wrong and I couldn't see her. She must be hanging out the washing, I thought, because the sheet wasn't there before. As I looked at the sheet I heard the distant engine of a car. I wriggled my body until I faced the opposite way, looking down the drive. Through the binoculars I could see a cloud of dust and Tannie Hettie's car. It was the day of her weekly visit.

I slipped the binoculars into my bag. I'd been carrying the bag around with me since I'd taken the binoculars. It was a bag Ouma had given me to keep my sewing in, but I didn't like sewing and had never done any. It came in useful now though. It was big enough to hide the binoculars in and put a jersey on top so they couldn't be seen. That way, I could carry the binoculars with me everywhere and no one would ever know.

I ran to the house. I liked to be there when Tannie Hettie was around, to see what she'd brought with her. She always brought dried fruit, and last time she'd brought things from the market people. I wanted to be there to unpack the bags.

Tannie Hettie and I arrived at the house at the same time. She parked next to Oom Piet's pick-up and got out of the car. She nodded to me and then at the pick-up.

'It's Oom Piet,' I said, answering her question before she asked it.

'Is it really?' She raised her eyebrows. She pursed her lips and looked at the pick-up. 'So it is,' she said.

I helped Tannie Hettie carry the bags into the kitchen. Oom Piet sat at the kitchen table, a cup of coffee next to him. He was talking in urgent tones to Mother, clasping her thin fingers between his two meaty hands.

Tannie Hettie waited at the door for them to notice her, and when they didn't, she cleared her throat sharply.

Oom Piet looked up and dropped Mother's hand.

'Hettie.' His round red face went even redder.

Tannie Hettie looked at him, a look that spoke of disapproval and wrongdoing, one that Mother used to give me whenever I was naughty.

'There's shopping that needs to be unpacked from my car,' she said in a voice that wouldn't allow protest, and handed him the keys. Oom Piet took the keys and slunk out of the door like a small boy who's just been caught stealing.

Tannie Hettie poured herself a cup of coffee. She sat down in the chair Oom Piet had recently vacated. 'You're looking better,' she said to Mother, 'but I think you've finally lost your mind.'

Mother looked up at Tannie Hettie and anger flashed across her face. She reached over and grabbed Tannie Hettie's hand. Veins stuck out along the top of Mother's hand; her fingertips were white, she was clutching Tannie Hettie's hand so tight.

'What do you know?' Mother hissed.

Tannie Hettie narrowed her eyes but she didn't try to

move her hand away, even though Mother's grip must have been hurting her.

'I know he's married,' she said.

Mother threw back her head and laughed, a manic, hysterical laugh. She let go of Tannie Hettie's hand, tossing it away like it was something horrible she no longer wanted to touch.

'Bella,' Tannie Hettie said in a warning tone, 'your child—' but she never finished the sentence, because Mother stopped laughing and with a sharp movement leaned towards Tannie Hettie until their cheeks were almost touching.

'I am thinking of my child,' she hissed, 'thinking of her and my future. Did Liesel and Marius think of my child? Why don't you ask them that, next time they're round for Sunday lunch?'

The colour drained from Tannie Hettie's face. For a moment she looked like she might cry.

'I'm just trying to help.' Tannie Hettie's voice sounded like the voice of an old woman, frail and unsteady. I was shocked, my world was disintegrating. Even Tannie Hettie, who had been the most solid person, steady and unshakable, was crumbling in front of me, and I couldn't stop it from happening. For the second time that week I felt myself disappearing, drifting away. If I couldn't even hold on to myself, how could I hold on to anything else?

Behind me I heard the front door close. Mother sat back in her chair and took a deep breath.

'I have no choice, Hettie,' she said, 'we have nothing left.' I looked at Mother and realized for the first time what the change had been the day Oom Piet came. Mother had stopped fighting. She was not getting better, she'd just given up.

Chapter Twenty-One

MOTHER WAS GOING out. Not just leaving the farm, but going out. I sat on her bed, watching as she chose a dress from her wardrobe, held it up against her, and studied herself in the full-length mirror on the inside of the wardrobe door. It was the dress she used to wear when Papa took her dancing, the clingy one the deep colour of roses that had no back. She threw it onto the bed and chose another, the black one with lace across the front and a red fabric rose in the middle. Mother also threw that one on the bed. She sighed and looked at me.

'What can I wear?' she asked, biting her lip. Mother had never looked so unhappy about going out before. Going out was something she'd loved when Papa was around. I knew Mother only had two going-out dresses, so I had to choose from the ones on the bed. I pointed to the red dress with no back, thinking that it was her favourite and maybe wearing it would make her feel happy. She shook her head.

'I can't wear that, don't be bloody ridiculous.' Suddenly Mother looked angry and I didn't know why; she snatched the dress off the bed and threw it back into the wardrobe. 'If I wear that, God knows what he'll think.'

Mother continued to look through the dresses in her wardrobe until she found a plain brown dress that had a belt through the middle. She held it up and asked me what I thought of it. I nodded, not wanting to upset her, but I thought the dress wasn't very nice. It was the plain kind of dress people wore on Sunday, a dress for singing hymns and saying prayers. It wasn't the going-out kind of dress – not that I'd ever been out, but I'd seen how Mother and Papa dressed when they went out, and I knew it wasn't like that.

Mother sat down at her dressing table and looked at herself in the mirror. She was tight-lipped and pale, and the light from the window played against the glass so I couldn't see her reflection if I tilted my head. With two fingers she stretched out the skin around her eyes, then she cupped her face in her hands and pulled her cheeks back. I wondered what she was doing; it made her eyes look slanty and her mouth extra wide. I wanted to giggle.

She caught my eye in the mirror. 'Do you think I'm old, Faith?'

I nodded. Mother was older than Nomsa and Nomsa was old. I knew this because I'd asked Nomsa and she was twenty-four. Mother was older than Nomsa, which made her very old. Mother narrowed her eyes and went back to stretching her face.

After she'd stretched her face enough, Mother took out her powder puff and patted it against her cheeks and nose. The powder on her pale skin made her look like a ghost; it clung to the fine downy hair above her lip and along her jawline like dry flour on bread dough. This was the first time I'd watched her dress in almost a year, and I wondered if the hair had grown since then, or if it had been there before and I had just never noticed.

'Run to the bathroom and get me some toilet paper.' Mother was holding the wand of her mascara out at me, the brush was caked with black clots. I returned with the wad of tissue paper I'd pulled off the toilet roll and held it out to her. She looked at me and shook her head. 'I only needed a little bit.' She sounded annoyed. I looked down at the thick wad in my hand, pulled off a small piece and offered it to her. She took it without saying anything else.

Mother was made-up and dressed, all that was left was shoes and stockings. She pulled a pair of beige nylons out of her drawer and ran them over her hand. 'Dammit,' she muttered, 'there's a ladder at the top.' She looked through the drawer for more, but couldn't find any others. She ended up wearing the laddered ones.

Finally, Mother slipped her feet into brown shoes that had a hole in the front for her big toe to peep through. The shoes had high heels that made Mother even taller. She looked at herself in the mirror and adjusted the belt on the dress. The dress hung on her like a sack and the tight belt made it look worse, showing up how skinny she was underneath.

She turned and looked at me, her eyelashes blackened and clogged with mascara, red lips like a gash against her ghost-powder face. She didn't ask me what I thought, she didn't have to. We both knew she wasn't the same as she used to be.

I AWOKE WITH a start, my heart pounding. I'd been having a nightmare, but I couldn't remember what it was. I lay in the dark, trying to cry out for someone to come and help me, but I was breathing so hard I couldn't find my voice. I felt sick, and before I could stop myself, I vomited on my bed. The heaving sent a sharp bolt of pain through my shoulder and down my back, making me cry out in a strange strangled voice I'd never heard before. I began to cry. I was scared, confused, but I didn't know why. I held on to my pillow, trying not to move because the pain was so big. I felt hot and sticky and soon I must have fallen asleep.

DAWN LIGHT SEEPED into my room. I'd pushed all my blankets back while I was asleep and now I was freezing cold. The bitter smell of bile filled my nostrils and I saw it was coming from my blankets, they were covered in dry vomit. Seeing the vomit made me retch again and this sent a pain through my shoulder. I rolled on to my other side; it didn't hurt so much, and after a short while I was able to wiggle my way out of bed. Standing up made me dizzy. I wanted to go and get Nomsa, tell her I was sick. I wanted her to make me better.

I was surprised to find Mother in the kitchen; it was early, too early for anyone to be awake. She was sitting at the kitchen table, staring into space. When I came in she looked up; her mascara had run down her cheeks, staining them, so they looked like ink paintings, the kind you do by putting ink into water so it runs and splits. She was still wearing the ugly brown dress, but it was torn at the neck and her lipstick had rubbed away. She looked at me with such sadness it made me cry.

Mother took a deep breath and pushed her chair back. She came over and stood in front of me.

'I'm sorry,' she whispered. I didn't know why she was sorry. Maybe she didn't love me any more because she just stood there, looking at me like I was the reason she was so sad.

'I want Nomsa.'

Mother began to cry, but I didn't care that I'd hurt her feelings by saying that. I didn't care about her any more.

I stood in the kitchen and screamed at her. I didn't want her to be my mother, this strange thin woman who wasn't there any more. I wanted Nomsa. Maybe Mother knew this, because she was crying. She sank down on to the kitchen floor and sobbed with me. We didn't touch.

Which one of us stopped first I don't know, but we did stop and the kitchen filled with broken silence. The ticking clock, the sharp snotty intake of breath, the drip of the kitchen tap.

Mother stood up and wiped her nose on the back of her hand. 'I need to clean you up,' she said. I nodded. I was too upset to object, I was cold and I wanted to get the vomit off me. She directed me to the bathroom, where she filled the big bath almost all the way to the top. She helped me out of my pyjamas and I climbed into the bath, trying not to jolt my shoulder. Mother reached out and touched my shoulder with her finger. 'You have a big bruise,' she said. 'Do you remember how you got it?'

I shook my head.

'Maybe you fell out of bed.' Her voice was soothing and,

like the scent of citrus, it made me feel like I did when I was a baby and she would rock me to sleep.

'It hurts.' My voice was shaky.

Mother picked up her face-cloth and dipped it in the bath. She ran it over my shoulders and back so softly that it was like she was stroking me with the tips of her fingers, like it was just the feeling of warm water running off my skin. Mother sat on the floor, stroking my body with her face-cloth until the water began to cool. She didn't say anything, and neither did I. I felt like my mother had come back.

I NEVER SAW Nomsa again, not properly. I watched through the window when Tannie Hettie brought the police and I watched as they took the stretcher away. It was covered with a sheet, one of the sheets that whipped in the wind when Nomsa hung them out, except this sheet wasn't clean and white, it had a dark stain. A stain like the one on the mattress blanket, the one Mother had wrapped the dead monster from the range in, the one she'd shot with Papa's rifle. The same rifle the police wrapped in plastic and took with them when they took Mother away.

Part Two – 1999

Chapter One

'Happy New Year!'

Mia erupts like a popped champagne cork. I peer at her over the top of my chipped orange tumbler. It's meant to be a Moroccan tea glass. Gold swirls decorate its surface, but I suspect it came from China City Cash and Carry, a cheap rip-off. She bounces round the room bestowing kisses, red skirt swishing round her ankles. At fifty-four she's got more energy than me; even her auburn curls, shot with grey, have a life of their own. I stifle a yawn and she descends on me, filling my glass with pink bubbly which spills over on to my hand. I suck at it quickly before it has time to trickle down on to my dress.

'Not exactly Dom, but it does the trick, eh?' She grabs me by the arm, pulling me up. 'To the balcony.' She pummels me forward. The room swims. Mia shrieks with laughter and pushes me out through the balcony door. I gulp the night air and, for a moment, the world settles. Then I feel woozy again.

The giant neon billboard capping the Ponte building draws my focus. Arcs of green and blue light build up from the bottom then somersault, lighting up the words YEBO GOGO! My stomach turns inside-out and I look away.

Fireworks begin exploding over Hillbrow, they flare into bright, multi-coloured light-flowers that cascade down like iridescent rain and fizz out, only to be followed by another party rocket whizzing into the sky. The whole world is filled with whistles and pops and whipcracks and explosions.

'That's a gunshot, definitely a gunshot.' Merv the Perv leans over and whispers in my ear with hot fumy breath. I stiffen and wonder how he can pick out the sound of gunfire from the cacophony of noise that surrounds us.

'Bullshit!' I look over at Mia, hoping for rescue, but she's too busy toasting the Jo'burg skyline to notice I've been cornered. Inside someone's turned up the music and Ketso's gyrating his hips in the middle of the living-room floor while Karl pushes the furniture back to make space for more dancers.

'Wanna dance?' Merv places his hand on my shoulder, making my skin crawl.

'With you?' I try to sound scathing but I'm too drunk and the words just slur.

'Course with me, baby, who else can teach you the moves?' He pushes up against me, thrusting his pelvis in a series of gestures meant to demonstrate the moves. The balcony railing cuts into my ribcage and for a brief second I consider throwing myself over to get away.

'OK then.' I duck under his arm and escape into the flat, making for Ketso. 'Save me,' I shout in his ear, gesturing at Merv, who is hovering just inside the balcony door, leering. Ketso laughs and swirls me around. Mia joins us, swishing her skirt and swinging her hips like she's twenty, like she's the same age as me, only I feel so much older.

'Phone's ringing,' Ketso shouts above the music.

'Where is it?' Mia looks around. We're expecting Molly to call. I stop dancing and cock my head, trying to make out the direction of the sound. 'Turn the music down.' Someone lowers the volume; for a moment we stand, frozen, listening. The phone trills from under the couch. Mia lunges for it and picks it up, still ringing. Then she sits down and grins: 'Everyone shout at once when I answer, OK?'

She picks up the receiver and holds it up.

'Happy New Year!' we shout.

'Happy New Year, Molly.' Merv, two seconds after the rest of us.

'Happy New Year, Mol.' Mia crooks the receiver into her neck and lights a cigarette. 'I'm sorry, who?' She waves her free hand up and down, gesturing for quiet. 'Yes, this is she.' I look over at her, wondering who's on the other end of the line. Her jovial expression melts, suddenly she's fifty-four again.

'No, that's not possible.' Mia drops ash on to her lap, brushes it off absently on to the carpet. She shakes her head. I watch the tendrils of smoke snake upwards from her cigarette past her furrowed brow with a deepening sense of unease.

'Yes, I'm sorry too. Thanks for letting me know.' She hangs up. For a while she says nothing; her hands clutch the phone on her lap, knuckles white. Someone on the balcony laughs, cutting into the uneasiness. Mia looks up, her face ashen, the flush of alcohol drained away.

'Faith, I'm so sorry, baby.'

I shake my head, my legs feel unsteady, my throat constricts.

'What?' I whisper, unable to get anything louder out.

She begins to cry.

'What's wrong?' Panic surges inside me. 'Is it Molly?'

She shakes her head. Cold relief.

'It's your mother.' I look at her, not comprehending. I haven't seen Mother in years. I feel all the eyes in the room on me. A hot flush rises up my neck. I want the cracks in the floorboards to expand and swallow me. All these people are here and someone calls about Mother. I take a deep breath.

'What about the crazy bitch?' I smile and shrug like I'm some cartoon character and I've just said aw shucks.

Mia reaches out to me. 'Faith, she's dead.'

'THIS WAY, PLEASE.' The man's tone is quiet, soothing, the tone of a man who is used to dealing with grieving relatives. He understands death, or at least understands the cliché of it. That's what this feels like to me, a cliché. If there's a handbook for morticians, he's studied it and knows it by heart. I wonder, briefly, if his suit is standard-issue funeral-director grey. He's obviously had it years, it no longer buttons up over his gut. I imagine him graduating: 'Congratulations, son, well done, and here's your funeral-director suit, wear it with pride.' I stifle a giggle.

He opens a door and leads us into a room with warm gentle lighting. On his advice we are dealing with the arrangements first, before the viewing.

'As I explained,' he continues to use his tranquil funeral-director voice, 'we have a wide range to suit all tastes and pockets.' He gestures to the display of coffins that run the length of the room. 'All handles and linings are interchangeable,' he adds and leaves us to make our choice, shutting the door behind him with a discreet click.

I wander up and down the display, running my fingers along the polished veneer of the coffins, caressing their smooth surfaces, peering into the open slice at the top to see the satin linings, white or black or red or light sky-blue, the linings that cushion and frame the head.

I already know which one I'll choose. It's the plain pine one, the one with rope for handles and nails to fix the lid on. The cheapest one. Not because it suits our pockets, as the man put it with such practised discretion, although it does, but because I can see no reason to spend most of my hard-earned cash on a pretty box to burn Mother in. If it were up to me, I would have let the state bury her in one of those prisoner graves marked with a concrete slab and a number.

I rap my knuckles against the top of the pine coffin. 'This one.'

Mia sighs. 'I was thinking of something with a little more dignity. Her life was so hard, she deserves something . . .' She makes a sweeping gesture with her hand while she looks for the word. I clench my jaw to stop myself from saying something nasty, something that will upset her. I take a deep breath.

'She would have liked this one, it's rustic, she liked rustic.' My voice sounds hard, sarcastic, not at all like the soothing funeral director's voice I'd tried to imitate. Mia doesn't seem to notice, or she's chosen to ignore my tone. She nods slowly.

I take her hand. I'm so much taller than Mia that I suddenly feel like I'm an adult and she's a child. I have my mother's height and, in so many ways, I look like her. At times I look in the mirror and feel like I am staring at her. I have her thick hair, though the colour is closer to Papa's, her thin, even lips, her straight nose. My hands have her long fingers, her square nails. I remember Mother as beautiful, but when I look in the mirror I don't see that beauty looking back at me. I lack whatever quality she had that made the features we share beautiful.

'This one,' I whisper, my hand absorbing the softness of the polished pine, 'I want to bury her in this one.'

THE CHOIR LEADS us in 'Amazing Grace', Mother's favourite hymn, according to Mia. I didn't know she had a favourite hymn; as far as I know she thought religion was nonsense.

The pallbearers wheeled the coffin up the aisle to the front of the church. Mia placed three sunflowers on top of it.

'Tasteful,' she said.

'Tasteful and rustic,' I said.

The church is strangely stifling, sweat trickles down the back of my neck, I dab at it with the wad of tissues Mia gave me, in case I needed to cry. It's an odd church: besides the fact that it's so hot, the ceiling is uncommonly low, which probably contributes to its airlessness, and it seems devoid of any religious references. There is a faint reek that catches in my nostrils every so often, reminding me of the dustbins at the backs of restaurants. It could be coming from Mother; perhaps she is starting to smell inside her pine box in this heat. The thought of Mother in the box sends a chill up my spine. Seeing her at the funeral home was weirdly disconnected from anything real. She was so thin, skeletal, like all her flesh had dissolved away and all that was left was her shrunken skin, clinging to her bones. She looked like Dead Rex, or his wife. She was pale too, like she hadn't seen the sun, ever. I suppose she didn't get to spend too much time outdoors. And her hair, chopped off. I wonder when they did that, cropped it so short. The beautician, if that's what they call the hair and make-up people in funeral homes, had tried to comb it so it lay flat against her head, like a 1920s flapper, but it had sprung back up in places, like it still had life.

That's not Mother, I thought, no way, it's somebody else, something else. A statue perhaps. Mother was never that still. But it was her, I knew that, even if her name was all I recognized. It was her. Was. Mother no longer exists. She's gone. Gone to hell to spend eternity with all the other murderers. God forgive her. I can't.

Chapter Two

'HOW ARE YOU feeling?' Mia hands me a cup of sweet tea, too sweet for my liking, I saw her ladle in the sugar.

'OK, I suppose.' I manage a smile, though all I want to do is to shout, to scream, 'Stop fucking looking at me!'

But I don't scream. I just smile, a watery, pathetic smile because everyone is looking at me, balancing their delicate white cups and saucers in one hand while shovelling miniature sausage rolls and triangle sandwiches into their mouths with the other. Their voices generate a low hum in the church hall as they exchange pleasantries about how lovely the service was, but all the time they're really thinking, I wish it was an open coffin, wish I could have seen what the mad murderess looked like. They want to know if I look like her, if I take after her, if I might be dangerous, if I'm crazy too.

'You sure? You look like you're about to explode.' Mia lights up a cigarette, causing the priest to cast a disapproving look in our direction. There are several NO SMOKING signs, but either Mia hasn't noticed or she doesn't care.

'It's no smoking,' I tell her. She drags deeply on her cigarette, causing the flesh around her mouth to pucker.

'I'm in mourning, let them try and stop me.' She offers me the pack and I take one, even though I don't smoke. Mia doesn't look surprised. 'Times of stress and all that,' she says, rolling back the wheel of her lighter. I lean in, dragging to ignite the cigarette and sucking the acrid smoke into my lungs.

Instantly, saliva floods my mouth and I want to throw up. I stand and look around, desperate for a sign to indicate the direction of the ladies' room. I can't find one so I head for the garden instead. I can puke in the rosebushes.

The slightly cooler outside air provides some relief after the stuffy heat of the hall and church, and my nausea begins to subside. I take refuge under a large tree and steady myself against its trunk. It seems so quiet in the garden after the conversational hum in the hall, so peaceful, yet I can still hear the traffic on the busy street at the front of the church.

I sit down on the grass, I'm exhausted suddenly, I feel like I can't stand upright any longer. I adjust my skirt so it covers as much of my legs as it can, lean back against the tree and close my eyes.

I don't know how long I've been there, in the shaded serenity of the tree, lost in the dappled light that plays against my eyelids, in the occasional birdsong, in the distant buzz of traffic. I don't know how long she's been standing over me before I notice her, or why I notice her – perhaps she blocked out the light with her shadow – but she's there and I don't need to open my eyes to know it's her.

'Mol,' I whisper. She says nothing; she doesn't need to.

WE HATED EACH other on sight. She hated me because I was stealing her mother, her room and even her bed. I hated her because I thought she could see inside me, and because I had never met a girl that hadn't tortured or bullied me. I was an only child, and so was she. We weren't used to sharing.

To make matters worse, none of Mia's cats liked me. The moment Mia led me through the door of her tiny two-bedroom flat in Troyeville, her cats spat and hissed.

'Merlin, Lancelot, Bratcat!' Mia stamped her foot, sending the three cats bolting in various directions, out on to the balcony, through the front door, into Mia's bedroom to quiver under her bed.

I stood in the hallway, feeling ashamed of the reaction I'd caused in the cats, convinced more than ever that I was a child born of the evil of fairies.

'Well, don't just stand there, come in.' Mia led the way into the cluttered sitting room, the parquet flooring clicking under her feet like loose teeth. I followed, reluctantly. I had still not accepted what had happened to me. I felt trapped in a nightmare, one in which I was unable to scream, where my voice had been stolen and the terror that something awful lurked around every corner squatted like a large toad in my belly.

I looked around the room, taking in the view of the jagged Johannesburg skyline. I had only been in Johannesburg a few hours and already I hated its broken sky. The room was small and cluttered, nothing like the ordered sparseness of the farmhouse. A large couch, covered with bright throws and beaded Indian cushions, took up most of the room. It was several months before I realized the couch was, in fact, beige and very similar to the one we'd had in the sitting room on the farm. I later learned that they were a set, from the days Mother and Mia shared a flat. Against one wall was a bookshelf; magazines and books spilled off it on to the floor, migrating across the room to make untidy piles all over the place. Every other wall was covered in paintings and drawings. The room seemed to be constructed from chaos itself.

A girl, around the same age as me, but smaller, came in the front door holding one of the cats. The cat seemed almost the same size as her; it looked awkward and uncomfortable in her arms, yet it was completely docile. She placed it on the floor and it arched against her legs, purring loudly. She looked up at me with large soulful eyes, and I felt as if they were chastizing me.

Those first few weeks of sharing were hell for both of us. We slept head to toe in a narrow single bed that seethed with resentment. After one week we were both covered in mottled bruises, me from the sharply delivered kicks born of Molly's anger at my presence, her from having to share a bed with someone plagued by violent nightmares, nightmares that left me feeling terrified yet unable to remember anything about them. Every night I would wake up screaming and thrashing about, while Molly yelled at me and delivered blows with her pillow and her small fists. We were alone in the flat: Mia worked at night at a jazz club, leaving us in the care of one of the black women who rented the tiny servants' rooms on the roof of the building. These women bathed us, put us to bed and left us, checking every hour or so to make sure we were asleep. No one ever heard our nocturnal wars.

Molly began to seek revenge on me in ways other than her kicks. She felt that she was suffering more than I was, that she had lost everything that was hers and, in her loss,

I had gained much. It didn't help matters that Mia was especially nice to me, and punished Molly if she caught her being nasty. Molly could not confront me with her anger, her jibes were lost in my silence and just served to push me further into myself. It was a no-win situation, but being children we hadn't realized that, we still thought there had to be a winner and a loser in everything.

Her attempts to drive me away became ever more inventive. She put salt into my tea, gave my clothes to the cats to sleep on, threw my toothbrush in the bin. It's ironic that one of these attempts finally brought us together.

I was finding it progressively more difficult to bury myself and my feelings. When I went to the bathroom I would only look at the floor, in case I caught a glimpse of myself in the mirror. I wanted to pretend I wasn't me, that everything that had happened had happened to somebody else. As long as I didn't see myself or hear my voice, I could hold on to the belief that I was someone else. I even kept King Elvis locked away in my suitcase because he belonged to that other person that bad things had happened to.

One night, after being woken up by another of my nightmares, Molly began to scream at me. Tears streamed down her face, she hit at me with her fists, but all I did was put up my arms to defend myself. Inside I was numb, safely hidden from her anger by the fact that I wasn't anybody, by my refusal to face up to anything. But unknown to me, Molly had discovered King Elvis while she was going through my things, looking for new ways to torture me. That night, unable to get a response from me, she decided instead to take her anger out on my bear. She ran out of the room and returned, seconds later, with a large knife. Opening her cupboard, she retrieved King Elvis and, throwing him on to the floor where I could see him, she drove the knife through him, straight into my heart.

I stared in shock at the body of my bear as Molly drew out the knife, white stuffing clinging to the blade like sinew, and plunged it in over and over again. Each time she stabbed him, she screamed in frustration, and each scream penetrated that place where I had buried myself like the blade penetrated the soft body of the bear. It loosened the hold I had over my pain and fear until it boiled over and exploded out of me. I screamed. It's impossible for me to tell how long I screamed, it could have been hours, or minutes, or even seconds, but at some point that scream turned into sobbing which turned into words. Words of rage, at Molly, at Mother, at Nomsa for being dead.

Somewhere in those words Molly began to fathom just how alike we were; everything she was so afraid of losing, I had already lost. I was the child she was afraid of becoming, the motherless child. Like me, her father was absent, far away and uninterested; Mia worked long hours, and when she was around she divided her time between parties and politics. She had little left over for Molly. Molly wasn't bad inside, she was just hurt and afraid, like me.

That night we wore ourselves down with screaming and sobs. By the time someone came to check up on us, we'd both fallen asleep where we lay, me on the bed, Molly on the floor.

A truce followed. Molly stopped kicking me and hiding my things, I no longer ignored her when she spoke to me. The body of King Elvis had vanished and, like everyone else who had disappeared from my life, I didn't expect him ever to reappear. A week later he did, his wounds carefully stitched up by Molly's small hands.

We shared the bed for a year before Mia managed to buy another one, but we slept head to head, toe to toe, spooning each other like lovers.

MOLLY SITS DOWN next to me and leans back against the tree. She lights a cigarette and takes a small, delicate puff. Everything about her is delicate, in complete contrast to me. She's lithe, with small hands and long tapered fingers, thin bony wrists, a somewhat elfin body, she seems slightly non-human, otherworldly. Even her large eyes, which protrude slightly, look delicate, like a deer's, but unlike a deer she's sharp and her gaze is intense, like she's looking into you and seeing all your secrets. I told her that once; she didn't deny it.

'Do you regret it?' she asks after we've sat in silence for a while.

'Regret what?' I pretend I don't know what she means, but some part of me knows what's coming.

'Leaving her to rot.' That statement from anyone else would have brought about a surge of anger in me, but from her it seems natural, not unkind in any way, the way I would have put it to myself.

I say nothing. I'm not really sure if I do regret it. I was eleven when I stopped going; there no longer seemed to be any point. It felt like Mother had said goodbye, like she wanted me to stop coming, get on with things. Then again, I could never be sure with her, she might not have wanted that at all. My stopping visits could have been what pushed her over the edge, made her lose hope and stop fighting the madness.

'I think you do.' Molly interrupts my thoughts to answer for me. 'Otherwise, why are you crying?'

Chapter Three

I FIND THE LETTER when I clear out our postbox downstairs. It's official-looking, though not very thick. The envelope is expensive; cream-coloured with a linen texture. It's addressed to me, care of Mia de Sousa. I'm unsure as to whether I should open it. I turn it over; embossed in dark green script is the name Michael Hurwitz & Associates and a post-office box address in one of Johannesburg's northern suburbs.

The letter makes me nervous. All official-looking letters have this effect on me. My only experience of them is limited to letters from the welfare, poking their noses into my life, wanting to interview me, make sure I'm happy and well placed in my foster home, reminding me I'm not normal, and letters from the prison services, regarding Mother.

This one must have arrived yesterday, during the funeral. I take that as a bad omen.

Back in the flat the kitchen clock displays the time, eight thirty-four a.m. Mia's still in bed. She doesn't get up until after eleven on a Saturday, and this is no usual Saturday, it's the Saturday after her best friend's funeral. I toss the letter on to the coffee table and make some tea.

Ketso has let me off work tonight, on compassionate grounds. Usually, I'd embrace the time off, it's so rare, but this morning the thought of the weekend stretching ahead with nothing to break it up fills me with dread.

Molly has chosen to stay at Tom's. She said she wanted to spend some time with him, but I know it's just an excuse, her and Tom have been over for months. It's because the nightmares have started again. I can feel it when I wake up, that sense of futility, that there is nothing to live for, that everything is lost. Sometimes there are snatches when I wake up in the morning, images. When I was little, I used to think I saw Mother, a glimpse of long white hair turning a corner on a crowded Saturday morning as we shopped in Eloff Street, or Nomsa, scarf wrapped around her head, laughing in a small crowd of nannies gathered on the corner. My heart would skip a beat and then speed up and drum out a rhythm of hope. But they were ghosts, briefly possessing strangers. The remnants of the dreams are like those ghosts, tantalizing images that slip away before I have time to fully grasp them. I haven't had the nightmares in years. Perhaps Mother's causing them from the grave, unwilling to be forgotten and left to rot. The thought chills me.

The envelope keeps catching my eye. I want to ignore it, pretend it doesn't exist, let Mia deal with it when she wakes up, but hard as I try to focus on other things, my mind always trails back to the envelope. I decide to go for a walk. It's just after nine and there's hardly anyone about. Some children play in the park, their brown limbs sticking out of ragged shorts and grubby T-shirts. They wave at me and I wave back. Children always know everyone in the neighbourhood, even if their parents don't. They're a great source of information around here; they listen in on everyone's conversations and, if you don't mind the facts being a little distorted by their imaginations and innocent misunderstandings, you can find out just about anything. I don't feel like chatting to them today. I'm probably the person they've got the most stories about, and interesting as it might be to find out how they've interpreted Mother's death, I'm still too raw.

I walk without seeing.

I know these streets, though they've changed so much since I first came here. The white walls and tiny well-cared-for gardens have been replaced with peeling paint and weeds. When I first arrived, Troyeville had a large Portuguese community; most of the children I went to school with were Portuguese. I felt so out of place amongst them, a blonde beacon in a sea of dark heads. The girls hated me for my fair looks. The boys all wanted to be my friend for the same reason, until they decided I was weird.

Most of the Portuguese have left. Houses that once contained small families now burst at the seams since the slum lords have taken over. It's a strange mix though: woven in amongst the slums are artists, musicians, writers. Open studios here have artists exhibiting their work while street kids, wise to the rich white patrons, flog their scribbles for five rand apiece.

This time of the morning, though, it's quiet, just me, the kids and a few drunks passed out under trees in the park.

I'm surprised when I look up and see a large woman and a man setting up a table on the pavement. The woman has a red doek wrapped around her head and is dressed in smart clothes – a brown skirt, made of a thick fabric that looks too hot to be worn in this weather, and a cream blouse – while the man, though not scruffy, is less smart. An electric guitar leans against the side of the table, and the man is connecting it to an amplifier that's running off a car battery. I stand and watch them awhile, curious. They place four chairs around the table, two a side, and the woman sits down at one closest to the wall. The man sits down next to her with the guitar and tests it. A loud whining pummels my eardrums; it sounds like the warm-up of a rock concert, but the man seems to be satisfied with the noise cutting into the early-morning stillness and doesn't adjust the volume.

I stand and watch them a while longer, but they don't do anything else. They seem to be waiting for something. My curiosity is piqued.

I cross over and just as I'm about to step onto the pavement on their side the woman looks up. I gasp, unable to control my fright. The woman's cheeks are scarred with deep, even lines, some kind of tribal marking, but it's her eyes that disturb me most; they're almost completely white, milky with cataracts. From watching her easy movements I hadn't realized she was blind. I want to turn away, feeling disturbed and embarrassed, but it's too late now, I don't want to offend her. The man doesn't look up; he seems totally unaware that I'm there, though I'm sure he can't also be blind.

'You are afraid of me,' the woman says. Her voice is like gravel underfoot.

'No,' I deny it, though I do feel a little afraid, especially now that she seems able to see me. She's addressed me in English, and her blind eyes appear to be looking me over; she must see me.

'Sit down, child,' she says, gesturing to the chair opposite her at the little table. There's something about the way she says it that makes me unable to refuse. I feel like a small child in the headmistress's office.

For a while the woman says nothing, she just sits and studies me. I smile at her, but she continues to stare, her face impassive. The man has still not acknowledged my presence; he picks dirt from under his nails, apparently completely uninterested.

After some time I begin to feel threatened, even though she's only staring at me. I clear my throat. 'What are you doing here?' I ask.

The woman takes a deep, sighing breath through her nose. Something about the breath makes me think she's annoyed at the interruption.

'You read the sign?' I look around for the sign, but can't see one.

'What sign?'

Without taking her eyes off me, the woman asks Joseph if he put up the sign. Joseph stops picking his nails and looks up.

'No, Mama, I forgot, it's by your feet.'

The woman reaches under the table and, after a brief rummage, brings out a piece of brown box-cardboard. On it, in black hand lettering, are the words

LET US PRAY FOR YOU

PROBLIMS SOLVD, MARIGE DIFFICULTYS, SICKNIS

RIO

Even though the idea seems comical to me, I don't laugh. The woman leans the sign against the wall and turns her attention back to me.

'I don't need any prayers, but thanks anyway,' I tell her. She says nothing and I get up to leave, but before I can her hand flies across the table and grabs mine in a vice-like grip.

'You do need it,' she says, 'there is bad inside you' – her voice wavers, a bit like a medium's voice in a movie seance, 'bad things have happened and need to come out. You don't let them come.'

My heart is in my throat, I'm suddenly terrified. The woman begins to sing and Joseph, as if on cue, picks up his guitar and screeches out a noise that sets my teeth on edge. I don't understand the words of her song, but I understand the tone. It's the wailing kind you hear in evangelical churches, the pleading, demon-exorcizing kind of song. The noise freaks me out. I feel like it's battering against my body, trying to get inside me.

As suddenly as it started, it stops. The neighbourhood seems unnaturally quiet, even the birds have been silenced. The woman leans forward, her hand still tightly gripping mine, and hisses the words 'Go home.'

There is a look in her blind eyes that reminds me of Mother, a madness I've forgotten, or chosen not to remember.

Chapter Four

I'VE LIVED IN Johannesburg for the greatest part of my life and I still haven't got used to the broken sky. Some part of me still wants to look up and see nothing but blue, without the interruption of telephone wires, buildings, houses. The sky looks more fragmented than usual, like the woman's wailing and Joseph's guitar have shattered whatever it is that holds things together, their noise has fractured the world.

'Go home.' Her words echo inside my head.

'Go home.' Fortune-teller words when they don't want to reveal what awful fate they have seen in the mulch of tealeaves at the bottom of your delicate porcelain cup. Omens, I can see them everywhere.

Out of the corner of my eye, I notice a small red dot travelling up my arm, like a shiny mobile mole. I flick at it with my finger and it takes off in a click-flurry of tiny black wings. Ladybird, ladybird, fly away home, your house is on fire and your children are gone. The red dot descends into a patch of grass and disappears among the blades.

I shudder, gooseflesh prickles my skin and I wrap my arms around myself. The morning sun is turning my skin pink, but it does nothing to dissolve my icy insides. 'Go home. Go home. Go home.' The words mock me, voices, the scarred woman's, the children's, Mother's, even the ladybird jeers.

I drift away from home, walking aimlessly in the opposite direction. I see nothing around me. My attention is so completely absorbed by her words that I'm surprised when I find myself staring into a shop window. The shop is tucked between a chemist and the entrance to a block of flats. It's so narrow that I wonder why I didn't walk past, five steps and I would have gone by.

The shop is familiar, though I'm not sure I've ever seen it before. The windows are thick-paned, painted white in places. Sun-molten glass slides down to greet a low concrete wall, enamelled shiny-green. The shop is all mining-town, a throwback, its only concession to modernity the security bars that cross-hatch across the front like graphic ink.

I am filled with an overwhelming urge to enter the thin shop, perhaps because it has distracted me from my grim thoughts, and I step through the open door into the cool, shadowy interior. An old Indian woman, wrapped in a burgundy sari, sits behind the counter, almost completely obscured by a curved-glass display cabinet of sweets. It's odd, the sweets, though they must be modern, seem to take on the air of another era displayed in the old cabinet. The narrow confines of the shop give it a strange perspective, the back wall seems far away but it's only a few metres. On the shelves are tins of food, soap powders, toiletries. It's a convenience store, though how they make enough money to survive, being so close to the newer, bigger supermarket, is a mystery. I close my eyes and take a deep sniff; it smells of laundry soap, wax floor polish, caramel and damp, a childhood shop smell.

The old woman watches me with sharp, bird eyes. I feel I need to buy something, I can't just stand here, taking in the atmosphere. I wander around, looking at the items on the sparsely packed shelves, pretending to be interested. I don't have much money; if I dig into my pockets I'll find fifty cents, a rand at the most. At the back of the shop I find wire baskets of vegetables, not very many, some potatoes growing eyes, a few spongy carrots and three hard, dark green gem squash.

I reach out and touch one. 'Gem squash Tokoloshe,' I whisper.

MOLLY AND I told each other scary stories to see who could hold her fear at bay the longest. Our fertile imaginations competed to create details more gruesome and monsters more horrible than the other could come up with. It was a game devised by me, perhaps as a way of exorcizing my demons, but it evolved into a competitive sport. We would spend hours under the bedcovers, whispering, the beam of Molly's torch scanning the far recesses of the bed for monsters. Most of our imaginings centred around Dead Rex and the Tokoloshe. Once I'd told Molly about them, there was no stopping her. They grew nastier, their actions more evil, more deranged than anything Mother or Mary, or even I, could have dreamed up.

At first Molly's stories would spark an argument between us: the things she invented were not possible, these creatures were, after all, my domain. But Dead Rex was capable of anything, I knew that, and it wasn't long before I began adding my own fuel to the myths.

Molly was not easily scared. She did not believe in these monsters, not really, to her it was just a game. Beauty changed all that.

Beauty lived in one of the rooftop rooms and sometimes babysat for Mia. Molly and I joked about her behind her back, saying her name should be Ugly or Melty-face, certainly not Beauty. Beauty was badly scarred, her skin had the same melted-plastic look as Sannie du Toit's scalded arm. Beauty's face was a criss-cross of scars, her eyelids, stretched taut, couldn't close properly, causing her eyes to seep while she slept. To add to the ghoulishness of Beauty's appearance, she had no hair, and although she kept her head wrapped in a headscarf, I had once seen her with it off. Her scarred bald head reminded me of the heads of the aliens we had seen at the cinema on a Saturday morning, and I became convinced that Beauty was not one of us.

Despite her appearance, Beauty was by far the most responsible of our babysitters. She stayed with us, watching television, until Mia came home or the broadcast ended, whichever came first. Perhaps she really cared for us, or perhaps she didn't want us to suffer the same fate that she had as a child when, left unattended, she'd lit the paraffin burner in her parents' shack and it had exploded, killing her younger brother and scarring her. More likely, the television provided the company she longed for, having no family, boyfriend or husband, like the rest of the rooftop community.

One night, during one of our scare competitions, Molly and I got into an argument about the Tokoloshe. Molly refused to be scared, insisting that the Tokoloshe didn't exist, it was just an imagined thing, like Father Christmas. Mia had accidentally disabused Molly of the idea that Father Christmas existed when Molly was three. I offered all sorts of proof, citing Mary and Mother, and Moses, who had been abducted by the Tokoloshe when Dead Rex stole the bricks from his bed. Molly called me a liar, saying she'd never seen a Tokoloshe and didn't know anyone who had. Our argument escalated until the bedroom door flew open and light flooded the room. We blinked back our tears, caused by both the sudden brightness and our anger. Beauty stood in the doorway, arms folded across her chest. She demanded to know why we weren't sleeping, and after some stalling, I blurted out that Molly had called me a liar. Molly retorted, saying that I *was* a liar, and a baby who was afraid of the Tokoloshe, and that Beauty should tell me that the Tokoloshe didn't exist. Beauty sighed and sat down at the end of our bed, considering us through eyes that had yellowed without the protection of healthy lids.

'There is such a thing as a Tokoloshe,' she said. 'Faith is right. In fact,' she continued after a considered pause, 'there are many such Tokoloshi.' Molly stared at her, mouth hanging open. I felt vindicated, if anyone knew about monsters, it was Beauty. 'But' – I looked up, hoping Beauty was not about to go back on her word – 'you have nothing to be afraid of. We are on the second floor, the Tokoloshe cannot get you here.'

Beauty got up from the bed, her movements slow, and left the room, switching off the light and closing the door behind her.

For some time we lay in the dark in silence, listening to

each other's breathing. Even though the Tokoloshe definitely existed, we didn't feel threatened. Until I remembered. 'Molly,' I whispered into the black, 'if the Tokoloshe can't climb the stairs, why do all the people on the roof have their beds up on bricks?'

Molly pulled the covers over our heads and flicked on the torch. Shadows played against her face, but even in the half-light I could see fear in her eyes.

Chapter Five

THE FLAT IS dead quiet when I get back, the only sign of life smoke tendrils hanging in the air. I step over the loose parquet tiles, not wanting to alert anyone to my presence before I've had time to hide the gem squash. Bratcat watches me through milky eyes; she's the only survivor of the feline trio, and she hates me still.

In the kitchen I bury the squash in the fruit bowl. I could just turf it in the bin, but childhood superstition and my recent scare make me want to keep it around as some sort of protection. Protection against what, though?, I wonder. Scarface and her inept musician? They didn't do anything to me, they're just roadside evangelists on the make. I shrug off my irrational fear of them, feeling stupid, almost a whole morning wasted wandering around terrified of nothing. Grow up, Faith, the days of evil fairies are over.

Feeling better, I throw myself down on to the old couch, displacing Bratcat. She glares at me, trying to look haughty and regal, but her pelt hangs from her arthritic bones like an empty sack, spoiling the effect; she looks more bag-lady than queen.

'Not long now,' I hiss, 'you'll be with your buddies

soon.' I flick her nose with a magazine, she chooses not to respond.

Mia emerges from her bedroom, dressed in a long black skirt and short-sleeved peasant top that shows off her cleavage, thong sandals on her feet, toes enamelled gypsy red, or whore red, outfit-dependent.

She swishes into the kitchen and switches on the kettle. 'Coffee, cooks,' she calls over the counter that separates the two rooms. Mia has called everyone and everything 'cooks' or 'cookie' for as long as I can remember.

'Please,' I reply, 'you making real?' Already I can hear the crunch of spoon sinking into instant-coffee granules. She doesn't reply and a minute later I'm holding a mug of steaming Nescafé. Mia plonks herself down next to me, rummages through her giant handbag and pulls out a new packet of cigarettes. With the one-handed skill of a practised smoker, she pulls off the cellophane wrapping, opens the box and offers it to me, all while sipping her coffee. She always offers me a cigarette, even though I don't smoke.

'It's manners, girls, manners that count,' she used to tell us, still does. It's her only piece of advice that's ever remained constant.

I shake my head but pull off the silver paper that seals the cigarettes in fresh.

'You're up early,' she says.

I shrug. 'Nice morning, thought I'd go for a walk.'

'Hmph,' exhaling smoke, 'meet anyone interesting?'

I look at her, wonder if she knows something, saw me with Scarface. I dismiss the thought, she would have still been in bed at that time. You're getting paranoid, Faith.

'Nope,' I say, trying to sound light.

Mia looks at her watch, reaches over and turns on the stereo. 'I want to hear the news,' she announces, 'they might have something on about your ma.'

I look at her, incredulous. 'Why?'

'Well,' she looks at me as if I'm an idiot, 'they sometimes have articles about famous murderers when they die, you know, and with the funeral being yesterday, I thought they might have covered it.'

I shake my head in disbelief: from grieving best friend to macabre celebrity seeker overnight. 'She's not a famous murderer, she's a crazy woman who shot her maid.' Crazy like you.

Mia arches a warning brow at me; sometimes it feels like she can read my mind.

'Besides, that's yesterday's news, it would have been on yesterday.' I draw the last 'yesterday' out, to demonstrate my incredulity.

We sit in a sulky silence, listening to Ruben Goldberg read out the latest crime tragedies, government corruption scandals, categorical denials, Y2K relief, nothing about Mother, the weather, and then the top forty countdown.

'I like this song.' Mia bops a little, bumps me with her shoulder to get me to join in. She doesn't mention the bulletin.

'I'm off to Ketso's braai. You coming?'

I shrug. The prayer stall is on the way to Ketso's house; maybe if I circle round the block, take the scenic route, so to speak, I can avoid it. I can't do that if I go with Mia.

'Later, I'm going to chill out awhile.'

'Fine,' she says, 'do you want me to get you some meat on my way? I'm getting for me and Mol.'

I nod, and hand over all the money I have in my purse, a grand total of fifteen rand and fifty-seven cents.

WITH MIA GONE I stretch out on the couch and flick through the magazine. It's not long before my eyelids droop, and sleep hangs over me like a thick blanket. For a while my thoughts remain focused on the article I am reading, but soon the magazine falls from my hands, though the words still run through my mind. There's a conscious part of me that knows I'm not actually reading, so I let go of the words, and they slip away, forgotten. My thoughts become fragmented, sliding around my mind, intangible, momentary, briefly incandescent. Light-shadow shapes play against my eyes; it feels like my body's asleep, totally relaxed, but my mind, still wakeful, is trying to see the world through the stretch of pink eyelid.

Sleep, unsleep, a halfway world.

Look, look, mosetsana, look what you done.

The voice rasps into my consciousness, malevolent and full of spite. My heart skips a beat, then begins to pound out an uneven rapid rhythm. I'm not asleep, I can't be dreaming. The voice, it's too real, too clear.

I try to force my eyes open, but they're shut tight, superglued. My chest begins to constrict with a suffocating weight, someone is sitting on me. I can feel their bulk pushing down on my lungs, a squirming balancing act, followed by a puff of hot breath against my mouth, sour and decayed. I struggle to breathe, try to turn away from the stench of rot that fills my lungs, but I can't move my head.

The something is sucking the air from me, draining me, sucking away at my existence. I try to twist out of its grasp, but I feel like a stunned fish on the end of a hooked line, wriggling helplessly.

One, two, threefourfive, Mary caught a fish alive.

The voice taunts me. It's inside me now, reading my thoughts. I struggle to fight it, I feel it digging into my mind. Panic sets in, I begin to thrash around in my sleep-paralysed body.

Wake up, I scream, voiceless. Wake up.

My eyes snap open and my voice returns with a strangled 'Nyargh.' My heart thrashes in my chest, causing a rush of nausea. I retch, grasping the couch for solidity as the room swims in front of me. I gulp the hot dry air and slowly the world begins to settle.

Calm yourself, girl, calm, just a dream.

I take slow, deliberate breaths, trying to still the pounding that pulses through me, making my temples buzz. I place my fingers against my throat and apply pressure to the jumping pulse points. Little by little, I begin to calm down, and soon I'm able to lift my head without a rush of nausea.

Then I hear the voice; it's small, tiny in fact, hardly there at all, not much more than an imagined whisper. The room is empty save for Bratcat, curled up on the armchair; she blinks slowly, accusing me of disturbing the peace.

Fucking cat.

'Koko.' The voice comes again, though this time it remains soft against my eardrums; it is sweetly pitched, having the resonance of a wet finger rubbed along the edge of crystal.

I sit up, feeling strangely disturbed by the voice; it's

soothing yet at the same time stirs up deep, unsettling emotions.

You're going mad, girl.

'Koko.' Again it comes and this time it brings with it a memory that hits me like I've been smacked with a brick. Nomsa. And suddenly, I can see her, the sharp lively eyes, the white teeth, the smile that speaks of a world of private jokes.

'Koko,' the voice calls, conjuring up her smell, Sunlight soap, Vaseline-oiled skin, iron-hot cotton sheets. I squeeze my eyes shut, trying to gain control of the rush of emotions. But the voice has opened up a floodgate of memories and, for the first time since she died, I can see her clearly.

So many hours I spent alone as a child, leaning against the cold tiles in the privacy of the bathroom, trying to conjure her up, willing my mind's eye to see the warm tones of her skin, or the swirling patterns of her plaited hair against her scalp. I was so afraid of forgetting her, scared that if I let her memory go, I would have no one, I would always be alone. I could never see her properly, not all of her, and what I could see was so fleeting that it still left me with nothing to hold on to. Memory is fickle and fades fast, soon she was just a faceless name, attached to a set of stories I told myself, alone in the bathroom. The loss of her memory made me feel small and insignificant and homeless, like I belonged nowhere. Now, years later, the sudden power of the returning memory makes me feel the same way. Fifteen years on I'm still displaced, unsettled, homeless.

'Koko.' The voice is right in the room now. My eyes snap open with a jolt, instantly focusing on a little girl who is standing just inside the door. Although she can't be any older than I was when I first stood inside this room, she shows no natural caution. Instead, she's craning on her tiptoes, trying to get a better view of me, like she's at the zoo and I'm one of the exhibits. I glare at her, feeling shocked and violated by her intrusion, but she seems unperturbed by my obvious hostility towards her and, instead of shrinking back, steps closer to the coffee table that separates us, examining me with a curiosity that I find infuriating.

'What are you doing?' I bark at her.

Her eyes widen with fright and she looks down at her feet, backing away a little.

'Sorry, madam,' she whispers, 'but I knocked.' I take a deep breath; it's the same voice that was calling me, not really calling at all, knocking. *Koko, koko.*

Faith, you idiot.

'And then when nobody came, you thought you'd just let yourself in?' My anger flashes up, irrational. I feel like she's made a fool of me, catching me on the verge of tears, though it's hardly her fault.

'The door was open,' she explains in the same small voice, only now it's beginning to wobble. I feel slightly deflated, Mia must have left it open, and it is reasonable to venture into a place if you've knocked and the door is open. Besides, she's only a little girl, hardly capable of murdering me in my sleep. I begin to feel mean for being so harsh with her.

'OK,' I try to soften my tone and sound less like a child-eating monster, 'what do you want?'

She shrugs, one of those maddening kid shrugs that tell you that they do know, but don't know how to tell you because you've just scared the bejesus out of them. OK then, as annoying as this is, it is my fault for barking at her. I try again.

'Are you looking for someone, one of your friends?' She could be in the wrong flat. Perhaps she was looking for one of the kids who live in another flat, a playmate, but she shakes her head. My patience is starting to wear thin. I'm not very good with kids, I have no natural rapport with them. Perhaps it was my isolated childhood that made me this way, but kids and animals, neither seem to take to me very well.

Then, as if she's suddenly decided to steel herself against me and get this encounter over with as fast as possible, she blurts out, 'My gogo sent me to fetch ten rand.'

'Your gogo?' I ask, wondering who this urchin's grandmother is.

She nods and begins to take on the defiant air she had when I first saw her.

'Ten rand.' Her head bobs up and down on the thin stalk of her neck, like a punctuation mark.

'Why?'

She shrugs like this is not her business and she doesn't care. I'm tempted just to give her the ten rand and be done with her, but good sense tells me that if I do that she'll be back with friends, and all of them will want ten rand.

'I'm not giving you money for no reason,' I tell her; 'the world doesn't work that way. You can't just come into someone's flat and expect them to give you ten rand because your gogo said so. If you or your gogo want money, you'll have to work for it like the rest of us.' I stop my lecture, feeling stupid; the child is obviously from a poor home – her skinny limbs and knobbly joints protruding from her grubby pink dress a size too small speak of a struggle I've never experienced and berate me for my insensitivity.

She pulls a face, and I'm unsure if I see a sparkle of a tear in her eyes, but then a little shudder runs through her body, like she's shaking off the hurt, and she gives me a disapproving look that makes her look like an old lady. It's comical, yet I don't find it funny.

'Gogo helped you this morning and then you ran away without paying.' Her voice comes out a bitter hiss and suddenly I can see exactly who her gogo is in the flat expanse of her face. She is a young, unscarred version of the blind woman.

Don't pay her, get her out of here. My inner voice of reason sounds small, useless against the fear that's soaking my brain.

The girl leans slightly forward, baring a row of small white milk teeth set in dark gums, and holds out her hand.

I pick up my purse from the coffee table and realize with sinking dread that it's empty. I gave all my money to Mia.

Chapter Six

THE ONLY CASH machine within walking distance is wedged between the Spar supermarket and the bottle store, in the basement of a small shopping centre. It's the kind of shopping centre that has failed to attract any real commerce, a white elephant, so to speak, where shops that have no real purpose open up and close down before you've had time to figure out what they sell. Only the bottle store and the Spar thrive; hence the white elephant remains.

It's a risky business drawing cash here on a Saturday afternoon, especially if you're alone, on foot, a woman, white. Drunks throng around the bottle store, alcohol-fuelled aggression sparks off fights, people are mugged, there is a very real threat of violence. As I walk across the parking lot, someone calls, 'Hey, baby, let me show you a good time.' Lewd laughter follows, but I don't turn around. Only an idiot would invite that kind of trouble.

In the parking lot, sunlight is cut into rectangular shafts by gaps in the concrete slab of shopping centre above. Every time I step into one of the isolated pools of sunshine, I feel like I'm being spotlighted. Everyone sees me: the harmless, who shake their heads and click their tongues before turning away, no one wants to be a witness; the leering catcallers; the opportunistic muggers. I've thrust myself into the underbelly of the world because of a little girl. I glance over my shoulder and catch a glimpse of grubby pink disappearing behind a support pillar, still following me.

I slow down as I approach the glassed-off confines of the cash machine. The glass, there to shield your secret PIN code from prying eyes, is open on both sides. Through it, I can see a man with his back to me and, as he turns to stumble out, I see he's pulling up his zip. It's a cash machine-cum-toilet. I take a deep breath and plunge into the funk of piss, stepping over the narrow stream that runs down the brick on to the pavement. My card is already in my hand, ready to slot into the machine. The screen is dark. I have to lean in close to read the dim text. I push the card into the slot, feeling for any resistance before I let it go, the machine swallows it easily. I punch in my number, hit ENTER.

Please wait while we verify your card.

Hurry up for fuck's sake. I can feel them closing in, I'm as edgy as the knife blade I imagine being pressed into me. I glance over my shoulder, but it's hard to see through the smoked glass in the half-light of the parking lot.

Finally, after what seems like enough time to be stabbed twice and call the police, a list of options pops up. I hit WITHDRAW CASH and another screen pops up. I hit the first amount, R20. Again, PLEASE WAIT.'

The machine begins to roll out my receipt, followed by my card, and finally my cash. I snatch the twenty-rand note as a hand closes over my shoulder.

'What the fuck are you doing?'

My heart stops. My hand freezes, ready to release the note,

but he doesn't take it. I edge my eyes slowly to the side and instantly recognize the sharp profile.

'Dammit, Ketso, I almost wet myself.' I'm so relieved, my anger and fear dissipate into a small laugh. Ketso shakes his head, but instead of the usual easy smile I'm used to being greeted with, his face remains dark. When he speaks, his voice is low, controlled. 'I'm in my car, I'll give you a lift.'

In the bucket seat of Ketso's old Merc, I feel small. I don't fit comfortably in most cars, my legs twist to the side like I'm a giant in a Dinky car. The Merc is more like a boat, a luxury liner designed for giants. I glance over at Ketso. His face is a tight mask, his nostrils flare and contract, like every inhalation makes him angrier. I twist in my seat, trying to make myself smaller, less noticeable. I have only ever seen Ketso angry once; it seems unnatural for someone who is usually so calm.

I look down at a patch of dirt on my jeans, then out of the window. His house can't be more than five minutes away by car, taking into account red lights, but it feels like I'm stuck in a time warp. Seconds tick by loudly on the dashboard clock.

'Where do you want me to take you?' he asks as he pulls off on the green, his eyes never leaving the road.

'Yours, I guess.' I shrug when I say this, but I don't suppose he sees it.

He doesn't reply, and minutes later we're pulling into his garage.

I follow him into the house, sit down at the long chrome kitchen table while he unpacks his bags of shopping. The house is quiet, though the sink is piled high with dirty dishes and the ashtrays overflow.

'Thought you were having a braai,' I say, after a moment.

'I was,' he says. 'I did.'

'So, where's everybody?'

'Everybody?' Ketso turns and looks at me for the first time since he picked me up. 'You mean Molly, Mia and Tom?'

He spins around and picks up a bottle of wine, uncorks it and pours two glasses.

'Mia's gone to get ready for work, Tom left shortly after he came, and Molly was worried about you, so she went home to find you. We were all worried.'

I rub the furrow in my brow. 'I told Mia I'd be along late,' I say. I can't keep the irritation out of my voice.

'Late? This isn't late, Faith. Late is fifteen minutes, an hour, tops. This is send out the search party.' He walks to the fridge and opens the freezer unit, takes out a tray of ice and slams it on to the counter.

'Then I find you, quite by accident, trying to get yourself killed. You know that's the same cash machine that Mina got stabbed at, and that was at midday, not five-thirty on a Saturday afternoon.'

My mind skips over everything he's just said and sticks on the part about it being five-thirty. I look up at the timer on the microwave oven; it flashes 17:46 in lurid electro green. I feel dizzy, it can't be that late. I look out of the kitchen window and notice for the first time that the light has the hazy quality of afternoon sun, though it's still hot. Ketso's voice becomes a hum that's indistinguishable from the buzzing of the kitchen appliances. I blink, so slowly that the world is dark for a moment and when I open my eyes, Ketso is really close to me. His hands grip my shoulders, and the microwave clock flashes 17:49.

'God, Faith, you just slumped.' I can see by his expression

that something is wrong. I know something's wrong. I could swear the clock said 17:46 a few seconds ago, and the whole day, gone.

Ketso touches my forehead with the back of his hand.

'You feel clammy,' he says, then turns and stands up, goes over to the sink and runs water into a glass. When he turns around, his face is once again tight.

'Are you taking drugs?'

The question hangs between us like the words are written on the air itself. For a long moment I look at him, waiting for the angry mask to break and reveal the punchline, but it doesn't come. I shake my head a little, try a small smile.

'Well, it fits, don't you think? Only a drug-starved addict would take the kind of risk you just have to get money, and then you pass out for a couple of minutes when you get here. You have no idea of the time. Where have you been all day?'

'I'm not on drugs, Ketso, and I've been at home. If you were so worried, why didn't you just pick up the phone and call me there?'

Ketso fixes me with a look, shakes his head.

'We did call, Faith,' he says after a long pause, 'several times.'

After discovering that the whole day has slipped past me, it isn't a great leap to believe that they'd called me. Cold fear slides into my gut.

'Can I stay here tonight?' My voice sounds small.

'Tell me what's going on, Faith.'

'I don't know.' I shrug. 'I think I'm losing it.'

He comes over and crouches down in front of me so we're eye-level.

'We can't do this for ever, Faith.' His eyes are pleading with me to go home.

'I know,' I say, 'just let me stay tonight.'

KETSO MOVED INTO our block when I was eleven. Things were changing, some areas were opening up, becoming mixed. Hillbrow was the first, Yeoville quickly followed, then Jeppe and Troyeville. Meetings were called by the body corporate, but the flow of change would not be stemmed, and no matter how hard people objected, they couldn't turn back the clock. We didn't mind. Molly developed an instant crush on Ketso, and we'd hang around on the roof, spying on him through my binoculars. My declaration of love followed shortly after hers, more out of a desire to be like her than any real feelings.

Ketso was a ladies' man, though at the time we never knew to call him that. We watched through the magnified circles as lovers entered his flat in the evening, watched as some left, dishevelled, in the morning. Some we never saw leaving: those, I presume, he didn't invite to stay for breakfast. But it wasn't only women, sometimes it was a man.

I never felt jealous, though, neither of us did; none of his lovers was around long enough for us to envy. We had something more, we had endless access to his collection of records and freedom to knock on his door at any time. He always let us in, maybe because we knew better than to knock when he had company. He chatted to us like we were adults, flirted outrageously and gave us Appletizer to drink out of champagne flutes. He was the first grown-up to let

Molly smoke in his presence, he gave us our first taste of sparkling wine when we were thirteen, our first drag of a joint at fifteen, and taught us how to kiss with tongue when we were sixteen, though he made us practise on each other rather than him. Molly said this was because had he kissed her, it would have been tickets for him; he would have realized how much he really wanted her. Maybe she was right.

At sixteen he gave us our first job, waiting tables in his restaurant. By then he'd moved away, bought his own house, but that hadn't stopped us going round.

Then school was over. Molly got her music scholarship, moved to Grahamstown. I stayed on, working for Ketso, but I was listless, bored. Without Molly to share secrets with, I lost interest in the boyfriend I had. I'd only gone out with him in the first place so Molly and I could double-date, she was so in love with Tom.

With Molly gone, Ketso made me the hostess at the restaurant, probably to make me feel better about not going to university. It wasn't something I cared deeply about though – school had never had any great appeal for me, perhaps because I'd started so late. Being the hostess made me feel sexy, something I'd never felt before. I got to glam it up. Molly had always been the pretty one and, had she remained, I was sure she would have ended up being the hostess. But she hadn't and, somehow, that made me sexy by proxy.

I'd only been hostess a week when it happened. I must have still been drunk on the feeling of sexiness, because otherwise I never would have done it.

We sat at the bar, side by side, sharing a bottle of wine

after everyone else had gone home. Ketso was so close I could smell his aftershave, his sweat and the sharpness of nicotine that clung to his hair and skin. He smelled like a man in a way that none of my schoolboy lovers had. They all smelled fresh, like clean laundry, too sweet. The smell coming off him was dirty, intoxicating, and I had this newfound bravado bred of high heels and low-slung dresses, plus the courage of two glasses of white wine.

I should have known better. Ketso wasn't the kind of man who would say no, who could say no, even if he'd wanted to.

In my fresh-out-of-school stupidity, I pushed him to a place he'd never wanted to go. All the years he'd resisted, held himself back when he could have had us both, slipped away when I leaned forward and flicked my tongue across his lips. It was a line he'd never wanted to cross.

'Faith.' It was a sharp sound, a warning, but I'd seen too many soap operas, read too many Danielle Steele sex scenes to pay any attention. Instead of backing off, I slid my hand up his thigh and began to massage the soft lump I found between his legs.

'Don't,' he said, but he didn't push my hand away and, like a date-rapist, I took that as a yes. With my free hand I pulled loose the straps that held my dress up, and it dropped down to my waist.

What followed was fast and furious and grinding. Ketso's body was hard and lean, nothing like the softness of the boys I'd slept with before. He pushed me up against the bar so that the wood pressed into my back. He didn't even bother to remove my pants, pushing them to one side and thrusting his cock against me until it found the access it wanted.

It was brutal, in every hard thrust I could feel his anger. His teeth bit into me where his mouth closed over my lips, like he was trying to eat me, like he was hoping, when he came up for air, I wouldn't exist.

I came, but it was hard and mechanical and soulless.

Then it was over. He pulled away, went round to the other side of the bar and poured two whiskies.

'You should clean yourself up,' he said, as he handed me one of them. I nodded as I took the glass, but he couldn't have seen it because he wasn't looking at me.

In the bathroom, I examined myself in the mirror. The skin around my mouth was raw and my lips were swollen. As I smoothed foundation on to my skin, I began to think that Ketso and I were the same. He couldn't love anyone. I wondered for a moment how he'd become that way, and then I realized, I didn't want to know.

THE MERC SLOWS down and slides to a silent stop in front of the dark hulk of Beryl Court. I slip out of the car into the quiet street. A distant dog barks, a lonely appeal for the night to end. I look back one last time as I enter the building, raise my hand, but the street lamp reflects off the windscreen, shielding him, though I don't need to see his face to know what expression it wears, regret and self-loathing.

I slip into the flat, taking care to avoid the loose tiles. Someone's left a lamp burning in the lounge. I turn it off; the night is clear and the moon round enough to spill a milky glow through the window.

I'd called, told them I was staying over at Ketso's to help

take stock at the restaurant. Said I wanted to work, to keep my mind off things. I need to shower, rid myself of the evidence of that lie, the smell that sticks to me, oozes out through my pores, but the noise would be amplified by the bathroom tiles and the late-night silence, so I slip into the tangle of bedsheets, noting the hunch of Molly's body in the other bed, and pray for sleep to take me fast.

I'm barely settled when she whispers, 'You in love with him?' into the dark. It catches me off guard. I should have known she'd be able to sniff me out. I try to let the tiredness take me without answering her, but the tension in the room keeps me awake.

'No,' I whisper back eventually, and instantly regret it. I hear her roll over and feel her eyes on me; even in the dark she can see into me. What's always felt like comfortable knowing begins to feel intrusive, perhaps because of the time we've spent apart, but I no longer want her looking into my soul, knowing my thoughts.

'He's can't love you, Faith.' This time more of a hiss than a whisper. 'He can't love anyone.' I'm surprised by her venom and the thought that she may be jealous flicks across my mind, but I know she's angry because I've lied, or rather because I didn't tell her: in Molly's mind that amounts to the same thing.

'There's nothing.' I turn to face her, to show her I'm not lying, and I can feel, even through the darkness that separates us, that she doesn't believe me. Though, on a level, I'm not lying, there is nothing. He doesn't love me and I don't have to pretend to love him.

She gets out of her bed and pads softly over to my side of the room. I sit up and shift over a little.

'You can't change him, he's twice your age, he's not going to change, not for you, or anyone.' She slips the 'anyone' in but I can't help feeling that maybe she thinks if it were her, he'd change. 'He's just using you.' She's pleading with me now.

I reach over and touch the softness of her cheek. For all the things that Molly can see in me, this is her blind spot. I can't bring myself to tell her that it's not him who can't love, not him doing the using. I'm the one that's taken his damaged soul and broken it so it fits into me. How can you tell someone who loves you as much as Molly loves me that I want this kind of punishment? She'd want to know why, and even I don't know the answer.

Chapter Seven

I STAND ON THE balcony with a cup of coffee, watching neighbours navigate their cars out of the tight parking spaces below, listening to their showers and kettles and clinking breakfast spoons, their morning sounds. Already the sun is too hot, its heat releases the heady smell of jasmine into the air, sickly sweet. The concrete under my feet is the only coolness on offer, the world feels frantic and feverish.

Sleep was an elusive ghost last night, haunting me only long enough for the nightmare images to flick across my mind's eye before I jerked awake, terrified of finding I'd lost time.

The shrill ring of the phone cuts into the morning buzz. Bit early, only eight-thirty, anyone who knows us well enough to have our home number should know better. I hear Molly answer it before I've had time to turn around, hear the annoyance in her clipped hello. I didn't realize she was awake.

'Oh right, yes well, she'll have to call you back.' She hangs up. I hear her making coffee, then the click of parquet tile and she's standing in the doorway behind me, I can feel her. She's waiting to see if I'll break the ice, speak first, but I don't turn, don't acknowledge her, I have the upper hand, I can pretend I don't know she's there.

She drops her teaspoon and it clatters on the polished concrete.

'Morning, Mol.' I don't turn around. She comes out of the flat and leans on the railing next to me. Like me, she's still in her pyjamas, but unlike me it bothers her to be seen that way by the neighbours. Molly, like Mia, has a strange sense of decorum. They're from the never-be-caught-without-a-clean-pair-of-panties school of thought.

'I'm leaving on Friday,' she says. I nod. 'I don't want us to be like this.'

'I don't either,' I say, hoping she'll let it go now.

'Then talk to me,' she says.

'Who was on the phone?' I ask.

She looks peeved that I've changed the subject and replies in the same clipped tones she used to answer the phone. 'Man,' she says, 'said his office delivered a letter last Friday. You weren't home so they left it. He wants you to call him about it.'

I'd forgotten about the letter. After a brief search I find it on the coffee table under a pile of magazines, unopened, the only difference a brown ring where someone's put a cup down on it.

A sense of apprehension descends on me as I look at the envelope in my hands, tightening my stomach and causing a twinge of nausea.

'Aren't you going to open it?' Molly asks.

I shrug, the envelope feels heavy, like it contains something more than paper and if I open it a Pandora's box of ghouls may come flying out.

'It's addressed to Mia really.' I look up at Molly, silently pleading for her not to push me on this.

'You don't want to open it.' I'm unsure whether it's a question or a statement, so I don't answer. 'Why?' she asks. 'You're being weird, it's just a letter.' Then the aggravation in her voice softens. 'What are you scared of?'

The nausea in my belly expands. I close my eyes and swallow hard. 'It's something to do with Mother, I can feel it.'

Molly nods slowly, and I begin to feel some of the closeness that has slipped away from us this past week returning.

'She can't hurt you any more, she's dead, you saw her body.' I'm unsure whether Molly's spoken the words or if they're in my head, but I nod in reply, holding the letter out to her. She takes it without saying a word.

I watch Molly's sharp eyes flick over the page. Her lips move silently as she reads, her eyebrows arch and she looks up.

'It's from your mother's lawyer. He wants you to contact him to settle her estate.' She sounds as surprised as I feel.

THE OFFICE OF Michael Hurwitz & Associates is in a converted house on Bolton Road in Rosebank. The reception area is light and airy, painted white with wooden floors sanded pale yellow. Even the receptionist, an attractive black woman in her late twenties, is dressed in a white trouser suit. There are only two things in the room which break the visual serenity: Mia in her black widow's weeds and a spiky pot plant that exudes an aura of barbed wire. As a child I loved Mia's sense of the dramatic: everything, from the first day of school to eating out at the Burger Ranch, was an occasion to be tarted up in high heels and lipstick. Since Mother's death, though, I'm finding it overblown and annoying. I pretend to read a magazine so I can ignore her.

We are called by a secretary who leads us up a staircase of the same pale wood as the floor, to the office of Michael Hurwitz. The steps are flat boards suspended on a metal framework that give the impression that they're floating in space; it makes them seem unsafe. I have a slight feeling of vertigo as I follow her up.

Michael Hurwitz himself is older than I'd been led to expect by the fashionable surroundings. He holds out a well-padded hand, first to Mia, then to me; he clasps my hand between both of his, conveying their clamminess along with his condolences.

We sit in leather seats on the opposite side of his large desk. Things in his office look more in keeping with what I'd expected, mahogany, green glass and leather. After a further exchange of pleasantries, he shuffles some papers and clears his throat.

'As you've probably already ascertained from my letter, you're here to discuss your mother's estate. Your mother had several assets, which, in the light of her death, and the absence of anyone to contest your right to inherit, will be passed on to you.'

He looks up over black-rimmed reading glasses to make sure I'm listening and I have the distinct feeling from the way he considers me that he feels a certain amount of dislike for me, like I'm a distasteful bug.

'There's a smallholding in the Northern Province, a house in Kensington and, of course, some personal belongings.' He flicks through the pile of papers in front of him and takes out a thick document held at the top with a paperclip. 'There are a few papers that need to be signed.' He hands me the document and then produces a copy for Mia and one for himself.

I look at the black type, unable to focus, then at the meaty face of Michael Hurwitz, then back at the type. He begins to read from the top line, droning legal jargon that seems to have no meaning.

I clear my throat. 'I'm sorry, but I don't understand.'

Michael Hurwitz stops and looks up. 'It's just the legalese,' he says, 'you don't have to understand everything, but I do need to read it to you. All you need to understand is that you're going to sign documents that will transfer your mother's assets into your name.'

I shake my head. 'That's the part I don't understand. I didn't know she had any.'

Michael Hurwitz puts the document down and takes off his reading glasses. He looks at me with the patient expression of someone used to dealing with idiots.

'Ah,' he says, 'I see. Do you know anything about your mother's affairs?'

I shake my head and look at Mia, mortified. It's beginning to dawn on me that she knows all sorts of things she's never told me.

'Faith was very young when it happened, and Bella didn't want her in court, to be part of things.' Mia looks at me with imploring eyes. 'I suppose I never expected her to die so young that we would be here.' She reaches over to take my hand, but I move it out of reach and make a fist in my lap.

'Well, then,' he says, 'let me try to explain her situation to you. I used to work for Legal Aid. We provided free legal assistance to people who couldn't afford it, mainly blacks in those days. Your mother was one of the few whites I did help. Normally, since she owned property, it would have been up to her to provide her own lawyer for trial, but her state of mind was such that it wasn't possible. The judge appointed a lawyer from Legal Aid, that was myself.'

He stops and takes a sip of water.

'Although I did find your mother to be, uh, mentally unwell, she had periods of seeming lucidity where she was able to instruct me as to her wishes. I was to try and locate your father,' he shuffles through his papers again and holds one out at arm's length, 'one Marius Albert Steenkamp.'

The sound of my father's name makes me feel cold, my chest leaden.

'And did you?' I ask. My voice sounds far away, like I'm sitting in another room.

Michael Hurwitz shakes his head. 'I don't think he wanted to be found, he simply vanished. I tried to trace him through his work, some friends, but came up with nothing. There was a letter, it's in the file somewhere, from your father to you. It had an address and some photographs, but unfortunately it came to nothing. I took out an ad in a few of the main papers, but never heard anything. Unfortunately, with the limited resources, I wasn't able to hire an investigator. She wanted you to live with him, on the farm, but that wasn't possible. Your grandmother, Albertina Steenkamp, was too old to care for you. The stress of the events made her very frail, and there was no other family. You would have become a state ward if it wasn't for Mrs de Sousa.'

I feel a twinge of guilt when he mentions Ouma. She died when I was nine, and all I felt was a sense of relief that I no longer had to go and visit her. She'd always been so strict about cleanliness and godliness, but after it happened she'd become a little demented. Visits were like nightmares, with Ouma a clinging ghoul. She would hold me against her and rock me back and forth, which would have been fine with the old Ouma, nice even to be shown that kind of affection, but the ghoul Ouma no longer bothered with false teeth or clean clothes. The smell of decay hung over her and her house, exacerbated by the stench of blocked drains that exuded from both the kitchen sink and her toothless mouth. She clutched me and swiped at things she couldn't see, afraid of demons both imagined and real. As I child I lacked compassion, I found her repulsive and hated visiting her.

Michael Hurwitz clears his throat to draw my attention back to him. I feel slightly startled that he noticed I wasn't listening.

'Would you like some more tea?' he asks. I shake my head. I want this over with, but Mia nods and he calls his secretary. I could kick her.

'What about her trial?' I ask when the tea arrives. I have a strong urge to know everything. As I child I imagined Mother being convicted, the judge's hammer coming down with an echoing bang. Murderer, he'd bellowed, I sentence you to life. The images in my head were pilfered from the horror comics Molly and I used to read, the judge a gaunt, beak-nosed man with tattered black robes billowing, Mother wide-eyed and cowering in the dock. Somehow these imaginings became my reality.

Michael Hurwitz smiles at me, the same sort of look he

gave me earlier, the one reserved for dealing with morons. 'Your mother never stood trial. She was declared unfit to stand on the grounds of mental incapacity.'

'I don't understand,' I say again, not caring whether he gives me the look or not: 'if she didn't have a trial, why did she go to prison?'

Michael Hurwitz shakes his head. 'Sterkfontein is not a prison, it's a hospital. Your mother was remanded there as a state patient for an indefinite period. It happens in most cases where the person standing trial is declared unfit. They remain there until they are declared well enough to stand trial or return to society, but in cases like your mother's, where she was declared mentally incapacitated at the time of committing the crime, release is unlikely, even if she had recovered.'

I sit back in the leather chair, unable to listen to Michael Hurwitz as he reads through the thick document that serves as Mother's will, though it's not. It's more him signing his powers over Mother's estate to me. I wonder if anyone lives on the farm now and whether they are happy or as haunted as we were. After they took Mother away, Tannie Hettie packed my things into a suitcase and took me to Ouma. I never went back, though there had been so many times I'd longed to go home.

'Will you go back to the farm?' Mia asks when everything is signed, hands have been shaken and we're back in the car, navigating the busy Johannesburg streets. I shrug, perhaps there's no going back, no regaining what's been lost. When I think of going back I feel tight inside, like there's something expanding in my body that I can't physically contain.

Chapter Eight

'WHAT'S THAT SMELL?' Mia asks, opening the door. The odour of burnt hair and a spicy aroma that reminds me of making campfires out of blue-gum leaves clings to the dense heat inside the flat. I wrinkle my nose and follow Mia in.

The sight that greets me leaves me speechless. Sitting cross-legged on the floor is Molly. Her head droops forward and even from behind I can see she's not fully conscious. The coffee table has been moved to the side of the room and on the floor in front of Molly is a piece of cloth upon which four wooden rectangular objects appear to have been thrown. A spiral of pungent smoke rises out of a saucer that has a burning coal as a source of heat with what looks like some sort of dried leaves and twigs smouldering on top of it. But it's the woman sitting on the couch opposite Molly that disturbs me most; it's the blind woman from the day after the funeral.

I swallow hard.

'Molly!' I call out to her but she doesn't respond. Then I realize her name sounds strange, all wrong, like it's not her name at all, and my voice, it's alien, strangled. I turn to Mia.

Her mouth is open, like she's about to speak but has forgotten what to say. As I look at her I realize there's something odd: she looks like Mia, but there is nothing familiar about her, it's like I've never seen her before.

The smell in the room is strong. I'm beginning to feel sick with it, dizzy and slow. Something in the air shifts and suddenly everything seems far away, like I'm looking at the room through a mirage of heat.

I take a deep breath to clear my head, but that makes it fuzzier, the air is too thick. My head feels heavy, like an oversized sunflower on a thin stalk, and my legs can't hold my weight, they're insubstantial, elastic. I slide down, the floor is soft and comfortable, I'm no longer afraid, the urge to sleep is overpowering. I close my eyes. Heat beats into me. I begin to realize I'm no longer in the flat, my fingers slip easily into the ground beneath me. 'I'm on the beach.' I hear my own voice, but it sounds far away. I take a deep breath, but there is no sweet-salt sea smell, there's only sand, like a desert, cushioning my body.

My skin begins to prickle, I can feel it turning pink, see the pink behind my eyelids, bleeding into red as the temperature increases.

You go burn in flame, mosetsana. It's the Sandman's voice. It gets hotter and I can smell my skin burning, but still, I want to stay in the heat.

'It's hot out there, take a hat.' Mother's voice. I open my eyes, I'm on the farm, standing in the back yard. I smile at her, try to take a step towards her, but my feet are stuck. I look down and realize the ground is tar, liquid and sticky. My feet begin to sink deeper into the tar, in seconds I'm up to my knees.

I look at Mother, she can save me. She opens her mouth and emits a loud sound, like a sizzle, water dropping into boiling oil. Mother begins to melt, her flesh drips off her, pooling at her feet like wax. Soon she is nothing more than wasted effigy, her hair gone, burned off in the searing heat.

'Why did you send me away? My little girl, why?' The accusation comes out of a hole in her face where her mouth should be. Then her face dissolves until all that's left is the hole-mouth. It sucks at me wetly. I begin to scream.

'JESUS! FAITH, STOP.' Hands clutch at me, pinning me down. I scream, try to throw them off, but they won't let go, they're holding me there for Mother's sucking mouth.

'Christ. Hold on to her.' I open my eyes and feel a jarring slap as Mia's flat hand connects with my cheek. I stare at her, wide-eyed, and she grabs me, holding my head in a vice-like grip.

'It's OK, OK, I'm here, you're OK, OK.'

'HERE WE GO, lots of sugar.' Mia hands me a cup of tea. I take it from her, my hands still shake. Molly has opened all the windows, cool air circulates round the flat. I cut a sideways glance at the blind woman. She sips tea out of a porcelain cup that is part of a set Mia's grandmother left to her, the heirloom no one's used since Molly and I chipped the milk jug during a re-enactment of the Mad Hatter's tea party.

'Here's the last one.' Molly retrieves the final rectangular tablet from under the couch and holds it up. I notice it has a picture carved into it, a crude rendering of a crocodile or something like it. The woman has not said anything since we arrived. She sits, sipping tea like she's Winnie Mandela, her face a picture of benevolence.

Mia clears her throat, smiles thinly. 'Well, aren't you going to introduce your friend?' I look at Molly, curious as to her connection with the blind woman. Molly returns my expectant expression with one of her own, and I suddenly realize that Mia's question is directed at me.

'My friend?' I falter.

'The child has had a shock, let her rest,' the woman cuts in before I can say anything else. 'I am quite sure I can introduce myself. I am Mrs Elizabeth Mabutu. I am a herbalist, a healer, perhaps you have seen my prayer stall, it's close to the park.'

The mention of her prayer stall makes me cringe, and I make a mental note to curb any future curious urges.

'Mrs Mabutu arrived just after you left,' Molly's eyes question me, 'said she knew you could pay your account today when you came home.'

Mia looks at me, eyebrows raised. 'You have an account with a herbalist?'

I open my mouth to deny it, but I can't find the words to describe my meeting with Mrs Mabutu, nor do I want to reveal the effect she has on me, the cold fear that she instils in me with her mad unseeing eyes.

'The child sought me out.' Mrs Mabutu smiles broadly, revealing a stretch of dark gumline fenced by teeth so small and white they could be a child's teeth. Her filmy eyes drift around the room, settling first on Mia, then on Molly and finally on me, where they remain, conveying a chill that makes gooseflesh prick my bare arms in spite of the heat.

'Her spirit is restless, she has buried it for too long in darkness. There are many restless spirits around you, child.'

'Like who?' Mia leans forward, eager to catch every word. 'Her mother died recently, is she one?' I shoot Mia a look, appalled, but she pretends not to see me.

Mrs Mabutu continues to focus her clouded eyes on me. 'Some are ancestors, but there are others. Some very bad. Your mother collected these spirits around her, they brought sickness to your house.'

I stand up, retrieve my purse from the counter; my legs feel unsteady, but I can't sit and listen to her any longer. I fish twenty rand out of my purse and hold it out to her. She makes no move to take it, and it takes me a moment to remember that she can't see it.

'Here's your money' – I can't keep the shake out of my voice as I touch her hand with the note – 'it's twenty rand. Please don't come here again.'

Mrs Mabutu's face hardens until it looks like a tribal war mask. 'To our people, to insult a sangoma as you have insulted me,' she shakes her head, 'it would be extremely bad. Your ancestors have spoken through me to try to help you. You are a stupid, stupid girl. I, though, cannot afford to ignore the ancestors, so I tell you this one final thing. Go home. It is only at your home that you will free your spirit.' Mrs Mabutu's fingers close round the note, she folds it up tightly and secretes it away in her bra. A tear I've been trying to hold back trickles down the outer edge of my nose.

'This is my home,' I tell her. I turn away and am shocked

to discover that, standing behind me is Mrs Mabutu's granddaughter. She is still wearing the same dress. She takes her grandmother's arm and they slowly make their way towards the door. Both Molly and Mia stand up, but neither says anything.

At the door Mrs Mabutu pauses and without turning back she says, 'You cannot make a new home for yourself while your spirit is buried elsewhere. If you don't return home to free your spirit, you will get sick. You already are.'

Mrs Mabutu and her granddaughter disappear through the door without issuing any further prophecies. When she's gone I turn to Mia and Molly. The shock I am feeling is reflected in their faces.

'I think you need to tell us what's going on,' Molly says.

Chapter Nine

MY HEART SLOWS down, but I still can't control the shake that makes my hands tremble and my legs weak. I take a deep breath, trying to push down the intense emotion I feel, but my breath shudders back out. I can't look at either of them, if I do, I will cry.

I feel a gentle touch on my arm. Molly's hand rests briefly on my wrist. 'Why don't you sit?' Her voice is almost a whisper. I allow her to lead me to the couch. We sit, three of us on one couch, and, for a while, we sit in a fragile silence.

Then Mia picks up her cigarettes and holds them out to Molly and me like a ceremonial peace pipe. Molly's thin fingers reach into the box and draw one out, I follow suit. Mia lights one for herself, then hands the lighter to Molly, who lights hers and puts the lighter down without offering it to me.

Soon smoke is winding its way towards the ceiling, imbuing the afternoon sunlight with a slow, magical quality. They hold the cigarettes to their lips, dragging deeply, easing the tension in the room.

After a while Mia begins to talk, her voice low. 'It's so

much easier to pick out mistakes in retrospect, to see where life got out of hand,' she sighs. 'Isabel couldn't have been much older than you when she met your father.'

I say nothing. Mia has never spoken about my father before, and for a moment it seems like she's not going to say anything more. Then she laughs, a thin nostalgic sigh of a laugh tinged with regret. 'I encouraged her to see him, she didn't want to, she thought he was too strange. He was quite strange. There was an odd look in his eyes, obsessive. Lots of men had that look, the ones who'd been to the border. He looked at Bella with those eyes, and it freaked her out.'

I see Papa's eyes in my mind. I always thought of his eyes as calm. Mother was the one with mad eyes. Like she's reading my thoughts, Mia says, 'After they married, it was like they swapped eyes. Like all the demons he'd brought back with him from Angola attached themselves to her. Started whispering. I didn't see it then, her going funny. Maybe I didn't want to see.'

'It's not his fault—' I stop myself, wondering why, even now, I want to defend Papa. Mother might have been too crazy to care about me, but Papa didn't have that excuse. He didn't want me to find him, even after.

'No,' Mia takes my hand, and this time I let her, 'perhaps it wasn't, but both of them had that obsessive side. They couldn't let go, Faith, it destroyed them.'

Molly balances the burnt-out butt, all that's left of her cigarette, upright on the coffee table. She looks at Mia, takes a deep breath. 'What happened to you earlier, I think she's trying to say that it reminded her of your mom.'

I don't respond. Molly goes on. 'You've not been yourself

since your mother's funeral. And then today, and that woman.'

I feel a tightness round my jaw. Mia's hand on mine begins to feel like a steel clamp. I turn my head so I'm looking at Molly; my face feels hard, like I'm made out of rock.

'I always thought that maybe if I'd spoken to her then, if I'd done something, got her some help, all of this . . .' Mia trails off.

I shake free of Mia's hand and stand up, my legs are steady now, no trace of their earlier wobble. I'm across the room in two strides, not enough distance to be free of their looks, but enough to face them. The creases in Mia's brow seem to be becoming permanent, like that's her only expression when she looks at me. She lights another cigarette and, suddenly, I hate her.

'I'm not like her, I'm not mad.'

Molly's face is a mask of sympathy that I can't bear to look at. 'What happened today, that woman did it to me, she did it to us.' Molly's mouth opens slightly, she shakes her head. 'You saw' – I look at Mia, she can back me up – 'when we got home, you were in some sort of trance, that woman, she did it to you too.'

'Did what, cooks?' Mia's voice shakes a little, betraying the fact that she's lying. I look at Molly now, her face is pale, drawn, her eyes edged with darkness. She looks like one of Mother's drawings, charcoal and white pastel. Then I remember how Mia looked just before I fainted, like it wasn't her. Every muscle in my body stiffens.

'I think I need to go for a walk.' Mia opens her mouth to

object, but I cut her off. 'I need some air, it's too stuffy in here.'

Molly gets up. 'I'll come,' she says.

THE PARK EXUDES an air of abandonment. The tennis courts, surrounded by a rusting wire fence, need resurfacing. The grass, where it hasn't been ground down to dust, reaches my ankles. Metal sculptures, installed by a long-gone community, have disintegrated, their strange animal forms more bestial for their decay than ever they were when their metal mouths gleamed.

Children, though, still eke out pleasure on the roundabout, which squeals in protest at every turn, still work their legs back and forth, back and forth, inching their splintering swings higher and higher in defiance of gravity, still push off violently from the ground, trying to unbalance whoever is brave enough to stand in the middle of the rusting see-saw, legs apart, arms windmilling in an attempt to gain purchase on the air. These children, whose shadows grow taller in the afternoon sun than their bodies ever will, cast lidded glances at us as we walk in uncomfortable silence through their midst. 'You're trespassing,' their eyes seem to say, 'this is our park, you don't belong here.'

But once, this park belonged to us. Once it was us taking turns to push the roundabout, our feet pushing off from the ground, us swinging higher and higher until we thought we might flip over the top bar, do the full 360 degrees, our bodies, for one split second, part of the vast blue sky.

But the children's eyes are right, we don't belong here any more. We can no longer abandon ourselves to weightlessness, free our bodies from gravity and in so doing forget ourselves. Perhaps, for me, this place was a temporary refuge from myself, a borrowed life, a childhood that Molly allowed me to share in. But we've outgrown childhood and, looking back at how things between us have shifted these past few years, perhaps we've outgrown each other.

'Do you even know me any more?' I put the question to Molly, the animal sculptures, the swings and the roundabout. For a long time the children's mocking laughter is my only reply and I begin to wonder if I've spoken out loud. I turn to Molly, about to repeat my question when she looks me straight in the eye and says:

'How can I know you, when you don't even know yourself?'

Chapter Ten

I WAKE UP feeling hollow. The heat has broken, replaced overnight by a soft and unrelenting rain. The radio clock on the bedside table displays the time with a faint red glow, 2.30.

The restaurant was busy for a Tuesday night. I fell into bed in the early hours, exhausted yet unable to sleep. Memories of the farm, memories which should have been good were they not tainted by bitterness, kept my mind ticking over, awake until the dawn broke, despite the lull of the rain and the comforting rumble of thunder.

The rain makes me feel melancholic; I can't be bothered to shower or dress. Instead I wrap an old gown around me, make coffee and settle down to examine the contents of the box file Michael Hurwitz gave me.

I flick through the pages of the farm's accounts and finances, my small knowledge of book-keeping does nothing to help decipher the rows of figures. After a head-splitting half-hour I'm no closer to understanding whether the farm is making a profit or deeply in the red.

Also in the file is a copy of the photo page of an ID book. Petrus Kgatle, the farm overseer. I peer closely at his stamp-sized face, trying to pick out defining features from the faded ink, but can make out nothing more than the shape of his head. From his date of birth I ascertain he is fifty-eight but, other than this, there is no information. Michael Hurwitz said he'd been installed on the farm after several failed tenants. That was the word he used, installed, like Petrus Kgatle was an appliance. Why the tenants had failed, again his word, he wasn't able to say and unwilling to speculate, though I suspect he knew, they must have given reasons. But, whatever the reasons, the fact remained, no tenant had stayed for longer than a year.

There had been an offer to buy the place, incorporate it back into the larger farm of which it had originally been a part, but the offer was extremely low, and Michael Hurwitz, on consultation with Mia, had turned it down, hoping for something better.

Whether Petrus Kgatle lived alone on the farm, or whether he had a family, the file did not say. His salary and other farm expenses were all paid from the money generated from Grandma English's house, a large property that was well placed in Kensington, sitting at the top of a kopje with a spectacular view and beautiful garden. I vaguely remembered the garden from my childhood. It was vast and green and had a shadowy pond from whose depths orange and white fish occasionally surfaced. Michael Hurwitz had acquired business rights for the property, and this had vastly increased its rental value.

Of course, Michael Hurwitz had waived his usual administration fee. He'd mentioned this as an aside, swiping a cotton hankie over his mouth as he said it. I'd narrowed my eyes, wondering why he would do such a thing, and noted the lurid pink spots that coloured his cheeks like the blush on an apple. Mad though Mother might have been, she'd obviously never lost her ability to charm men. I wondered what he'd think if he'd seen her when she died, whether he'd have waived his fee for her then.

I leaf through the rest of the documents in the file. Certified copies of the title deeds for the farm and the house, even my parents' marriage certificate, dated 1975. Marius Albert Steenkamp and Isabel English, even their names seem mismatched, incongruous that they should share a page, let alone a marriage.

At the bottom, under the documents, is an envelope. My name is at the top, my first name, Faith, no surname, but the address is not the farm. It's a residential address in Potgietersrus. My hands shake, this must be the letter Michael Hurwitz mentioned. Papa's letter. He never said it was addressed to me. I hold the envelope to my nose and sniff, I don't know why, it smells only of old paper, slightly dusty. There is no trace of Papa in the smell. I urge the contents out, a one-page letter and two photos.

One photo is of a house, nothing special, whitewashed with fading red roof and a small garden, though I can't tell whether the roof is really faded or if it's the photo. The second is a close-up of Papa's face. For a moment I look at the image, unsure of what to feel. It's been such a long time since I've seen him, the reality of what he looks like doesn't connect with the image in my head. Somehow over the years my father has transmuted in my memory; features pilfered from others, a schoolteacher's nose, an old boyfriend's eyes, have combined with his and made him different. The real him, staring at the camera, is a stranger to me.

Slowly, though, as I stare at the image, the memory comes. Standing in my mother's room, in front of her dressing table, looking for her powder compact. There was an envelope in the drawer. Though I can't be sure the envelope is the same, I'm pretty sure I've seen this picture before.

With trembling hands I unfold the single page. It is dated 12 July 1985, the winter of Nomsa's death. I take a deep breath and read.

Dear Faith,
You must be pleased to hear from your old pa after all this time, even though it's just a couple of weeks. I know being a kid makes it feel longer, I remember that myself, but one day, when you're a grown-up, time will fly by.

Things have been a bit difficult for me, what with fighting with your ma. I've needed time to get back on my feet, get some money together for a decent place. I know you probably want me to come home, but that's just not possible any more. I've heard your ma's not well, and I don't think I help with that, so it's best if I stay away. This doesn't mean I don't care about you, you're my kid, and I'll always care. I just need some time away. One day maybe you can come visit me in my new house. I've taken a picture for you so you can see where I'm staying for now. There's also one of me so you can see I'm OK, your ma didn't do my head too much damage, so don't worry about that.

Look after yourself and your ma.
Love, Papa

I feel sick. For years I believed Papa didn't know about Mother's illness, that if he'd known he'd have come for me.

But he had known, and he hadn't come. I look at the single page in disbelief, turn it over and stare at the other side, perhaps hoping for something more to materialize from its blank face. Then I read it again, and again, hoping to see something I've missed, discover some new word, some indication of his love, but it remains the same. The words 'I'll always care' a hollow greeting-card platitude.

A pain, buried so deep inside me that I didn't know it was there, constricts my breath. I feel a convulsion stiffening my body. My hands spasm into tight fists, crumpling my father's letter. I squeeze the page, screwing it up into a tight ball in my stiff hand, and when I can get it no smaller, I let out a scream and hurl it across the room. It hits the wall with the softest sound, gentle and unsatisfying, and lands on the floor in front of Bratcat. She half opens her eyes and looks at the crumpled letter. It holds her attention for the briefest moment, then she closes her eyes again, like the ball in front of her is of no importance, not even arousing her curiosity enough to swat at with a paw. Her disinterest mocks me. 'So what?' she seems to be saying. 'Your papa didn't love you. Surprise.'

Chapter Eleven

THERE IS NO point to my life, it lacks meaning, direction. I look around the room that I share with Molly, look at the two single beds against opposing walls yet not so very far apart that I couldn't reach across from mine and touch hers and realize, not for the first time, that this is not a room meant for two.

I'm always slightly surprised when I catch a glimpse of myself in the mirror; the person that looks out at me isn't the person I expect. I feel smaller than her, feel like what I am should take up less space than my framed reflection. My mirror image is a reminder that I don't fit, that this life is not mine. I'm like Alice, grown too big.

I am a spectator. Since the day I stepped on to the train bound for Johannesburg, I have done nothing to alter the course of my fate. My entire childhood was spent playing a game of follow-my-leader, acting out a part in a life that wasn't my own. And then Molly left for university, leaving me to drift along like an abandoned paper boat set sail on a lake. I have drifted out of reach, sodden and heavy with water, soon my own weight will drag me under.

For years, all I longed for was to return to the farm,

breathe in the hot smell of citrus, or even taste the dust-grit of the drought years on my teeth. I can't remember when I gave up hoping, when I buried myself so deep that I ceased to be. There is something inside that is beating to get out, some violence that is buried, an anger that, if I remain here and ignore it, will end up harming more than Bratcat. There is something inside of me and it's out of control. A thing that has been suffocated for too long and now claws its way up, gasping for air. It's the voice that whispers spite in my dreams, a darkness that attached itself to me long ago, before I was aware of dark things that grasp. I feel it beating against my ribcage, like a giant irregular pulse. If I don't do something soon, it will be all of me, and I will be like Mother, a nothing locked inside my body, waiting for death.

I was eleven the last time I saw her alive. I sat in the visitors' room and watched as a nurse led my mother to a seat opposite mine. The visitors' room was a small lounge that smelled of stale cigarettes and waxed linoleum heated by the sun that poured in through the barred windows. The walls wore bits of graffiti in shiny haloes where attempts had been made to scrub them away. The bits that survived were faded and mostly illegible. I made a game of making sentences from the bits I could read. JESUS DIED tagged on to the lewd 4 FREE SEX. SISTER BONGI IS joined with JOU MA. I sat staring at the wall, making sentences for the entire visit. Mother didn't seem to mind, in fact she too stared at the wall. Not once did her eyes focus on me, not one word formed on her lips. Every so often she'd make a small moaning noise that would startle me and it would take all my concentration not to look at the shrivelled woman in stained baggy trousers. If

I didn't look too closely, I could pretend I didn't know the person sitting opposite.

At the end of the hour the nurse, who had been sitting in the corner reading a book, led my docile mother back out of the room. Only then could I look at the spot where she'd been. I reached out and touched the place where she'd sat, feeling the warm imprint her body had left on the vinyl. All that was left of my mother's humanity was in that seat.

When the nurse returned to escort me, her eyes were full of pity and that pity judged me, tainted me with the madness that had eaten Mother. I stepped out into the scorching sun, cheeks burning with shame.

'How is she?' Mia asked. I shrugged my shoulders.

'OK, I s'pose.'

The following month I made an excuse not to go. And every month after that until Mia stopped asking.

I PULL THE old blue suitcase off the top of the wardrobe; it's covered in a thick layer of dust that tickles my throat and makes me cough. It's the same suitcase that the black porter carried on to the platform in Pietersburg, where I was left to guard it, bewildered and afraid, while Ouma bought my ticket to Johannesburg. I didn't know where I was going, what life held for me. To me it seemed life had suddenly enlarged, grown too big to contain in my head.

When you're seven, you never think the world is bigger than the places you've seen, and even if you know it is, you don't really understand. My world, which had been no bigger than a child's jigsaw puzzle, with large pieces that fitted easily together, was about to expand into one with thousands of tiny pieces that took ages to assemble and, always, when you finally finished, had pieces missing.

Ouma said goodbye to me, pressing me to her so my cheeks rubbed against the soft downy talc-scented flab of her upper arms and I was enveloped in the sickly-sweet smell of her White Linen perfume. I could visit, she said, I would like it in Johannesburg, it was for the best. I said nothing. I hadn't said anything since the day Mother had been taken by the police. I was holding my fear at bay by closing it off inside myself. I was afraid of what might come out if I opened my mouth.

The conductor led me along the narrow train passage to a sooty-smelling compartment with green leather seats, sat me down next to the window and left, promising to collect me once we reached Park Station, Johannesburg.

I looked around, took in the face of the thin woman opposite who smiled at me, widened her eyes and tilted her head. I focused on the hairy mole on her cheek as her lips moved, letting out a stream of questions that I didn't want to answer.

'What's your name?

'Shy, hey?

'Are you by yourself?

'Are you scared, is that it? Nothing to be scared of.

'Cat got your tongue.'

She reached up and touched the mole on her cheek, slowly becoming aware of my focus. I watched as the smiling expression re-formed itself into something else, something disapproving and annoyed. I continued to stare at her mole until she held her book up in front of her face like a shield.

Then I stared at its pink cover, with its flourish of gold lettering, its swooning woman, its dark-haired man. I stared because I didn't want to look out of the window. I didn't want to see Ouma waving from the platform.

When the whistle blew and the train began to move, my eyes flicked to the side and I saw the ghosts that had been following me, a snatched glimpse of Nomsa, of Papa, of Mother's white hair. I looked back at the book cover and dug my nails into my palm. I was not going to cry.

Finally we left the town behind and I let myself look out of the window. The train chugged towards Johannesburg, smudging trees against the vast empty landscapes between towns and their corrugated-iron-shacked townships, and I felt myself shrinking. I was just one small being in an ever-expanding world, a tiny speck with nothing to hold on to. Everything I knew was behind me, growing more and more distant with each passing tree, and everyone I knew was gone.

I closed my eyes, not wanting to see how big the world was, how far away from anything familiar this train was taking me. I wanted to be forever surrounded in comforting darkness. In the dark I could pretend that the chugging of the train was the heartbeat of someone I knew, in the dark I could be anywhere, with anyone, because darkness is the same wherever you go.

I GET OUT of the taxi and slam the door. 'My bag,' I say to the surly driver. He cuts me a look and pops the boot, leaving me to wrestle with my suitcase alone. Once my luggage is safe between my legs on the pavement, I stick my head into the passenger window. My nostrils suck up the odour of car freshener mixed with hair oil mixed with stale sweat. I hand him fifty rand, he gives me back ten, five rand short. I point at the meter: 'It's thirty-five,' I say. He shrugs, turns the key in the ignition and pulls off slowly, giving me time to retract my head before he accelerates and leaves me standing with anger swelling in my belly at the entrance to Park Station.

Chapter Twelve

I WAKE TO A rattle as the compartment door is slid open and the conductor sticks his head in. 'Potgietersrus,' he announces and slams the door shut. I yawn wide, stretch sleep from my limbs and push the scratchy Spoornet blanket away. The only light comes from outside, slipping between the gaps in the blinds, but I'm loath to turn the light on and further disturb the other passenger. I slide out of my bed and feel my way along the edge of the empty top bunk until I can make out the hump of my suitcase. I fumble for the handle and edge it down, taking care to not make any noise. Once it's safely on the floor, I turn to open the compartment door and notice that the other passenger, a black woman around my age, is staring at me, the whites of her eyes luminous in the tight shadows. For a moment we are suspended in the sleeping silence of the train, and I'm filled with a strange sense of recognition. Then she shuts me out and the feeling is gone.

The platform is deserted. The other disembarking passengers hurry quickly through the station and out into the early-morning dark. A pre-dawn chill is settling, bringing with it the damp scent of dew-wet world.

Ten minutes pass. I check my watch frequently, but no one appears. Perhaps he's waiting outside. I leave my suitcase, tired of the effort of dragging it around and, since there is no one to steal it, it seems safe enough.

The parking lot outside the station is dark and empty. Nothing moves in the pre-dawn stillness. Even the stationmaster snores softly in his office. I return to my suitcase and drag it into the waiting room.

The waiting room smells of piss and is no warmer than the platform. I open my suitcase, take out a cardigan and drag the suitcase back to the platform. I sit down on a bench to await the arrival of Petrus Kgatle.

I open my eyes to the *shup-shup* of broom against concrete. I'm stiff with cold. I squeeze my eyes against the sharp grey dawn, breathe deeply, then look at the man wielding the broom. He is sweeping the platform several metres away from me, but I can tell he's watching me, his eyes hooded and curious. My watch tells me it's six forty; I've been here over three and a half hours with no sign of Petrus Kgatle. He is obviously not coming to pick me up.

The stationmaster is still asleep and I have to tap the glass several times before he becomes aware of my presence. He wipes the sleep out of his eyes and shuffles over, seemingly unperturbed at being caught sleeping on the job.

'I need to get to Zebediela,' I tell him.

He looks at me for a moment, his expression blank, then shuffles to the other side of the room and opens a filing cabinet. He shuffles back and slides a pamphlet through the window, then sits back down in his seat. I look at the pamphlet. It's a timetable for local trains which I study for several minutes before realizing that no train goes to Zebediela. I return to the stationmaster's window and find he has nodded off. After several loud taps on the glass, I manage to rouse him.

'There is no train to Zebediela,' I tell him, waving the timetable at him.

'No train?'

'No, no train.'

He shrugs and closes his eyes. I feel a surge of frustration. I bang on the glass with my fist, his eyes open halfway.

'I need to go to Zebediela,' I almost shout at him.

He shakes his head and drops his feet off the desk, sits up. 'Ay,' he says, 'I gave you the timetable.'

'Yes,' I reply, 'but there isn't a train.'

He gives me a puzzled look, shakes his head and sighs. He gestures to me to give him back the timetable, which he studies for a moment, then he shuffles back to the filing cabinet and puts the timetable back. 'You can't go by train,' he says. 'Why don't you drive?'

I'm tempted to point out the obvious but can see that it will get me nowhere. I abandon the stationmaster and sit down on my suitcase. A feeling of hopelessness seeps into me. Perhaps I will simply wait for the train back to Johannesburg and go home.

There is nothing for you there, a small voice in my head tells me, and I know it's true. I doubt Mia would welcome me back, not after our sharp words.

I feel forlorn and grubby; my pores are black with soot, my nails thick with dirt. I watch the cleaner sweep the platform, his *shup-shup* moving ever closer to me. I'm too tired to move, even when it seems his broom is going to sweep over my feet. Then the *shup-shup* stops, and I feel he is watching me. I look up at him and manage a thin smile. He smiles back, revealing a dazzling row of white teeth that make me feel even grubbier. I move my feet, waiting for him to resume his sweeping, but the *shup-shup* doesn't restart. I look up at him again and see he is studying me, his brow furrowed in concentration.

'You can catch a taxi,' he says when he sees he has my attention again.

I'm startled by his voice. It's deep and melodic and slices through the morning stillness like glass cuts flesh. 'To Zebediela,' he continues, mistaking my surprise for confusion; 'there is a rank outside the station.

'Taxi rank,' he adds softly when still I don't reply.

I manage to nod. His attention is making me feel overwhelmed, close to tears. I'm uncomfortable under his scrutiny.

'You come from there?' he asks.

I shake my head. He leans on his broom and waits awhile, his face soft and paternal. Then he asks, his voice lowered, sensitive to my discomfort.

'You visiting the big baas there? He forgot you were coming?'

I sigh. 'No, I'm going to a small farm, it's close to the estate.'

He thinks for a while, then the expression of warm sympathy on his face narrows. 'You're going to Legaê la Morwêdiake?' His voice drops to a whisper when he says the name. I look at him, confused, and, as if he reads the confusion on my face, he says, 'My Daughter's Home.' I nod. He steps backwards and looks at me, his eyes dark, suspicious. 'Ay, that is a bad place. Why you want to go there?'

The expression on his face tells me I should lie, make something up, but I'm too tired to think of anything.

'You're the madam from there, I remember you, the white-hair madam. From the newspaper.'

I'm startled by his assumption, but before I can protest at his mistake, he resumes his sweeping and moves off, muttering to himself. His broom *shup-shups* double time and in less than a minute he's swept a clear path all the way to the far end of the platform. I'm left staring at his back, with the realization slowly forming in my head that, in the minds of people, killers don't age.

THE TAXI DROPS me at the junction where tar meets the dirt road that leads down to the farm. I offer to pay the driver extra to take me all the way to the house, but the other passengers cast him tight looks and he refuses, shrugging his shoulders good-naturedly as he gets my suitcase down off the roof where it's been tied on with the rest of the passengers' luggage.

'Šala gabotse,' he waves out of the window.

'Sepelang gabotse,' I mutter without meaning it as I watch them drive off unevenly.

I set off down the dirt road, carrying my suitcase with both hands, cursing Petrus Kgatle with all manner of evil. The bush around me hums into the hot, still air; the vibration of life, of birds and insects, forms the background sound that

African silence is made up of. I had forgotten this noise, and even as the early-morning sun beats down on the top of my head, yellow and hard, even as my shoulders ache with the strain of carrying my suitcase, even as my tired body groans with each uneven step, my soul sighs with relief.

My progress is slow, weighted down with the trappings of my Jo'burg life, I have to stop and rest every few metres. After fifteen minutes of going nowhere, I sit down on my suitcase in the middle of the road and take in what has changed in my absence. The red road that stretches in front of me is ungraded; it's so deeply rain-rutted in places that deep dongas have formed, like miniature grand canyons. Mother would not approve, she considered keeping one's road well graded simple good manners. How could you expect your neighbours to visit if they were certain to ruin their chassis?, I remember she once said to Papa when he groaned about being sent out on the tractor on a Sunday. During the drought years it was easy to keep the road smooth. I take the state of the road as a sign of good rainfall.

The bush too shows the signs of a wet season. It's thick and thorny and gives off the pungent smell of khaki bos; crushed beetles and wet earthworms and dung; and lion-yellow grass; dry sticks and wheat chaff.

The sun-glare has bleached the sky a pale almost non-blue that goes on for ever, uninterrupted, and combines with the bush smell, the African silence, the vibrating heat, to create an infinity that makes me feel tiny and much bigger than I've ever felt before. I could sit on my suitcase in the middle of the road for ever, or at least until the heat sucked all the moisture out of me, dried up the expanding sweat-circles on my T-shirt, shrivelled and blackened my eyeballs to raisins, turned my skin to parchment, me, a sacrifice to the African road.

Suddenly I feel happy and the feeling strikes me as being something alien, something I've not felt in a long time. It's the simplicity of being, a non-thinking happiness that comes when you've blotted yourself out, when you are nothing. But it's fleeting. As soon as I shift, even just to balance out my weight, the heat-haze-sleep-spell breaks and the reality of my situation floods the feeling out.

I move to stand up and my body protests, my back aches, my eyes tear against the glare, my shoulders bunch defensively. I look down the road and I'm fearful of what lies at the end of it, perhaps this was a bad idea, the idea of digging around in the memories of the farm weighs my stomach with dread, I should have stayed in Jo'burg.

As much as I would like, I can't remain sitting on my suitcase in the middle of a dirt road, slowly roasting in the sun.

I sigh and stand up, ignoring the protests of my tired body. I can't face dragging the suitcase any further. I think of black women and how they carry heavy loads on their heads, baskets of wood or buckets of water; a black woman would make light work of my suitcase. With muscle-groaning effort I lift the suitcase up and place it on my head. Stabilizing it with my hands, I try to find its centre of balance, but it slides from side to side, unevenly weighted, and I feel like my neck might snap at any moment.

I drop it back on to the road, where it lands with a thud and sends up dust. It's now red-coated and looks battered and old and tired and abandoned in the middle of the rain-rut-road. I rub the back of my neck with my hand and massage hot sweat and dust grit into my skin. I feel like the suitcase looks and I want to curl up in the middle of the road and wrap my body around it and comfort it, press my ear to the sun-warm earth and let giant ants swarm over me and dung beetles shape me into balls like they do with cow shit and roll me away in small bits.

'Dammit.' I kick the suitcase, my fragile empathy worn thin, my mood ropy. I pick it up and try fling it into the bushes, but it lands less than a metre away and the catch pops and the lid bounces open and then shuts again, snap.

It looks like a giant mouth, chewing my belongings. I pick it up again and throw it, and again the lid bounces open and snaps, this time catching the sleeve of one of my shirts between its thin lips like a piece of spaghetti. I laugh. I laugh until my stomach aches and my sides scream and my lungs gasp for air between convulsions. I laugh until tears run down my cheeks and snot runs out of my nose and I want to be sick. I laugh and my *ha ha ha* cuts the bush vibration up then gets sucked into it, just another bird call, another animal sound.

I laugh and laugh and then I cry and feel foolish and wipe my nose against my arm like a child and then I feel appalled and bereft and mad.

I abandon my suitcase on the side of the road and walk the rest of the way without it.

Chapter Thirteen

I WALK FOR TWENTY minutes and the veldt gives way to the cleared expanse that is the farm. I'd forgotten how far back from the main road the farmhouse was, how isolated; now that isolation feels threatening.

I can smell the orchards, the hot citrus scent of the waxy leaves, the ripe fruit. I close my eyes and imagine I can see the bright orange globes against the dark green of the leaves. With my eyes closed other memories come and I can almost hear the sound of singing, like the harvest pickers would before the drought came, like the house girl would before the rain stopped, like Nomsa would before Mother killed her. The sudden thought of Nomsa catches me and twists sharp in my gut. I take a deep breath to ease the knot and notice another smell, the fermentation of rot underlying the sharp acid citrus, a foetid-yeasty-bloated smell. Like death.

My stomach squeezes, saliva squirts into my parched mouth and I'm forced to spit. It's then that I notice the singing is not inside my head, because it stops as my spit hits the ground.

The figure of a woman stands in the near distance, cut out against the glare of the sun. I use my hand as a sun visor to try to pick out anything else about her, but she's too far away. She seems to shimmer against the glare, a dark mirage.

I raise my hand and wave, but she doesn't respond. She sees me though. I sense her gaze, sense my presence is unexpected to her, disturbing, and I wonder again at the isolation of the farm, perhaps she's not people at all, perhaps she's other. The thought chills me, plucks my flesh.

Suddenly, she turns and runs around the house.

'Petrus.' Her voice cuts like a siren, sets off dogs barking. I laugh at myself: fairies, you're a grown-up now, Faith, remember. I walk on, glad there is someone other than Petrus, who I've already decided is going to be difficult, on the farm.

The barking sounds closer and, rounding the house, I see a pack of dogs running towards me. I freeze. I know dogs well enough to know that if I turn and run they will chase me down. I stand my ground, hoping that they won't smell my fear, people say they can.

A sharp whistle pierces the air and the dogs stop, go back, their excited barks intermingled with submissive squeals. The whistler is a man, I presume it's Petrus Kgatle. He walks towards me, even from here I can see his step, slow, deliberate. The dogs have swallowed him into their pack, they surround him, tails wagging, but their energy is bound by his presence. One of the dogs breaks away, begins a mad dash towards me, but another sharp whistle brings him in line, he stops, lies down in the dirt, rolls over, whines, waits.

The man makes his way a little way down the drive, not far from the house and stops, beckons me and waits.

I brush my hair back from my face and walk towards them. I know I must look a sight, my face streaked with dust and sweat, my hair wild, my clothes rumpled and grubby. Not a great first impression.

As I draw close, Petrus steps out from the dogs, who pant and whine with impatience. I wipe my hand on my jeans and hold it out, aware of how sweaty it is, but he makes no move to take it, and I'm forced to withdraw it.

'You Petrus?'

He narrows his eyes at me, they're dark, almost black, the whites brownish yellow. His face is sun-darkened, the skin on his cheeks thick, almost black, like tree bark.

'I'm Faith,' I introduce myself, determined not to let his unfriendly attitude put me off. 'This was my parents' farm,' I add when I still receive no response. He remains silent and I begin to wonder if he even understands me; perhaps he only speaks Afrikaans and Sotho. I'm about to repeat myself in Afrikaans when one of the dogs sticks his nose between my legs.

The dogs – I can see there are six now they aren't charging at me – are sniffing around me, jostling for a turn to shove their nose into my crotch. As I push one nose away, another takes its place. All the dogs are black and skinny and have a ridge of vertebrae running along their backs. Two are definitely female, and have distended bellies and long teat-like nipples, pregnant or recently pregnant.

'You should have come next week.'

I look up, my cheeks hot from the sun and embarrassment. 'Sorry?'

'I told Baas Michael you should come next week.' His voice is like rubbing gravel in your hands, slowly. He shakes his head and I get the feeling that everything this man does takes time. 'Ja, next week would be better.'

'Well, I'm here now.' I can't keep the annoyance out of my voice. 'I did call and Mr Hurwitz said it was arranged. He spoke to you, you were supposed to fetch me, from Potgietersrus. Did you forget?'

He grunts. 'Ay. He did tell me.' Petrus turns and begins to walk back towards the house. 'Next week is better.'

I follow him, determined not to be put off. The dogs sniff at my feet, excited, whining, tails wagging.

Petrus circles round the house, through the yard, and makes his way along a path that leads past where Mother used to grow her vegetables. The ordered rows of tomato plants, squash, cabbage, carrots have been replaced by tall maize plants and weeds. I try to remember where this path leads, but it's unnecessary to dig into my memory, as we soon come to the workers' compound, where Moses fashioned whistles out of the stems of pumpkin plants for me.

I look around, it's both familiar and unfamiliar, like déjà vu. The compound has changed, the original buildings are there, but several huts have been added. Three women sit together in the shade; they stop talking as we approach, I'm aware of their black-eyed stares. No one returns my smile.

Pungent woodsmoke spirals up from a cooking fire. A small boy, wearing only a dirty T-shirt that reaches halfway down his belly, stands looking at me, his upper lip crusted with snot. The dogs, their sense of excitement dissipated, leave me and settle in various shady places around the compound. Their tongues hang out, drip saliva into the dust.

I hold up my hand. 'Dumêla.' I'm acutely aware that the only Sotho words I know are hello and goodbye, but I need not worry. The women murmur a greeting, nod, but don't engage with me further.

Petrus disappears into one of the rooms and I'm reluctant to follow him. I smile awkwardly at the women, but they avoid my searching glances and I'm left with only the interest of the small boy. I give him a little wave. 'Dumêla,' I say in my toddler voice. I get down on my haunches and hold out my hand. He sucks on his fist, watching me through round and wary eyes, his drool making his umber skin slick and shiny.

'Dumêla,' I try again, moving towards him. He lets out a frightened yell, takes several unbalanced steps backwards and falls on to his bum in the dirt. He begins to cry.

'Ay.' The youngest woman, who must be his mother, gets up from the group and lifts the boy roughly by the arm on to his feet. This makes him cry louder, and she admonishes him in harsh tones, picks him up and takes him to where the other women sit. She says something in Sotho and the other woman nod. 'Êê.'

'I'm sorry,' I try, but the women just click their tongues and murmur amongst themselves.

Petrus re-emerges from the room with a bunch of keys. He comes over and holds them up. 'These are all the farm keys,' he says. 'I will get someone to help clean the house. Mpho,' he shouts. The young mother gets up and hands her child to one of the other women.

'My daughter,' he says, 'Mpho.' I hold out my hand and she touches it briefly, unsmiling. 'She will clean for you.' I look at Mpho's sullen expression and I'm gripped by a sinking feeling that her help will not make my life easier.

Chapter Fourteen

THE KEY DOES not turn, it sticks and scrapes and I imagine I can see the rusted lock teeth straining to release their oxidized bonds. Petrus rattles the key from side to side, then grips it in both hands, twists and, slowly, it gives.

The kitchen is dark, the air dank and heavy with the smell of mildew. I'm surprised at the low light, considering the brightness of the morning, until I notice the windows, opaque with dirt. Nothing seems to have changed, or my memory deceives me into thinking it's the same. The range still squats, the wooden table still sits squarely in the middle of the room, though the wood is mildew-black in places, and the clock, though silent, still hangs on the wall, its face coated with thickened grey dust. There are even a few pots on the shelf above the stove.

It feels like a tomb.

'How long since anybody was here?' I ask Petrus, my voice low so as not to disturb the hush. He makes a dry, guttural noise. '1987 I come. Baas Michael, she come once to show the people who want to buy, but nobody come again.' The offer to purchase in the box file was dated

12 September 1987, no one had been here since. Thirteen years this house has stood empty, and by the looks of it no one's come near it in all that time. It strikes me as odd that Petrus wouldn't have moved into the house. Why choose to live in the compound with its huts and cramped rooms when there is a house with running water and a generator for electricity?

'Didn't you want to live in the house?'

Petrus looks at me, brow creased, lip curled. He shakes his head and offers no explanation.

The tap at the kitchen sink is dull, the inside edged with rust. I turn it, it resists, scrapes, opens a little. Nothing comes out. I sigh.

Petrus makes a dry guttural noise, like his throat is full of rust. 'I disconnected the pipe from the water tank,' he says, 'we must check the pipes before we put it back. For rust. And washers, the taps will need new washers.'

The passage is just as dank as the kitchen. Patches of damp have seeped up from the ground, the plaster is crumbling in places. The floorboards are rough and splintered, having swelled with moisture, then dried out, then swelled, unprotected, unpolished, unloved.

All of Mother's paintings have gone, and I don't know if I feel relieved by their absence or bereft. The walls still show signs of where they once hung, a faint grey edge where dust gathered round their frames, permanently marking the paint, a slight difference in the colour of the wall where the paint was protected by canvas from the grime of life. The lighter squares are visible only at a certain angle and could be mistaken for a trick of the light by someone who'd never seen the grim portrayals of Mother's fantasies that had once covered them.

All that remains in my bedroom is the bed, upon which the mattress moulders, and the cupboard. Grandma English's rocking chair is gone, as is my suitcase of treasures. I try and remember what happened to it, did I take it to Johannesburg? I can't remember it as ever having been anywhere other than under the bed in this room. It's one of those things that you forget about completely until something stirs it up in your memory and suddenly its absence seems inexplicable and a minor tragedy.

The door to Mother's bedroom is closed, and I leave it that way, not ready to face it, not with Petrus hovering around me like I'm a thief that he needs to watch lest I steal something.

In the lounge someone has taken the trouble to cover the furniture with sheets, like they do in the movies where Victorian summer homes stand empty half the year, the furniture dressed like Hallowe'en ghosts. All my life I thought it an English thing to do, that no one else did it.

I pull the ghost costume, grey with solidified dust, off the couch. I uncover the lamps and the cabinet and the armchair where Papa liked to sit. I uncover the toad phone, its coiled black wire frayed at the end, robbed of its oily sheen by time.

All the wooden furniture is dull, lifeless, though in better condition than the kitchen table. Someone has taken the trouble to put mothballs on to the couch and armchair, under the cushions, down the sides, and the smell of damp is accompanied by a faint, almost-not-there smell of naphthalene. The curtains have been taken down, the windows are opaque with dirt like the rest of the house, the rug is rolled up against the wall. Cleaning thirteen years of dirt out of the house seems like an impossible task and I'm too tired to begin to contemplate it.

I sink down on to the couch, cover my face with my hands. I feel on the verge of tears, exhausted and raw. I haven't cried since I left Johannesburg; my anger at Molly and Mia, at our ugly parting, has fuelled me, kept me going. But the realization has finally dawned on me that, for the first time in my life, I am truly alone.

The dry guttural cough that Petrus makes before he speaks makes me look up. He stands in the doorway, his face gruff. 'We must open the house, take the furniture into the sun, clean. Mpho has gone to get my wife and sister, there is too much work for her alone.' He turns to leave.

'Petrus.' He stops. 'My suitcase, I left it at the side of the road.'

He makes a sound in the back of his throat and leaves me.

WHILE PETRUS'S WOMEN move the furniture out of the house, I open the door to Mother's room. Like the sitting room, all the furniture in here has been covered with sheets. Two of the sheets hang strange and tall over objects I don't recall. They look like they could conceal something humanoid, and the memories of being afraid of fairies hiding almost anywhere resurfaces and sends a shiver down my spine. Determined not to let Mother's flights of fancy affect me any more, I take an end of one of the sheets with nervous bravado and tug sharply, pulling the covering off in one go.

A frightened shriek escapes me and I stumble backwards

into the other covered humanoid shape, sending it crashing to the floor.

I grab on to the footboard of the bed to steady myself and confront my reflection, wild and scared-looking, in the standing mirror in front of me. A small relieved laugh escapes me as Mpho looks into the room. Her immediate surprise wipes the sullen expression, the only one I've seen when she's looking at me, off her face. 'I just knocked over the, uhm, lamp,' I say, looking down at it to check what the second humanoid thing was. She sucks in her cheeks a little and nods, the sullen mask returning.

Once my drumming pulse is back under control and I've righted the lamp, I go through Mother's drawers and wardrobe. They're empty, all her clothes have vanished, all her make-up and other beauty paraphernalia gone. There's just old newspaper lining the bottom of the drawers, watermarked in places.

Outside the sun beats down on the musty furniture and mattresses. Inside Petrus's women scrub the floors, clean windows, air the place out. If it wasn't for the damp, the crumbling plaster, the rusted pipes, the mildew, it might be as it always was. All the furniture, with a few exceptions, seems to be the same. It's just my family and our personal belongings that are missing. It almost seems as if the house has been waiting for us to come back, frozen in time, patient.

Petrus has gone off in the van to fetch my suitcase, Mother's van. That, at least, he's maintained quite well, the signs of wear and tear minimal compared to the rest of the farm.

The three women don't speak to me or respond to my attempts to make conversation. They seem to regard me with resentment, only grunting or nodding replies to my questions. They hardly speak, and when they do it's to each other, huddled together in secrecy, their voices low.

I'm in no mood to try to break through their barrier of resentment, so I wander off, leaving them to work alone. Out in the back yard the sheets, washed in cold water in an iron tub much like the one Mother used to bath me in, hang on the line. The sheets remind me of Nomsa. Her room is padlocked from the outside, the curtain drawn over the window and, for now, it will remain that way. I have no desire to look into her room, gripped by an illogical fear that the room, like the house, will be the same as the day we left.

Instead I open up the generator shed and discover it too has been neglected. I cannot help feeling a certain amount of resentment myself for the way things have been left to decay. Perhaps that is why Petrus did not want me here, did not want me to see that all these years he and his family have been living off our land while he has been neglecting his duties. Perhaps, had I arrived next week, I would have found the place deserted, my farm overseer absconded in my mother's van.

I sit down on the back step in the sun and try to figure out what to do about Petrus. I'm loath to confront him, acutely aware of my vulnerability in this isolated place. For the same reason I feel I cannot ask him to leave. I know, though, that somehow I need to assert my authority, need to get him to help me fix the place up, make it habitable, get the farm up and running.

I don't know yet what sort of a man Petrus is, whether he is a good man or a man who will see my weakness and, like a lion stalking prey, choose a moment to close in for the kill. Though they are helping me now, I cannot help feeling that their help is grudging.

What were you expecting, Faith? I say to myself, wondering exactly what it was I expected. That the house be the same, beds made and ready for me to drop into, the farm productive? I am unsure how I will be able to make this place work; my funds are limited, just the rent from Grandma English's house and what's left in my bank account.

But Mother made it work, she ran the place single-handed. The thought that she managed without Papa for so long, without workers at times, makes me think I could do it too, though I know nothing of farming. It's strange, all the time spent in Johannesburg I felt out of place, the simple country cousin. Here, where I thought I belonged, I'm city folk.

Chapter Fifteen

THINGS I HAD FORGOTTEN.

The way dusk shrouds the farm with the mysterious glow of twilight that paints the sky in hazy pinks and oranges and deep purple-blues, and makes silhouettes out of the solid things so that they become black holes against the last-light.

The fertile soil-heat that escapes from the earth as the ground cools, releasing the rich smell of night, a loamy perfume lost under the tar and concrete of the city.

The nocturnal insects that rise out of the bush in a cloud of powdery wings as the light fades, ready to feed and mate and commit suicide in candle flames and cooking fires and high-voltage bug zappers.

The symphony of night-crawlers and frogs and scavenging jackals yip-yipping that makes the world hum and vibrate and makes you realize in the density of the new-moon night that there is no such thing as silence.

Then there is the creeping of shadows and creaking of floorboards, the thick darkness that envelopes me and won't be cast back even when I light one candle from the packet Petrus gave me, its small circular glow a focus for my eyes and nothing more.

The almost-whispers of trees stirred by the evening breeze, the voices that once belonged to fairies but have lost their magic for me, and yet, if I close my eyes I can just about make out words.

And the gnawing hunger that hollows me out and makes me bone-cold in spite of the warm night, that reminds me of bad times, a sensation that memory has dulled into unfamiliarity yet I know belongs to this place and to me in it.

The night is only just dark, the horizon still indigo, yet I'm ready to curl up on the bed under the sheets that, though washed and smelling of detergent, have resisted the bleaching power of the sun and remain a dull grey broken only by age-yellow patches, like liver spots. I am ready to let the night suck me into her dark arms when I become aware of Petrus, standing just outside the doorway. How long has he been standing there, watching me? His silent approach makes me nervous.

'Yes, Petrus?'

'I have brought you something to eat.'

He comes into the kitchen and places a plate on the table along with a plastic Coke bottle he's filled with water. The smell of meat stew makes my mouth water and I have to use every bit of my willpower not to pounce on the plate like a starved dog.

'Thank you.'

He grunts and turns to leave.

'Petrus.' I am made suddenly brave by this human gesture. It makes me feel there is a chance to make things work in this isolated place among his strange and sullen clan. 'I need to go into town tomorrow, to buy things. I'll need the van.'

Even in the limited light I can see him stiffen. My resolve

wavers and I know if he refuses I won't have the strength to insist.

'I can take you,' he says and disappears into the night.

I AM UP with the first dawn light, having slept fitfully. I woke often and stared into the oppressive dark pressing in on me from all sides in the wide bed that was once my parents', imagining someone in the room with me. The darkness itself seemed to have a presence, the inky blackness shifting like an oil slick around me, sometimes silent, sometimes accompanied by creaking and scuttling. I felt six again, lying awake, afraid of the things I might see in the dark, and the new fear that Petrus might sneak into the house in the dead of night and slit my throat. No one would care.

In the kitchen I use a little of the water from the Coke bottle to rinse the sleep from my eyes and brush my teeth. Turtle doves sing encouragement to the workers and I feel the knot in my stomach release, relaxing into the peaceful warmth of the morning.

I am determined not to let Petrus push me around and, feeling stronger even after a restless night, I resolve to go to town alone. The van is, after all, mine, as is the farm, and the sooner I make him realize that the better.

I dress quickly, make a list of things I'll need, toilet paper, bedding, food, cleaning products, light bulbs, soap, just about everything I can think of. With my extensive list complete, I can see no point in waiting around and allowing the day to waste. I make my way to the compound. Smoke from the cooking fire adds to the early-morning haze, tainting the new day with an acrid pungency. One of the older women is squatting by the fire stirring a black pot of porridge. She is still in her nightie, and has a blanket wrapped around her fastened with a large nappy pin. She scowls when she sees me.

'Petrus here?' I ask without bothering to greet her. She doesn't reply, gets up and disappears into one of the rooms. Minutes pass. He emerges bleary-eyed, wearing only trousers, his upper body and feet bare.

'Good morning,' I greet him and don't wait for a reply before continuing, 'I'm going to town now, I need the van.'

He rubs a hand over his face, stretches and walks over to a bucket of water. He splashes water over his head and I watch as the drops catch in his greying beard and trickle down his neck. He stands up dripping. 'It's too early, wait and I will take you.'

'I'm going now,' I insist, 'I've got things to do.' The woman re-emerges from the room and stands, defiant, next to Petrus. 'The keys.' I hold out my hand. The woman mutters something under her breath. Petrus grunts.

'You need to get washers, for the taps, and pipes, and oil for the locks, and diesel for the generator. And gas bottles.' He pauses to gauge my reaction, and I see that he can continue with his list if he feels he needs to, but he doesn't. I get the point. I look at the ground, a hot blush warms my face, I feel like I've been admonished. 'I will take you in one hour, the shops won't be open now.' He turns and says something in Sotho to the woman, to which she clicks her tongue in annoyance and glares at me.

'Maswabing is making the porridge, you can eat with us.' With that he disappears back into his room and leaves me with the woman. I consider going back to the house and waiting there, but I don't want to offend Petrus further, so I hover around the fire, watching Maswabing cook.

'Maswabing is a beautiful name,' I say. She looks up from her pot and frowns at me. 'What does it mean?' I continue, determined to make this woman warm to me.

For a moment she contemplates me, as if she's trying to decide whether to speak to me or not, then she says, 'It means sadness.'

'Oh, sadness. It's still lovely.'

She stops stirring the porridge. 'My mother had five daughters before me. My father wanted me to be a boy, and when I wasn't, he took another wife. My mother had to leave us on the farm with my grandmother who was too old for children and go and find work in Johannesburg. My name is not because life is lovely, life is not lovely, life is hard. Ay.' She shakes her head and I realize I've caused her great offence.

'I'm sorry.'

'Sorry? For what are you sorry?' Maswabing suddenly stands; though she is a small woman, anger makes her tower. 'You come here and expect us to clean for you, to fix your house, and then you want to take our transport. And tomorrow, maybe you come tomorrow and say we must leave your land, land where we have lived for more than ten years. Eleven, twelve, thirteen,' she holds out her hand and snaps off the numbers on her thumb and two fingers. 'And if we don't go, will you shoot us?'

I feel the blood drain from my face. She takes a step closer to me, lowers her voice. 'Ja, we know why you went away, what you did here. We know. You come back to live in that house, but soon you will be gone from there. Like that white man who come before us, to live in that fancy house. That is a bad place.' She spits on to the ground. 'No one can stay there. It is full of spirits.'

'Maswabing. Enough.' Petrus's gruff voice betrays an anger that his blank face masks. I know, though, that his anger is for no other reason than she has betrayed their feelings towards me and in doing so jeopardized their livelihood.

The baby starts to cry in one of the huts and I hear his mother try to quieten him. One of the dogs whimpers and paws the ground, all the others have raised their heads, alert to the tension.

My blood is buzzing with anger and adrenaline; it takes me some time before I can control my emotions enough to speak. When I finally do speak, my voice shakes. 'I'll wait for you at my house to bring my van so we can go get supplies for my farm.' I speak to Petrus, but accentuate every 'my' for Maswabing. I shoot her a look to make sure she understands before I turn and leave.

Chapter Sixteen

I SIT ON THE kitchen step in the early-morning sun and wait for Petrus, trembling with anger. The light glints white off the darkened window of Nomsa's old room, and I feel it's accusing me in the same way Maswabing did, and I say over and over to the dusty yard, 'It's not my fault. It's not my fault.' But somehow I feel the yard doesn't believe me, and the more I say it, the less it rings true in my own ears.

My past life here seems shrouded in mystery. Why did I believe? And what exactly was it that I believed? What was real and what imagined? I still struggle to separate what memories are true from the ones that she planted there. Even now in my mind I can see Mother's fairies, imagine their slim, bony forms, their slick skin pulled taut over sinewy muscle and protruding, bulbous joints. I can place them in scenes from my memory, though I know logically they were never there. I can't recall for definite ever having seen one, something I thought at the time was due to a lack of privilege, but somehow their forms are as solid in my mind as any other real-life being who ever entered my world.

'It's not my fault.'

After the brightness of the sun, the house seems dark and my eyes struggle to adapt to the gloom. I pick up my list from the table, and looking it over I realize how ill-equipped I am to lead a life on this farm. I left Johannesburg, half distraught, half anticipating adventure, the first time I've ever been out on my own, so to speak. I realize now it's not as easy as I thought. Just because I spent my first seven years in this place doesn't mean I know it, and what I do know might be a fantasy based on confused memories.

And yet, for the first time in years I feel like I might belong somewhere. Buried inside me, somewhere, must be the knowledge of this place. There is an invisible cord that binds me to it, it has featured in my dreams and in my mind, it is the only place that has ever felt like home. If I cannot peel away the layers that are not me here, if I cannot discover, buried after years of hiding, a soul I can claim as my own, then I have no hope.

In the bedroom I dig through my suitcase until I find the letter Papa sent. The address is the only link I have to my past life, the only link I have to a father who abandoned me and yet, in spite of that, I still want to go there.

I catch a glimpse of myself in the mirror, a mirror that manages to capture all of me in its long frame, not break me up into smaller pieces. My face is tight, cheeks hollowed out, eyes sunken. My hair, oily and unkempt, is ropy. I narrow my eyes at my reflection and it seems the wild-looking woman caught in the glass is not a version of myself I know, not me at all. The person framed by dark wood in the age-clouded mirror is Mother, in her room, on her farm. Am I so much the product of her, so much my mother's daughter, that I don't exist at all? Perhaps there is no Faith, no person separate from the source, just a genetic imprint of her, her exactly, fated to follow her in life, and maybe even death. Perhaps every action perpetrated by Mother was also by my hand. That is what the people of this place see, not the little girl returned, but the murderer, untouched by time.

I pick up a shoe and hurl it at the mirror. 'You're not me,' I scream. But the shoe bounces off the glass, leaving it intact, leaving the reflection that I don't want to claim as my own, staring back at me through over-bright blue eyes.

WITH THE LAST of the water contained in the plastic Coke bottle, I wash my face for the second time that morning, perhaps this time hoping to remove the signs of madness that seemed etched on to my reflection. I drag my brush roughly through my hair, pulling it away from my face and twisting it into a single plait down my back. With a clean top and clean jeans, a spray of deodorant, I imagine I look normal, respectable, that no one will be able to see Mother inside me.

The van pulls up in front of the house shortly after nine. I hear its arrival, though Petrus does not get out or turn the engine off. I wait a few minutes, a small revenge for his tardiness, then, eager to escape the claustrophobic presence of the house, I give in.

The day is already hot and the small cab stifling. I feel uncomfortably close to Petrus. I can smell the odour of sweat and woodsmoke and home-grown rolled in newspaper that clings to him. He does not apologize for being late, nor does he mention the incident with Maswabing.

The road to town is both familiar and strange and I'm glad I did not insist on driving, though I was tempted to, just to assert my right. Places on the outskirts of town I remember as uncultivated expanses of veldt, occupied only by lonely umbrella thorns and fever trees, are now crammed with tin shanties, some of whose residents watch us pass with shiftless eyes.

Even the town itself has changed, though I hadn't expected it would be untouched by the passage of time and politics. A low green-roofed shopping complex, with shops that sprawl on a single level centred round a Checkers, has replaced the market. The open-air parking lot, though, is edged by purpose-built concrete stalls on which women hawk vegetables on coloured plastic plates; small pyramids of tomatoes, onions, bananas, sometimes sweets or bright orange corn chips that look like artificial mopani worms; or men shove sunglasses, toys and mobile-phone car kits into my face. Is this where I once hid under a blue metal trestle table, is this the same place we sold our vegetables? It doesn't seem possible, yet it must be. I wander through the shaded brick paving between the shops, looking for something familiar in a place I'm almost sure I once knew well. One small shop, Saartjie's Jam, gives me a glimmer of hope. Inside the shelves are lined with bright jars of fruit preserves and pickles, but the woman behind the counter is young and has never heard of Tannie Saartjie. The owner is a man, she tells me, but she doesn't think his mother is called Saartjie.

'An aunt, maybe?' I ask, but she shrugs and serves another customer. They talk in lowered voices and cut sideways glances at me, so I leave the jar of marmalade I was pretending to examine on the counter and leave.

I find Petrus waiting for me in the hardware shop where I left him. A white man wearing a blue dust jacket over his khaki safari suit is leaning over the counter checking the items Petrus has brought to the front by pointing at them with a short pencil, mumbling to himself and licking the tip of the pencil before writing in an invoice book. It takes him several minutes from the time I arrive to finish his inventory and when he does he tears the page off and pushes it towards Petrus. Without looking at it Petrus nods at me, alerting the man to my presence for the first time.

'Môre, mevrou.'

'Sy's Engles,' Petrus says. The man looks at me as if he's seeing something altogether different from the first time he looked.

'Oh, ja. That's five hundred and sixty-six rand, altogether,' he says, taking the invoice off the counter and holding it out to me.

I glance over the list, mentally trying to calculate if I can afford it and still make it through the month until the next rental payment from Grandma English's Kensington house comes through. I feel the man's eyes on me and look up to catch him studying me, his brow creased in concentration.

'You been here before?' he asks. I shake my head. 'You look familiar,' he says, and I can see the cogs of his brain turning over, trying to place me. I look away, pretend to look at one of the miniature Maglite torches he has displayed on the counter.

'I just moved here yesterday.'

'Ja, where?'

I hesitate, not wanting to tell him in case it sparks off something in his memory. 'Just a small plot, near the estate,' I tell him, hoping he won't ask anything further. He narrows his eyes, and I can see he is close to recognizing me, or at least mistaking me for Mother, when Petrus clears his throat.

'Time is short, we need to get back and there are things still to do.'

I smile at him involuntarily, surprised he has saved me.

'Ja, well, how do you want to pay?' says the hardware man.

WHILE PETRUS LOADS the van with the supplies I've bought from the Checkers, I go to the post office to apply for a telephone on the farm. The only phone at the moment is Petrus's old mobile, a brick of a phone with a short battery life. There are problems picking up a signal on the farm and I decide it will give me some security to have a line to the outside world, though I'm sure no one will call me, even if I do give out the number, which I probably won't.

Like everything else the post office has changed, but it still retains its inky smell.

'Three months,' the woman behind the glass partition tells me, stamping my application and attaching the fee. I look at the name tag pinned to her shirt, Elsie van Wyk. I explain my isolated situation to Elsie, trying to appeal to her as a woman, but she seems immune to my pleading. 'That is how long it takes,' she explains, her voice dragging with boredom, 'there's a waiting list.'

I'm about to give up when I hear a familiar voice. A

woman has entered the office behind the glass. Though older, her hair shot with grey, her bony frame is unmistakable. Her name is out of my mouth before I have time to think about what I'm doing and Tannie Marie Bezuitenhoud looks up at me. For a moment her face clouds with confusion, but as she studies me a light of recognition goes on behind her eyes.

'Well I never,' she exclaims, coming over to stand behind the listless Elsie van Wyk, 'if it isn't little Faith.' I smile thinly, remembering that this woman is the town gossip and news that I am back will spread like wildfire now that she knows. 'And don't you look just like your ma, ag, this is a surprise.' She beams at me with an enthusiasm I know has nothing to do with me as a person and everything to do with me as a newsworthy item. 'And your ma, how is she, poor woman?'

'She died.' I hope my directness will put her off, but she's not easily deterred.

'Dead. How very sad. She must have been very young. Prison couldn't have been easy for her though, what with her delicate health.'

Elsie van Wyk's ears prick up and her face takes on the animation of interest.

'She didn't go to prison.' I give Elsie a look that I hope will scare her back into bored disinterest, but she is either too stupid to notice or my looks don't have the same impact that Mother's did.

'Is that so?' Tannie Marie looks at me expectantly, but I refuse to be drawn out further.

'Well, it was good to see you. I must be going. I just came in to apply for a phone line for the farm.' I wait to see if she takes the bait.

'The farm? You moved back there with your husband?'

I'm tempted to say yes and introduce her to Petrus, just to see her face, but common sense gets the better of me. 'No, I'm not married. I'll be running the place alone, for now. I would call you when I've done it up and invite you over, but there's no cellphone signal and it'll be three months before Telkom can come.' I shrug.

Tannie Marie picks up the application. 'Can't have you on that farm alone with no phone for three months, what with the blacks killing farmers all over the country.' She mouths the word 'blacks', like it's some dirty word she doesn't want Elsie to hear. 'Leave it to me.'

Back in the van with Petrus I wonder if it was worth letting Tannie Marie see me to jump the queue for a phone. Everyone has to know I'm back sometime, perhaps it doesn't matter if it's now.

'You have everything you want from town?' Petrus interrupts my thoughts.

'Just one more thing,' I reply, digging in my bag for the envelope.

Chapter Seventeen

THE ADDRESS ON the envelope leads us to a small house, painted a garish peach colour, that squats low in a residential tree-lined street. I compare the house to the one in the photo, but it's not the same.

Petrus waits in the van while I push open the low gate and head up the path to the front door. There is something vaguely familiar about the place, but perhaps it's just the sort of house, small and unprepossessing, built en masse after the war to house veterans and their families.

I ring the doorbell and 'Greensleeves' chimes through the house. A small dog yaps within, followed by the clatter of heels on tile, then a yelp of pain.

'Bladdy dog. Lizelle! Fetch this dog, there's someone by the door.'

The door swings open and I'm confronted by a blonde woman wearing shorts and a stripy pink shirt which she's unbuttoned halfway and tied in a knot in the middle to reveal her belly. Her skin is tanned to an uneven golden brown and puckers round her navel. She looks at me, her eyes travelling up and down my body before she settles on my face.

'Ja?'

She has a strong Afrikaans accent and I'm surprised that she addressed Lizelle, whoever she may be, in English before opening the door. I open my mouth and realize I have no idea what to say. In coming here I expected to find someone I knew, expected that I would know them and they know me. I have nothing rehearsed.

'What's wrong?' she says. 'Cat got your tongue?' I look at her sharply; there is something about her that I recognize, but I can't place.

'I'm sorry, I think I've made a mistake. I thought I knew the people who lived here.'

She narrows her eyes at me. 'No,' she says, 'I don' think I've ever laid eyes on you before.'

'Well I was quite young the last time I was here.' There seems to be nothing to lose by asking her a few questions. 'Maybe you knew my father.' She cuts me off before I've had time to explain further.

'Your father?' She looks at me closely. 'I don' think so. I've known some men but hardly any of them would have been old enough to be your father. I don' really go for old men.' She smiles, deep furrows form around her mouth.

'How long have you lived here?' I ask, hoping perhaps that someone had lived here before her who might have known Papa.

'Just about all my life. I grew up in this house.' My heart sinks, this seems to be going nowhere.

'Hey, don' look so worried,' she says, seeing my face drop, 'maybe my mother knew your dad.'

'Your mother?' I ask.

'Ja, Hester Els.' The name is not instantly familiar. 'Hettie,' she says, 'most people called her Hettie.'

'Oh, yes,' my heart leaps, 'I knew her. Is she here?'

The woman shakes her head, and I suddenly realize she referred to her in the past tense. 'She's in a old people's home, got old-timers,' she leans forward and lowers her voice, for whose benefit I'm not sure, 'you know, she's gone a bit funny, in the head.'

I'm starting to dislike this woman in spite of the fact that she seems willing to talk to me. I'm sure it must be visible on my face, but she doesn't seem to notice, because she carries on.

'If I ever get like that, I'd rather you shoot me, put me out of my misery. But you can't just do that, go around shooting old people' – she laughs as if the thought of geriatric target practice amuses her – 'oh no, you have to fork out every month so that there's someone to feed them and change their nappies, just like babies.'

'Poor Tannie Hettie.'

'Poor her nothing, what does she know? Poor me. They expect me to fork out for extras as well. Twenty rand to get her hair done in blue rinse and curlers. Twenty rand! What does she care if her hair's done, she just sits there staring out the window speaking kuk. But Lizelle, see, my kid, she wants me to pay for it. I says to her, "Where must I get an extra twenty bucks every week for blue rinse?" You do her hair when you go. She likes to visit her ouma, poor kid. I'm Liesel, by the way.' She holds out her hand and I'm forced to shake it.

'Faith.'

She narrows her eyes at me, drops my hand and looks at me as if she's only just seen me. 'Your father, do you see him a lot?'

I shake my head, surprised by her sudden interest. 'I haven't seen him since I was seven. Did you know him? Marius Steenkamp.'

For a long moment she seems to be considering something, then her face closes and she changes the subject.

'I must get going, things to do.' She's dropped the chatty tone, her voice now cold and uninviting. I decide not to press her about Papa further. She seems to be the kind of person who would slam the door in my face if I annoyed her.

'I'd like to see your mother, visit her if I can.'

'She won' be able to tell you anything. Like I said, she's not all there.'

'Not for that, just to visit. She looked after me quite a bit when I was a kid, I'd just like to say hello.'

Liesel shrugs. 'Well I suppose there's no harm in it. She's in Piet Potgieter.'

I thank her and am about to ask where that is when she closes the door. I'm left looking at the varnished wood, wondering how someone like Tannie Hettie could have landed up with such an uncaring daughter. Then I feel ashamed; maybe people thought the same of me.

THE DUTY SISTER glares at me over the top of the magazine she's pretending to read, and I wonder if it's because she recognizes me or just because I have arrived during the lunch hour. I page through an old copy of *Fair Lady*, not reading or seeing anything, my thoughts on Tannie Hettie, trying to prepare myself.

It's fifteen minutes before a nurse comes to lead me up some stairs and down a long corridor, the antiseptic odour of Dettol and ammonia mingling in my nostrils, their sharp astringency barely masking the smell of incontinence and age.

Strains of Mozart and white noise float out of one of the many rooms that lie on both sides of the corridor. We pass an elderly lady slowly going nowhere, her Zimmer frame caught on the edge of the door. She lifts it an inch off the ground, then places it back in the same spot, unable to work it free of the doorframe.

'Shouldn't we help her?'

The nurse shakes her head. 'Alzheimer's, don't want her wandering away unsupervised, she'll just hurt herself.'

She raps sharply on a door near the end of the corridor and opens it without waiting for a reply. I hover outside, uneasy about entering without being asked, but even from where I'm standing I can see that this is not going to be an easy experience. A hunched figure, partly obscured, sits by the window in a chair. The nurse goes over to her and taps her on the shoulder.

'Mrs Els' – her voice is loud, like she's addressing someone who is either deaf or stupid or both – 'someone to see you.' She gestures for me to enter and I step tentatively through the doorway.

The room is bright and has three beds with metal sides that lift up to prevent the sleeper from falling out. Each bed has a locker type of bedside table on one side and a chair on the other.

'You can use one of the other ladies' chairs, they're down in the lounge. Mrs Els didn't want to go, did you, Mrs Els?

'She's a bit depressed,' she says to me in an aside.

The nurse leaves us. Tannie Hettie continues to stare out of the window and for some time I hover behind her, out of her sight, unsure of what to do. Part of me, the cowardly part that couldn't look at Mother when she sank into herself, wants to turn and run from this room, pretend I've never been here. Part of me wants to reach out and stroke her flat, unbrushed hair, hair that hasn't had the twenty-rand rinse and set, and tell her how sorry I am that it has come to this. Then I remember the Tannie Hettie I knew, the gruff woman who would have hated my pity.

I drag one of the chairs over to the window as quietly as I can. For the first time she seems to notice my presence in the room and turns her head slightly so she can see me.

'Who's that? Hendrik, is that you?' Tannie Hettie's face has softened with age, her once-round cheeks hang from her face like small empty sacks.

I sit down next to her and she eyes me with suspicion.

'It's me, Tannie Hettie, Faith, remember?'

She turns away from me and looks out of the window again. For a long time we sit in a silence that is uncomfortable for me and I have no way of telling how it is for her. I look at the clock and see that almost twenty minutes have passed with neither of us saying anything. I wonder if there is any point to me being here.

'There's no birds in this garden. They said there would be birds, in the brochure, but there's no birds. Not very nice for a honeymoon. I try to put out seed,' she makes small jerking movements towards the window with her empty hand, 'but still they don't come.' Her voice is thin, reedy, almost as if she's not addressing me but is somewhere else, speaking to someone else.

'Tannie Hettie, it's me, Faith, remember?'

For a moment she says nothing, then, 'Faith's such a skinny thing, never got enough to eat, shame, poor child.' She begins to knead the crocheted blanket on her lap. Encouraged that she remembers me, I reach out and touch her hand, but she jerks away, eyeing me through watery grey eyes.

'Tannie Hettie, it's me, it's Faith, I've come to visit you.'

'Faith's not here, she's gone away.'

'I'm back now, Tannie Hettie, I've come to visit you.'

Tannie Hettie begins to make tiny rocking movements, her hands clenching the blanket, her knuckles white.

'Don't stir the pot. Leave it, I told him, she's just a girl. He's a bad man, I told you that, Bella, he's a bad man.'

'Who, Tannie Hettie? Who are you talking about?'

She rocks a little faster. Her heel begins to tap out a rhythm against the leg of the chair. It has become obvious that I am upsetting her and will achieve nothing for either of us by being here. I push my chair back.

'I'm going to go now. Bye, Tannie Hettie.' I sit for a moment longer, wondering if there's anything else I can say, something that will make it seem OK, but there's nothing that will make a difference to either of us. I stand up to leave.

'You did right by the child in the end, Bella, what you did for her. At least you gave her that.' Her voice is stronger, almost like the old Tannie Hettie. For a moment her eyes seem to focus on me.

'What do you mean?' The strangeness of her words seems to contradict her sudden lucidity. 'What do you mean, Tannie Hettie?' But she turns away and once again looks out of the window, like she's forgotten me.

The hopelessness of trying to get her to explain herself to me is plain. I stand and wait, hoping she'll say more of her own accord, but the seconds pass with nothing.

Then someone knocks gently on the door. ''Scuse me?'

I turn and see a girl, around eleven or twelve. Her appearance startles me and, for a moment, I feel like I'm looking at myself ten years ago. I realize I'm staring at her when she looks down at her shoes, embarrassed by my scrutiny.

'I'm here to see my ouma.'

'Oh, right. Well I was just leaving.' I pick up my bag from the back of the chair. I find the girl's appearance disturbing, and need to collect myself before I look at her again. Put it down to wavy blond hair and environment, I tell myself. I give her an uncertain smile and gesture for her to take the chair.

As we squeeze past each other, she looks up at me and I notice her eyes are light brown. They catch the light and seem to reflect an almost yellow glow, something which makes me feel strange in the pit of my stomach.

'Hello, Ouma,' she says as I leave the room.

'Is that you, Faith?' Tannie Hettie's reedy voice follows me and I feel a prickle of tears, a well of pity for the girl. That was me once.

Chapter Eighteen

My sleep is restless, punctuated by dreams. In one I am walking down the passage, following a voice that cries for help. The voice seems to be all around me, first coming from the left, then the right, then in front, sometimes a scream, sometimes a whisper.

There is a place inside myself that knows it's hot, the night stifling, close, yet my feet feel like ice. I look down and discover that my feet are not my own, they are small and bare, their skin plump and smooth like a child's. Flannel pyjamas rub against my ankles; I can feel the texture of them on legs that are not my own.

The passage goes on for ever.

One moment it's the passage of my childhood, walls lined with fairy paintings that seethe and undulate, the canvas bulging as faces and hands try to press out towards me. I pass Mother's room, it's dark, yet I can still see her lying on the bed, asleep, as if the night glows indigo.

Another moment the passage is damp and dark, the walls bare. I can hear the slap of my feet against the floorboards. It is so dark, I am blind.

Someone's crying. Someone's moaning.

Then I'm outside. The ground sends fresh ice into my already chilled soles; it feels hard and frozen. Nomsa's room is in front of me. The window bleeds an orange glow from the gaps in the curtain. In a second I am so close to the door I can see the paint which peels away like scabs.

My hands, small child hands, reach out and push against the door. I feel like I'm pushing through viscous sinew, and then the hands I am looking at are my own, pressed against the padlocked door of Nomsa's room as the dawn light breaks.

I WAKE UP late, exhausted, my nose plugged by the heat of the day. I lie, staring at the pattern in the pressed ceiling, not seeing it at all. It occurs to me that I have vague recollections of my dreams, that I can recount them to myself, though they make no sense. Perhaps it's the air, more oxygen than in the city, less pollution.

I drag myself up, trying to shake the disconcerted feeling that the night's vivid dreams have left me with. I remember standing in front of Nomsa's door, my hands pressed against wood. I could feel the rough edges of the peeling paint, but was I really there, or was it part of the dream?

In the kitchen I stick my head into the bucket of water that I fetched from the borehole last night. The water is cool and clears some of the sleep-heat fog away. I look to the kitchen clock, but it's still three-fifteen, the same time it was when I first saw it, in spite of the new batteries. The seconds hand jerks against the minutes hand, stuck, and I am struck by a feeling that the farm will not be budged from its past.

I wrap my dripping hair in a towel and give myself a quick once-over with a damp face-cloth. I wonder how long it will be before Petrus fixes the water. Once dressed I set out to take stock of the farm, to try to figure out a plan. After yesterday I have become increasingly conscious of how ill-prepared I am for this. I'm unsure if this is even what I want, though it seemed I had little choice when I came here; where else was I to go?

Since the orchard should be the farm's main money-spinner, I head there first. The low gate is open, its hinges rust-encrusted and immovable. I wonder why the gate and fence are necessary in the first place, so low anyone could climb over.

Then I notice the smell, the rot-odour that I noticed on my first day back. Rot masked by citrus, only this time it's stronger.

The trees have grown tall and stretched out so that their branches have meshed together in places; they look like one green mass, the pathways that once lay in neat grids between them no longer immediately obvious. Long grass and weeds cover the ground, fruit flies have infested rotting fruit. I press down on one of the decaying brown orbs with the toe of my shoe and it collapses, spewing a cloud of small black flies.

I push into the mass of trees, ducking under low branches. Nature has encroached on the orchard, claiming it back, shrubs and weeds compete for space with the trees that once had this land all to themselves. Stopping to examine the leaves of some of the trees, I notice they're yellow and I wonder if the trees are dying. Their fruit is misshapen and has ripened only on one side. But there are bound to be problems. I can't let a few sick trees get me down.

I walk further into the canopy that the trees have formed, enjoying the shady respite from the heat. It's quiet and cool, the smell of the oranges refreshing, though every now and again I catch the sweet odour of decay.

I wander around aimlessly, looking at leaves and fruit, my mind empty of thoughts. Perhaps this is what Mother felt when she escaped to the orchard, this sense of being lost to the world, protected by the trees. I watch for a while as a thick black line of ants marches up the trunk of one of the trees and disappears into the foliage, then, for old times' sake, I interrupt their line with a leaf and watch them panic and spread out, frantic to reconnect. But I've lost the remorselessness of childhood and I'm quick to drop the leaf and let them be.

Stepping back from my focus on the ants, I turn to leave and realize I don't know which way I came from. It reminds me of the last time I came in here, and I feel a tight squeeze of fear. I shake it off, I'm not a kid any more. Logic tells me that this is not a very big orchard and if I just walk in any direction I will soon get to the end. I begin to walk, nerves on edge in spite of logic. Leaves brush against me, making me jump, and I notice for the first time that webs constructed by long-legged spiders stretch diaphanous across the paths.

The smell of decay is becoming stronger, the air seems thick with it. I take shallow breaths, not wanting the sweet taste of rot in my mouth. Suddenly, I come across the source. The remains of a goat lie, partly obscured, at the foot of a tree, flesh eaten away by maggots. All that remains is the poor creature's matted fur, shrunken over bone. I stare at it, my curiosity at its presence here overcoming my need to get away from the stink. I don't remember having seen any goats on the farm and Petrus has not mentioned any, though, now that I think about it, it would be unusual for him not to have any.

I step around to the other side of the tree, to get a better view of the animal. Its leg lies at an awkward angle, trapped by the snarled roots of the tree. It must have lost its footing in the roots and broken its leg, though that seems strange for a goat.

The tree catch it, mosetsana.

The trees whisper, their leaves rustle, like there's someone moving through the branches above me.

'Who's there?' My voice slices into the hush and disappears, swallowed up by the dark foliage. 'Don't be stupid, just birds,' I whisper to myself, but I can't shake the feeling that someone's watching me.

I force myself to keep going in the same direction, holding down an urge to run that makes my muscles twitch. I'm soon free of the trees and following the fence round to the gate, relieved and victorious.

'I beat you,' I shout at the trees, not quite knowing if I mean them or the fairies. Then I feel stupid. 'I don't believe in you any more, but I still beat you,' I shout again, pleased for the first time in three days that there's no one around to see me.

BACK AT THE house I find Petrus fixing the pipes to the water tank. He nods at me from his elevated position on the roof. Being in the orchard has made me think about Mother again, and I find that I have a strong urge to find out what happened to her paintings. After several frustrating minutes of trying to explain to Petrus what I want, he tells me everything is in one of the sheds, or maybe the garage. It was before he came. When he came the house was like this, everything that is inside now was inside then. I don't know whether to believe him or not. It seems unlikely that his family, after so many years of being here, would not make use of some of the things from the house. Then I remember the women's reaction to the place; superstitious lot, perhaps he's telling the truth.

Armed with Petrus's bunch of keys, I find paintings stacked against the wall at the back of one of the sheds, behind some cardboard boxes. The boxes smell of mould and some of the corners have been chewed, possibly by mice. Propped up against the wall, on a makeshift shelf, is a rectangular piece of glass, covered with blobs of paint that have dried to a plastic skin. I run my fingers over Mother's old palette, revealing bright colours underneath the dust. Memories begin to flood back.

Papa knocking up a wooden plank for a shelf; I passed him the nails.

Sitting on a chair, trying not to fidget, while Mother sketched me, eyes narrowed in concentration, measuring off my features on her pencil. She would fling the double doors open to let in the light; she was always complaining that there wasn't enough light in the shed, wanting Papa to make the window bigger. But all he ever made was the shelf.

I remember Boesman lying in front of my chair, my feet resting on him, absorbing the heat of his body, toes wriggling restlessly. Sitting still for long periods made me feel cold, no matter what the weather.

A watermark stains the back wall against which the paintings rest, indicating a leak in the roof. It still feels damp and I realize water must trickle down every time it rains. I pull the paintings away from the wall, one by one, and place them around the shed.

Mould blooms cover Sillstream's face and part of the background like fibrous fur. I scrape what I can away with a piece of cardboard, but she is left blackened and cracked, her smooth silvery skin for ever marred.

Tit Tit Tay's support has warped, twisting the canvas so that it's stretched too tight in places, flaccid in others. She looks caught in the throes of a painful convulsion.

Each painting I place against the wall is damaged in some way, mostly by the water, but some have been chewed by mice as well. They are split, warped, the paint cracking, mouldering, with a fungus that is spreading across them like a cancer, and yet I find them as fascinating as they are disturbing and I cannot stop looking at them.

Dead Rex, though, is missing, and I feel a mixture of disappointment and relief at his absence. I do find some drawings of him in a portfolio among other sketches, mostly of me. I lay the sketches out on the floor. They have escaped the water damage for the most part, but the paper has discoloured. I stand in the middle of the shed, sketches of myself fanning out around me, almost covering the entire floor. Some of the drawings of me are in similar poses to some of the paintings of the fairies.

I look from one painting to the next and see, for the first time, that each fairy, though their hair, skin and eye colour and expression are different, has the same face. The child-girl face that looks at me across time from the sketches I posed for also looks out at me from within the frames of the fairy paintings. Their poses mimic quick studies of me at play, running, jumping climbing, swimming in the reservoir. It makes me realize just how isolated Mother was, how lonely she must have felt.

'She really knew how to paint, your ma.'

I swing round and see a man standing at the door. The glare of the light behind him cuts out his shape, highlighting the edges, and makes it difficult to see his face. 'I heard you'd come back, didn't think you would. But there we are, you just can't tell what's going to happen until it does.'

I squint, trying to make out the visitor. The tone he takes with me is one of familiarity, but instead of putting me at ease, it knots my stomach and makes the hair at the nape of my neck prickle. 'Is there something I can help you with?' I ask, my voice edged with tension.

'You don't remember me,' he says, stepping into the shed. 'It's me, Piet, your oom, remember.'

Chapter Nineteen

THE YEARS HAVE not been kind to Oom Piet. His belly hangs over his belt, flaccid and deflated, his nose and cheeks are red, the kind of red you get from too much drinking, too much meat, and mapped out with small purple veins. What's left of his greasy hair is brushed over to one side in an attempt to cover his sunburnt scalp.

We size each other up. His eyes travel over my body in an easy, familiar way that makes me squirm and turns my stomach. His examination of me is so intense that I can almost feel his meaty fingers probing, squeezing my flesh. The tip of his tongue pokes out from under his moustache, moistening his lips and galvanizing me into action. I fold my arms across my chest, protecting my breasts from further scrutiny.

'What do you want?' I ask, forcing his eyes up to my face. He retracts his tongue and smiles.

'You're not very friendly. Then again, you were never the friendliest when you were a little girl. Some things never change, huh?' His voice is jovial, Father Christmas, but there is an edginess there, a tension that heightens his tone like a violin string tightened to snap. He is as unsettled in my presence as I am in his. I can see it in his eyes though he smiles wide.

His close proximity makes me feel slightly nauseous, the way a bad smell would, but my reaction to him is out of proportion with my reasons for disliking him. It's been a long time, this is a small community and people are more neighbourly here. I should try be more civil. I force my mouth into a smile, but it feels like I'm just baring my teeth at him, like a dog.

'I apologize, I'm just surprised to see you, that's all. How have you been?' It's a stupid question, considering the amount of time that has passed, but it's the only thing I can think of with all my nerve endings on red alert.

'Ja, no. Well. Can't complain.' Oom Piet moves further into the shed, close to me, and I'm acutely aware of how much of the space he takes up. He points at one of the paintings. 'That's a bit of mess.' He walks over to it and runs his hand over the mould, stepping on a sketch of me as he does so. I watch his boot crush my face and suddenly the cold hand of fear closes over my throat and I can't breathe properly. I need to get out of the shed.

I step towards the door, but as soon as I move he stands up and blocks my path. He narrows his eyes. 'You OK?'

I nod, try to take deep, inconspicuous breaths through my nose into my hot tight lungs. I ball my hands into fists so they don't shake.

'Sure? You don't look so good, is something wrong?'

'It's just the paintings, they upset me.' My voice is strangled.

He nods, looking down his nose at me. I feel a surge of panic, he doesn't believe me, he can see I'm scared.

But I have no reason to fear him. You're being silly, Faith.

'I'm not going to hurt you. Do you think I want to do something to you?'

I shake my head and push the panic down, try to smile. 'The paintings, I'm just creeped out by them, that's all. Would you like a drink?' I indicate the door. The urge to duck and run is making my feet vibrate. I half expect his butcher's hands to close around my neck and shake me like a chicken. Oom Piet doesn't even blink as I flinch past him, and within a second I'm out of the claustrophobic confines of the shed into the bright day.

I gulp the humid air, try to expand my fear-squeezed lungs, calm my pounding heart, and notice Petrus, leaning against the wall of the house smoking a roll-up, his gaze focused on the shed. I raise my hand and he nods and looks away. Behind me the shed door closes. Oom Piet gives me an uncertain smile, and I stretch my mouth, closed-lipped, into something that can pass for friendliness. As we start towards the house, Petrus flicks his butt to the ground and crushes it under his foot.

'So, you're back. What brought you?' Oom Piet stirs the third heaped teaspoon of sugar into his coffee.

I shrug, not wanting to reveal that I had no where else to go. 'No particular reason; my mother left me the farm, so here I am.'

Oom Piet looks up sharply. 'Your ma's dead?' I nod, wondering if the news upsets him; he doesn't look bothered.

'I'm sorry,' he says, not looking particularly sorry, 'it must have been hard for you.'

'We weren't close.' My tone is abrupt. I don't want to talk about Mother, but Oom Piet is thick-skinned and doesn't take the hint.

'So were you with her at the end?'

I glare at him, what kind of a question is that? 'No.'

He takes a sip of his coffee and stares into space for a moment, like he's considering something.

'Your ma, did she ever say anything about me?'

I snort and hot coffee goes up my nose. 'Believe it or not, she never mentioned you.' I feel a surge of anger at his arrogance, after everything he still thinks of himself as some sort of Valentino. 'Why would she?' I can't keep the sarcasm out of my voice.

Oom Piet clutches his cup so tight his knuckles go white and for a moment I think he's going to crush it. Slowly, he lowers the cup to the table and stands up, walks to the door and looks out. Tension hunches his shoulders, his hands are clenched into fists. I take a deep, slow breath and wonder what he's thinking, if he wants to hit me. I remind myself that I'm being silly, but my nerve endings buzz, unwilling to calm down.

'So how long you back here for?' The question makes me jump and I'm glad his back is towards me.

'I don't know. How did you know I was back anyhow?'

Oom Piet turns and looks at me, then comes back to the table, perhaps encouraged by the friendly tone I tried to force.

'Liesel told me you came by to see her.' His answer

surprises me, but I try not to show it. I can feel his eyes on me, waiting, for what exactly I'm not sure, then he goes on: 'Said you were asking about your pa.'

I look up sharply, wondering if this is perhaps the reason for his visit. He was a friend of Papa's, maybe he's come on his behalf. He's cagey though; perhaps Papa doesn't want me to find him, or wants to know what my reaction will be if I do. Maybe that's why he's asking about Mother.

I shrug. 'Just curious, I guess.' My voice shakes and I need a second to try and steady it. 'You still see him?'

Oom Piet snorts. 'Me? What would I want with him?'

A bitter hate that has been buried for fifteen years swells up inside me. After everything it seems to be more a case of what would Papa want with him. I feel a sudden sense of loyalty to a father I haven't laid eyes on in more than a decade.

'No, I don't suppose it's easy to keep friends while chasing after their wives.' It's out before I have time to think about the can I'm opening.

Oom Piet shakes his head and whistles in disbelief before his eyes narrow and he leans towards me. A thin mean smile twists his lips.

'Listen, girlie, I haven't seen your old man since, you know, what happened. No one has. Hettie was the last person to see him round here. Went to tell him about – you know, the thing, and after that he just upped and left. It had nothing to do with me. He knew I was fooling around with your ma. I told him, us being friends and that, and truth be told, he didn't seem overly bothered.'

Oom Piet's words sink into my brain like a slow-motion lead bullet. 'So he knew.'

'Knew what? About your ousie getting killed?' I nod, unable to speak. 'Ja, he knew. Hettie told him. Your ma, she didn't want him to know about it. Tried to make her swear not to tell him, both of us, but Hettie couldn't hold back. Truth be told, she blamed him for, you know, what happened.' He sips his coffee, wipes his hand over his moustache.

'Why?'

'Why what? Why didn't she want him to know?' He shrugs, but his eyes shift and I can see there's something he's not saying.

'Tell me,' he says after a significant pause, 'how much do you remember, about that night, about when your ousie died?'

I look at him, stunned. 'Not much, just remember you and my mother went out, then – ' her name catches in my throat – 'then Nomsa, Nomsa put me to bed and when I woke up . . .' I trail off.

Oom Piet is watching me with an interest I find disconcerting, like he's trying to see into me, to see something that he knows is there but I can't fathom.

'When you woke up, what? What do you remember seeing?'

'Nothing. I woke up and she was dead.' I want this conversation to end, I don't want to remember that morning, it's too painful to go over now, not here, not with this man.

'You didn't hear something, wake up in the night?'

I shake my head. Tears spill down my cheeks. I don't want him to witness the fresh pain that has risen up and cut me like all of this was yesterday. I get up and look out of the window at the orchard grown wild, try to focus on the trees instead of the pressure of the emotion expanding inside me. Then, like a pin inserted through tape into a balloon to let air out slowly, it dawns on me that this line of questioning is weird. No normal person would bring this up. No one, not even those closest to me, would dare dig into that night. The tears dry on my cheeks, I turn and look at Oom Piet like I'm seeing him for the first time and I see fear. Fear in the way he cannot meet my eyes, fear in the way he jollies himself up like he's a safari-suited Santa, carefully masked, well disguised, but there.

'What do you think I heard, Oom Piet?'

He shrugs, looking into his opaque brown coffee like it has depths he can hide in.

'You know something.' I look at him in disbelief, I can see he knows something. 'Were you there?'

His head jerks up and he looks at me, eyes narrow. 'No. What gives you that idea? Of course I wasn't there.' Small beads of perspiration appear on his brow.

'You do know something, I can see it.' Even as the words come out of my mouth I know I'm being reckless.

Oom Piet stands up and leans on the table so he's almost looming over me. 'I wouldn't go around saying things like that. I wasn't there, I don't know fokol, you understand? Nothing.'

My heart is in my mouth, blood rushes in my ears. I nod and he sits down.

'Look,' he says after a short-lived silence, 'it's getting on, I must get back to the shop. I can't leave my boys alone too long, they'll do nothing all day if I don't watch them.'

He stands up and I'm relieved to see him out. Once he's

gone, I pour what's left of his coffee down the drain; my hands shake.

HIS VISIT LEAVES me disconcerted and I wander around the house, unable to settle in any room, without the focus I need to tackle the many jobs I have set myself to fix the house up. Around five in the afternoon, Petrus comes in to tell me the gas is hooked up and the water will be fixed by tomorrow. Only when it begins to get dark do I remember I wanted him to help me get the generator up and running.

I light a candle and resign myself to another dark night.

The darkness does nothing to ease my restlessness. In the dim flickering candlelight I can do nothing but think. I run over everything I can remember about Nomsa's death with the reserve of someone testing the sharpness of a blade. I go over it, slowly at first, testing each memory for its ability to drive a sharp pain into me, then more quickly as I reach the numbness brought about by repetition, until I feel nothing as I conjure up the fragmented memories, image by broken image.

My mind turns constantly to Oom Piet, to his questions. I go over every word, mumbling them into the darkness, trying to extract that vital something that I know I'm missing, that piece of this puzzle that will somehow make everything fit, but it is elusive and I'm left frustrated and raw, like a crushed nerve, cut off from the intensity of the pain that pulses from its pulpy centre yet acutely aware of it.

I am certain that he was there that night. Logic dictates he must have been, otherwise how did Mother get home? I think of her torn clothing; he must have been the one to tear it.

'He's a bad man, I told you that, Bella, he's a bad man.'

Tannie Hettie's words echo round the room. A few days ago they seemed to be nothing more than the muddled rambling of an old lady, though now I'm left to wonder who she meant. I want to go and see her again, ask her about him, but even as I think it, I realize it's futile; all I can achieve by visiting her again is to upset her further.

Questions, questions, questions. I fall into a fitful sleep on the couch with the questions going round and round and round.

I FOLLOW THE voice down the passage on small cold child-feet. My feet. I am seven and I am not dreaming and knowing this makes me proper-awake not half-mucky-eye-awake. Somebody screams fear-screams muffled-by-the-wall screams inside my heart cutting-screams. Faster my feet slip-slap against the floorboards and my blood rushes and my temples pound and my heart beats so fast it makes me dizzy with the fear-panic-sick. Because I know. I know the feet are mine and I know I'm seven and I know it's night and I know that the screams and the moans and the pleading is Nomsa and I know that I must help her. I must save her.

And I am outside pushing the peeling-paint door and it opens and I can smell paraffin and sweat and something else something thick and blood-sweet that turns my stomach and makes the fear-panic-sick rise up bitter in my throat.

And I am inside and I can see by the orange glow that

flicks and dances making light making shadow that there's a hump on the bed covered over with a blue mattress blanket and the candle-flicking-orange-light changes the colour into a funny deep purple and when I look again I see the funny-deep-purple is a spreading seeping dark stain. And I know that blanket. And I know that stain.

I reach out, take the edge of the blanket, pull it slowly away. It feels slippery-toad-slimy, slides out of my grasping fingers on to the floor and wriggles under the bed, disappearing into the shadows.

And I see her, I see the light dancing over Nomsa, body-broken, bent forward over the bed. Shadows lick legs hanging over the side, schoolgirl innocent, pigeon-toed feet only just touching the ground. Her pushed-up skirt sits bunched around her waist like a tyre. The light shadow plays over twisted arms, elbows on backwards, dances over open-wide eyes, all white. Licks her head. Part gone. Gore spread like finger-flicked spatter-paint on the wall behind her.

'Nomsa,' I whisper, 'wake up.'

Her eyelids close and open, slow and sedated, and then fear-wide they're alive and bright with terror her mouth twitches opens screams.

'No, baas, no.'

I WAKE UP, heart pounding, sick with the dream. I stare into the dark, eyes wide, unable to still the panicked gasping breaths that aren't deep enough to calm me and they come, like a movie projected on to the thick wall of night, like lost bits of puzzle. Oom Piet's eyes-bulging face. One delicate arm, twisted, broken. His trousers round his ankles. Her skirt. They begin to mesh, become scenes which are cut, sliced, edited together until I am seven and watching Oom Piet do a bad thing to Nomsa through an open slice in the peeling-paint door.

Chapter Twenty

THE MEN FROM Telkom come and they look at me with my tear-swollen eyes and rubbed-raw face and wonder what bad thing has happened to make me look like this. But they don't ask and they avert their eyes; it's not polite to stare. They install my phone in the hope that I will call someone who will come to my assistance. That is what they tell themselves will happen as they drive off, pushing down the guilt because they don't feel human enough to pry, to ask the simple question, Are you OK?, and they feel better because they have done all they can for me. They feel relief, I will not call them.

'Do you think something happened to her?' one asks when they reach a distance far enough away so it will seem irrational to turn around.

'It's none of our business really,' the other shrugs.

They say these things as I wait for my line to become active. 'Your phone will be connected in the next thirty-six hours, ma'am, sign here.' My rage grows.

The time comes when I pick it up and hear the dial tone, and I dial 1023, wait in the automated queue for my turn and when the woman's voice asks, 'What number?' I ask for all the names and addresses of all the butcheries in Potgietersrus. There are five listed.

J & S Butchery
TAN Butchery
Potgietersrus Koelkamers
Hypermeat Products
Rembrandt Butchery

I dial each one and ask to speak to Piet. At the first three there is no one called Piet and I scratch them from my list. At the fourth a man comes to the phone, but his voice is unfamiliar. I ask him the price of steak and he tells me it's R45.99 a kilo, but I could've asked anyone, why did I want to speak to him? I hang up.

At the fifth, a woman answers and when I ask to speak to Piet, there is silence. 'Who is this?' she asks, her voice edged with suspicion.

'A customer,' I reply after a long pause. In the background I can hear her calling him, and I can hear the bone saw grind to a halt, and I can hear footsteps coming towards the phone.

'Ja, this is Piet, what can I do for you?'

I hang up.

I PARK THE van across the road from Rembrandt Butchery and watch as people go in and come out with blue and white striped packets. It's late morning and the shop is busy; the customers, mostly women, come in a steady stream that seems never-ending.

I sit in the van until after lunch, windows open wide for air, waiting for a lull in business, then I get out of the van and cross the road, entering the shop when there's no one else there.

Oom Piet looks up as I come through the door, opens his mouth as if to say something, maybe hello, but nothing comes out. It just stays open like dead fish lips stuck for ever in a futile gasp for oxygen. Maybe it's the look on my face but, without me needing to say anything, he knows.

I walk around the shop, dragging my fingers over the sides of the open refrigerated units, over plump packages of meat that are cool to touch, neatly arranged in rows, fillet steak, stewing beef, chump chops, boerewors. I come to the end of the unit and stop, then I turn to him and smile. His fat face breaks into a grin that is hopeful, full of relief.

I step up to the counter, to the part where he's been chopping up steak and wrapping it in waxy white paper, lean over, so close to his cheek I can smell the Brylcreem in his hair, and I whisper, 'I remember.'

The smile drops from his lips as fast as the colour drains from his cheeks leaving him grey against his blood-smeared butcher's whites.

Behind me I hear the tinkle of the bell over the door and I glance back and see a woman enter the shop. She walks up to the glassed-off counter where meat marinates in steel dishes, greets Oom Piet, oblivious, all smiles and small-talk. A nod is all he can manage in return as he goes over to help her, cutting a sideways glance at me that is supposed to shut me up.

I amble over to where she is pointing out her choice of cut in lurid yellow marinade, right up, next to her, and I say, 'I remember what you did.' My voice bounces off the white-tiled walls. In the back someone starts up the bone saw. The woman looks at me, frowns, my proximity disturbs her, I can see it in her eyes, most people don't like to smell the ketones on a stranger's breath, she's no different. She shuffles away from me a little, turns to Oom Piet. 'Everything OK?'

His head, skin the colour of used soap suds, bobs up and down behind the glassed-off counter. 'Ja, just excuse me for a minute.' His voice is hoarse, breathless; he clutches the counter for a moment, knuckles white against the purple abuse of his hand, before disappearing into the back. It crosses my mind that I may be giving him a heart attack, but I don't care.

The woman's curiosity gets the better of her and she glances at me. I catch her eye and twist my mouth into a vicious smile that's all teeth. She makes a quick escape to the refrigerated units where she picks up a pack of meat and pretends to read the label.

Oom Piet returns with a black man who has bits of gore sticking to his white overall. 'Help this lady, eh, Joseph, then close the shop.' He lifts a hinged panel on the counter and beckons me with a sharp tilt of his head. I follow him through the thick strips of clear plastic that act as a barrier, separating the air-conditioned shopfront from the back, and immediately feel the temperature rise a few degrees. The air in here is dense and fleshy and suggests meat on the verge of turning. Large double doors open on to a yard, presumably to circulate air, but let in only corpulent flies that buzz black over slicks of congealed blood as we walk over the floor, disturbing their feasts. A bloodless sheep's carcass hangs from a hook on the ceiling and I notice it's relatively free of flies; perhaps they are too fat to lift themselves that high on their brittle wings.

A stainless-steel counter dominates the room where a black man divides a carcass, pushing large joints of meat on to a zigzag-toothed blade that moves rapidly up and down, sending tiny bits of gore flying to the floor. It sounds like an angle grinder as it connects with bone, then eases into a wet vibration as it tears easily into flesh. Another man stretches clingfilm that reflects light like flies' wings over thick chops nestling in polystyrene.

'Take a break,' Oom Piet shouts over the din of the saw, 'bugger off down the road and go smoke cigarettes.' The men give me approving full-white-teeth smiles as they leave that give me the impression I'm not the first woman to be invited to the back. The thought makes me feel sick.

Oom Piet leans against the counter, sliding a hunk of meat to the side. Newly separated joints ooze blood that runs in slow rivulets down the steel surface and drips on to the floor, pooling round Oom Piet's white rubber boots. I watch as a red drop hangs off the end of the counter, growing bulbous and heavy before it lets go and bursts on the smooth concrete floor.

'What do you want?'

I look at Oom Piet's grey face, full of hatred and revulsion. The answer is simple, I want revenge. I want everyone to know what I know. I want to ruin his life, make every day that remains to him a misery. I want every person he cares about to know what sort of a man he is, and I want them to hate him. Hate him as I hate him. I want him to suffer.

'I remember,' I say, my voice calm with power. I know and there is nothing he can do about it, nothing he can do to stop me from telling everyone what he did. For days I have thought about this moment, considered all the years he must have waited for me to come back, for me to remember, and now here I am, watching him, waiting for him to break, to crumble in front of me, like a dog with a snapped spine, like a life in ruins.

He folds his arms against his chest. 'Ja, you remember, you said. Now what the fuck do you want?'

His voice rises to a shout and he slams his fist down on to the counter. The corners of his mouth are white with spit, rabid. I laugh, hollow and without humour, and glance over my shoulder towards the clear plastic barrier, my meaning obvious.

'Your customers can hear you,' I mock.

Oom Piet flares his nostrils, his irises dark circles surrounded by white. He steps towards me, clenches a fist, but there is a tremor in that balled hand that he can't hide. I smile, vicious, twisted and full of revenge. I watch him squirm for several minutes, listening to Joseph and the customer lady exchange banter; even the flies stop buzzing. Then the bell tinkles and the customer is gone. Oom Piet exhales loud and slow. Joseph comes in through the plastic barrier and sees us. He stops, unsure of what to do.

'Clear off, Joseph,' Oom Piet growls.

Joseph backs away through the barrier, but before he disappears I repeat myself, loud enough for him to hear.

'I remember what you did to Nomsa.'

Oom Piet waits until he hears the bell over the door, then he says, 'I heard you the first time, now what the fuck do you want?'

'What do you think?' In a strange way, I'm enjoying this.

'You bring a gun?' he asks, watching me like I'm a Rottweiler ready for attack. His eyes flick to the knives hanging on the wall behind him, butcher's knives, ground down to dull, paper-thin edges. I follow his gaze, then notice the double-sided meat-hook above his head. I hold up my hands. It would be stupid to make him think I've got a weapon; he's jumpy enough as it is without thinking I want to harm him physically.

'No gun,' I say. Oom Piet seems to relax a little, but the tension that leaves him crawls up my back, stiffening my muscles. Was I stupid to come here alone? What if he killed Nomsa as well as raping her?

'Then what do you want?' He reaches out and takes one of the knives off the wall and begins to clean his nails with the pointed tip.

'I want you to pay for what you did.' It comes out a whisper, the voice of a terrified little girl.

Oom Piet stares at me for a moment, then starts to laugh.

'You want me to pay. Pay how? You want money?' I shake my head, tears prick my sinuses. 'What then? You want the police should come and take me away, lock me up, like that mother of yours?' I glance over at the door, ready to bolt, but in one quick movement that seems impossible for a man of his size and health, he's across the room and grabs my shoulder with vice-like hands. The knife he's holding clatters to the floor, where it spins a few times before settling, the sharp tip pointing towards us. 'Let me tell you something, girlie, there's no evidence any more. What evidence there was against me is long buried.' He lets go of my shoulders, pushing me into the counter. The edge cracks into my spine, sending a horizontal band of pain up my back. 'Your mother took care of that.'

Tears blur my vision, obscuring the wide pores that pock his nose and cheeks, but I can still smell the stink of his breath, feel it against my skin. I shake my head, turn away from him, but the significance of his words can't be erased. The buzzing of the flies increases, becomes so loud it almost blots out the sound of my voice.

'My mother protected you,' I rasp. 'Why? Why would she protect you?'

Oom Piet snorts and lets go of me; I gasp for air, trying to clear the fog that's descending rapidly.

'She didn't protect me, girlie, she protected you.'

He is saying other things, things that reach into the core of me and rip me apart, things I don't want to believe but I can feel, in the soul of me, are true. His voice stretches, elastic, far away, like I'm underwater. I reach for the counter, my hands slip in the pools of coagulating blood, unbalancing me, I slam down on to the floor, jolting my knees so hard I bite my tongue. The pain is sudden and intense and has the effect of clearing the fog, making me fully alert, if only to the pain. I taste the copper salt of my blood, it makes me feel sick. I put my hands down on to the floor to steady myself, stop the world from spinning around me. Fear keeps me from giving in to the darkness, I'm afraid if I pass into it I will not be allowed back. Slowly, the nausea subsides, the world settles and the darkness clears.

I look up at Oom Piet, towering over me, his face twisted into a victorious sneer. He shakes his head and walks out, leaving me alone with the flies. I sit for a long time, unable to move, then I peel my hands away from the sticky floor and turn them over and I look at the blood that stains my palms red and I wonder why I never saw it before.

Chapter Twenty-One

MY HANDS TREMBLE as I push the key into the padlock that seals Nomsa's room. My fingers are tacky with blood, and I leave a red smear on the lock, then the imprint of my hand on the paint-scabbed door. It swings wide and I step inside. The interior is shadowy and dim; the sudden contrast from the outer brightness robs me of my sight. While my eyes adjust I breathe deep the cold smell of crumbling concrete, brittle fabric, disturbed dust. I'm half expecting to find her concealed under the mattress blanket, for her long-dead eyes to hold the accusation of murder.

But the room has been stripped bare of everything that was her. All that remains is the bed, raised on paint tins and bricks in an unsuccessful attempt to keep the Tokoloshe away. And, on the bed, propped up against the wall, is the missing painting of Dead Rex.

The scream builds up from a place that is deeper than my gut, making my innards feel like they will explode with the pressure of it. Inside me it grows, expanding outwards until I feel so tight I'm sure I will burst. There is a pop, pain slices through me like I'm being cut with a butcher's knife, and I open my mouth to let it out, but nothing comes, only the dry rasp of expelled air.

DAYS BLEND, ONE into another, broken only by indigo nights which stretch eternally. I can no longer tell the difference between sleep and waking. I see them all the time, swirling around me in the dark, a thick and soupy vortex, pressing against my feverish retina in the light, the silvery eyes flash like darting fish, their magenta voices whispering, 'Killer.'

Sometimes it's only me and him; the others can't bear his company. He sucks me down, into him, where I clamour fearfully in his belly with disjointed creatures I try not to believe exist, things that have one arm or empty eye sockets or are nothing more than a head. But there is not enough space for me, I am still too whole, and the others push me out, forcing me up the tight passage and through the sharp teeth until I spill out, slick and gasping, back into the here.

There is someone that is not them that knocks on the door every day, or perhaps it is the same day, over and over. She comes to me and hovers over the bed, she is both familiar and strange, I know her name but can no longer remember it. She pulls me up and tries to force soup into my mouth with a spoon that is metallic and tastes of blood. I retch and the soup dribbles out, its nourishment of no use to me.

My body shrinks, sweats, wastes away. It's no longer the house for my soul but is my soul, a shrunken husk devoid of life.

The woman comes again but this time it's different (perhaps

the day has changed), there is someone with her, a presence that hovers by the door. She presses her hand against my brow and I reach up to hold it there, cool against my hot skin, but my synapses misfire and my arm remains firmly pressed against my side, only the ghosts of my limbs move, ineffectual. Her palm lifts away and takes the coolness with it.

'She is very sick, we should get someone.'

'Êê. A doctor.'

'No. A doctor cannot help this one. She is already in the spirit world, she hears only the voices of her ancestors. She cannot eat anything. I try to give her soup, but she spits it out like poison. I think she will die soon.'

'We cannot let her die.'

'She is not our responsibility, what can we do?'

'If she dies they will blame us.'

'What do you suggest then? You have called Mr Hurwitz?'

'Êê, they say he is on holiday and will be gone some time. They say this is not their case, it is a charity case of his, there is nothing they can do. They say we should call her family.'

They fall silent. The fairies swirl around, playing discordant music on the taut cords of tension that web between the two visitors. It makes me restless, my feet twitch and jerk like a puppet dancer. The visitors retreat, leaving me alone with my tormentors, who use the web of their tension as a net to catch me up.

Day comes and soft powder wings flutter against my face, taunting, teasing, mocking. Like moths, their wings leave behind a dust that tickles, then itches, then becomes unbearable.

'Killer,' they whisper in my ear with soulless breath.

'Killer,' they shriek like night birds, clawing me, trying to rip me into small pieces to be devoured and regurgitated into something that is like them. The nothingness that is them.

I fight against them, keeping the swelling thing that pushes my organs to bursting inside. They clamour for it, ripping at me, trying to get it out. But it is all of me, all I know, and to release it would mean I no longer am.

COOL DAWN LICKS my brow. There is a new presence in the room, someone who has not been here before. The woman I know but cannot name has brought him. He is old and gnarled and brown and stooped and looks like a tree spirit but doesn't feel like one of them.

He moves around the room, hunched over, sprinkling powder that glows faintly as it hits the ground, then fades to nothing. His dry, papery skin brushes against me as he moves over me, pressing his hands over my swollen belly, probing me with knuckle-knotted fingers. His breath, sweet with age, hangs in the air, mingling with the smoky scent of the incense he's lit and placed around the room.

They don't like him, I can feel it. They swarm around me, hissing, but part like the Red Sea to let him through, taking care not to touch him. Their anger beats the air like a drum. The thing that swells my belly responds, pulsing inside me, beating against my skin.

'How long has she been like this?' the old one asks, his voice tremulous.

'One week, maybe more. We don't know how long she was sick before we found her, maybe two or three days.'

'There is a thing inside her, a thing that has been there for many years, maybe since she was a small girl. It grows. She will not let it go; for some reason she wants to hold it inside her, even though it will destroy her. If we are to help her, we need to get it out.'

They press against my face. 'He lies,' they hiss in hot yellow squirts that splash against me and burn my skin like uric acid. 'Lies, lies, lies,' they chant.

The old one moves slowly around them, protecting himself with a switch which he flicks from side to side. They flinch and hiss.

'You must leave, my daughter,' he says to the woman, 'there are things here that I cannot protect you from. You must leave me with her for three nights and three days. Bring food and water and leave it at the door.'

The old one spreads out a mat on the floor next to me and lays out his things, bones, powders, strange viscous liquids. I watch him out of the corner of my eyes that ache with the fevered effort. He prays and chants and mutters to himself and they laugh at him. Their laughter is soulless and mean and fills me up.

The first night is black.

The old one pulls back the sheet and lifts my shirt and spreads a cold black tar over my stomach. It sinks into me, coating the swelling thing, containing it. I cry and kick against him, but I am too weak and can do nothing to stop his magic destroying me. The blackness spreads throughout my body, down into my limbs, numbing them, up into my heart until it no longer beats, over my lungs so I no longer breathe, into my eyes and my mind and I am sucked into a void in which nothing exists.

The second night is red.

Feeling begins to seep back into my fingers. My dead mind yawns and stretches and looks out. The light against my eyelids is red, like looking into the sun. My skin is tight and sensitive, roasted red. I twist, my body jerks, the spasms begin and, like a pupating worm, I begin to change. My outer shell hardens, cracks, falls away and I am left, small and pink and raw, squirming on the bed like a new baby grub. The old one digs his hands into my soft fleshy abdomen where the swelling thing lies, hard and dead now, and draws it out. I reach for it, wanting it back, but they swarm in and snatch it from him, fighting for it like crows fight over stolen meat.

The third day is white.

I open my eyes. They're gone, for the first time I can remember they are not there and I'm alone. I'm an empty shell, hollow and vacant, yet somehow I feel free. I am no longer a creature of their design, no longer their puppet. I am nothing now, a blank canvas, and the only one who can scar my surface with paint is me.

I look up at the old man, who hovers over me like a concerned parent. His face is mapped with wrinkles, his eyes shine out from between folds of skin. I feel we have spent an eternity together in this room and I know he has seen the things that I have seen. We have a shared past, yet I have never seen him properly before, never looked at his face and seen the features that distinguish him from every other creature that walks this earth.

I open my mouth to speak, but my tongue is swollen, my lips cracked and dry; I can't form words, but he seems to understand. He reaches out with his gnarled hand and pats me on the forehead.

I watch him gather his things, roll up his mat, pack away

the three bottles of medicine he has fed me from over the past nights, black, then red, then white, and he leaves me, completely alone, for the first time ever.

His loss is final and reminds me of all I have lost in my brief life. The tears flow easily, for Papa and Mother and Nomsa, for Ouma and Grandma English and Tannie Hettie, for Boesman, for Molly, for the fairies, and finally for my small self that died with Nomsa. My grief pours from me, making the first marks on my fresh soul, and outside it begins to rain.

Chapter Twenty-Two

I SIT ON THE stoep, watching the heat of the day pass into evening. Even though it's hot, Maswabing insists on covering my legs with a blanket, making me feel like an old woman. Her manner is still abrupt, but she doesn't hate me any more. She fusses over me like a hen, making sure I eat, insisting I clear my plate of every bit of food. I think she sees me as a kindred soul, feels united with me in suffering. I don't want to tell her that I no longer feel punished, that I am whole and healed and more than I have ever been, in spite of my wasted body.

I have started to put the weight I lost over my period of illness back on, though my legs still look like knobkerries and my elbows poke out. I can even go for short walks now. My energy is returning rapidly; soon I will be back to my old self, physically anyway.

I close my eyes and listen to the voice inside me, my voice. It tells me that now is the perfect time, I should wait no longer. I stand up slowly, stretching my muscles; my joints crack and pop, it feels good to be alive.

I dial the number and listen to it ring. Even though I have been building up to this moment, my heart still pounds in my throat. Perhaps it is too much to expect, after all these weeks of nothing. I come close to hanging up.

'Hello?' her voice barks down the phone line, sharp and annoyed, and I wonder what I have interrupted. I have to swallow hard to control my emotions.

'Mia, it's me,' is all I can manage in the end.

'Faith, oh my God, where are you? We've been so worried. Mol, quick, it's Faith.' I hear scrambling in the background, the click of another receiver being lifted, then they both begin to talk at once, excited and emotional and tearful. I wonder what ever possessed me to doubt them, to flee the safety of their friendship. Of my family.

The Baby Snatcher

He watch them come, those who love mosetsana, and he watch as they unite, a power circle of three. His nose wrinkle in disgust, he gag and choke. He like not love, it starve him and he be too thin and hungry now to be doing with love. But soon, he knows, they will burn his image, set fire to the mad woman painting that has trapped him in this place too long, he will be free. For now, there is nourishment in what the others have snatched from mosetsana. Good eating, and he know where to find it.

Twist and slip through the wire fence. He smell the stink of goat-dead and it please him. The sad one give him appeasement, the sad one know how to protect her own.

He find her easy-peasy, her lullaby give her away. He shape himself round gnarled tree knot and watch, patient. He wait fifteen long year, what be his hurry now?

Tit Tit Tay clutch the swollen-hard-black she stole from mosetsana to her monkey breast, croon and sing like it be child. She look around, look straight at him, but she see no Dead Rex, so well he conceal himself. If she look careful, maybe she notice the leaf that wither and drop like autumn come to soon, but she be too wrapped up with swollen-hard-black, she don't care for nothing else. Careful, like she hold a delicate porcelain baby, she nestle hard-swollen-black between tree roots, cover it with leaves for warm, for disguise. Then she off into the night, thinking her baby be safe under that gnarled-knot tree.

Dead Rex reach down with bony-fingered hand, extend easily all the way to the root, and lift up hard-swollen-black. He hold it to his nose. Sniff. Sniff. The shell of sangoma muti contains it well, no smell escape.

He drop down and open wide, wider than eating a man, and place hard-swollen-black between his teeth. He bite. The shell crack and like juicy bird egg the nourishment leak out. He lick it, like it be sweet flower nectar. Iguana tongue slither in, slither out. Iguana tongue tease out memories long-time buried, taste them. Taste the cold on mosetsana's small feet. Taste the burnt sulphur of gunpowder on her hand. Taste the fear in her heart and the scream of her soul when she realize it be not easy to shoot straight.

Guns have life all their own, Dead Rex could tell mosetsana that, but then Dead Rex need to eat.

Hard-swollen-black be almost empty now. He savour each drop, stop the last hate juice from the crack out flowing with his finger bones. It be long time since he ate such things, long time since this place began to change and the fear-hate eased and hope came.

It be not so easy now to find fear-hate to eat. Things be different, hope replace bitterness, hope replace fear. But there will be them that hate, and Dead Rex will look hard to find them. When he do, he will swallow them down, and he will be fat with them once more. And when he fat, his belly will bloat and he will regurgitate hate into the world and it will grow and feeding will be plentiful again.

Mosetsana's fear-hate be finished now. Dead Rex drop the hard shell to the ground, crush it under splayed foot into tiny bits that disperse like dust on the wind.